Chaos and Cranberries

A CHRISTMAS MYSTERY

CHARMING MYSTERIES AND PINEY FALLS
MYSTERIES CROSSOVER

JOANN KEDER

ISBN: 978-1-953270-12-2

Edited by Michele Gwynn

Cover Design by Molly Burton with Cozy Cover Designs

Publisher: Purpleflower Press

Copyright © 2022 by Joann Keder

All rights reserved.

No part of this book may be reproduced in any form or by any electronic or mechanical means, including information storage and retrieval systems, without written permission from the author, except for the use of brief quotations in a book review.

"You aren't wealthy until you have something money can't buy."
-Garth Brooks

For those who love holidays and those who tolerate them for those they love.

Characters

CHARMING MYSTERIES

Feather Jones—hairdresser, paranormal investigator
Tug Muehler—her boyfriend
Jayden Ko—Feather's mentor

PINEY FALLS MYSTERIES

Lanie Anders Hill—marketing manager at the Fallen Branch Resort
Cosmo Hill—Lanie's husband and owner of Cosmic Cakes and Antiquery
November Bean—Lanie's best friend
Truman Coolidge—Cosmo's best friend
Wendell—front desk manager, Fallen Branch Resort
Sylas—Lanie's Cousin
Tidbit—his wife
Eloise—their daughter

Chapter One — Feather

"I'm sorry, could you repeat that?" Tug Muehler, normally calm and composed, leaned over the check-in desk, grasping each side with his muscular arms. To the average person who didn't know his kind and gentle demeanor, this could be interpreted as an act of aggression.

"I suh-suh-said, sir," the dark-haired front desk employee stuttered, taking a step back. "The Fallen For You you requested is not available."

Feather Jones glanced around the spacious lobby. The cabin-themed Christmas decor was a feast for the eyes. Swoops of garland dotted with sparkling lights framed the perimeter. A giant tree, at least twenty feet tall, adorned a sunken sitting area in the center of the lobby and a fire crackled in a huge stone fire place.

"It's okay, Tug. Really. We get to spend Christmas week in the Fallen Branch Resort. Does it matter which room we're in?"

The employee eyed her up and down with disapproval. Feather wrapped her arms tightly around her body.

Her appearance was more on the eclectic side, and she realized for some people it took some getting used to. She changed the color of her short, spiky hair to match her mood. Most recently, it had been jet black with yellow accents. To celebrate their planned holiday trip, she dyed it Christmas red on top with evergreen on the bottom layers.

She stood just over five feet tall, and the combat boots she wore religiously clomped when she walked. Her face resembled what Tug endearingly called, "The shape of a pixie's. Cute and to the point."

"No, babe, it's our first Christmas away from Charming together," Tug insisted. "I researched for an entire month, trying to find a special place to bring you. The reviews said the staff were extremely accommodating. It was supposed to be a romantic getaway from all of the stresses in Charming." He glared at the clerk. "And now they're trying to cheat me out of my money."

In stark contrast to Feather, Tug looked as though he stepped out of a fashion magazine. His chiseled features and sharp jaw were what some men spent thousands of dollars to achieve. With thick hair the color of brown sugar, muscular tanned arms and intense green eyes, he could have chosen any beautiful woman he wanted.

Tug Muehler only had eyes for Feather Jones.

"Suh-suh sir, that's not it. We'll refund your money and even give you a discount on your next visit. The room was available when you booked, but it's since become...uninhabitable."

Feather nudged her boyfriend out of the way, positioning herself between an angry Tug and a flustered front desk clerk with a name tag that read, *"Hi! I'm Wendell. Your comfort is my number one concern!"*

"We'll take whatever you have, then. Forget about the Fallen For You. It's late and we're tired. We'd just like to go to bed, if you don't mind, Wendell." As the owner of Feather Works Salon, she knew the headache angry customers caused. The last thing she wanted was for Wendell to go online and complain about Feather and Tug. If potential customers for Feather Works Salon found evidence of Feather exhibiting poor behavior, chances were, they would take their business elsewhere.

"That's the tha-tha-thing, ma'am. Since it's Christmas, we're fully booked. I could call over to the Spruce Bark Motel and get you a nice room. It's not as high-end as this place, but Ed Junior will take good care of you." Wendell's eyes darted back and forth, as though he was working hard to keep unpleasant thoughts at bay.

"No thanks," Tug snickered. "I saw that dump on the way into town. It's one step away from a bad horror movie."

"Could you give us a little more information on what happened to the room, please?" Feather marked off the days on her Hair Stylists of the Month calendar, knowing they would spend the Christmas holiday being pampered. That dream was fizzling away right in front of her eyes.

"I'm sah-sah-sorry, Miss. I'm not allowed to divulge that."

Wendell glanced down, shuffling papers in front of him. The heading on each of them read, "Pool and Gym Rules."

Feather slid the sleeve of her Christmas sweater up to her elbow, though she really didn't need to. She knew what was happening.

"You have a great aunt who lived in the Fallen Branch cult, before they disbanded it."

What little color he had drained from Wendell's gaunt face. "How did you know that?"

"She hated your mother's Christmas pies. She used to throw them away after your mother left. You promised you'd never tell."

He took a step backward and collapsed on the chair behind him. "I don't know what kind of magic you're practicing, young lady. This is not the puh--puh-place you want to make enemies."

She rubbed her arms as her boyfriend noticed the little hairs all standing at attention. He squeezed her shoulder and nodded. Just then, a middle-aged woman with blonde hair and a dazzling smile approached them.

"Hi, folks!" she greeted them, before pivoting to the clerk collapsed in the chair.

"Wendell? Is there a problem here? I was about to head home for the night. I thought everyone had checked in for the holiday."

Wendell's demeanor went from "shocked" to "I feel faint."

"La-la-lanie! Weren't you called to the Fallen For You-suh-suh-suite?"

"I heard the page, hon." She brought a large, white watch up to her face. "I didn't realize so much time had passed. I was on the phone with my caterer, finalizing plans for Christmas Eve. What did you need?"

Wendell stood and mumbled words to himself, shaking his head. Finally, he gestured toward Tug and Feather.

"The-the-these...people are the ones who rented the *Fallen for You* Suite and I was explaining to them we have nothing else available. Someone sha-sha-should have called them after–"

"After what?" Tug asked impatiently. "What happened in the room? Because I can tell you right now, I would pretty much sleep there if the roof was missing. As long as I have a bed and covers. We're beat."

A stout man in a police uniform approached the desk. "Glad I happened to be here testing out the new tiki bar. Non-alcoholic, of course." He winked at Lanie.

"Ba-ba-boysie? You've been in the Fallen For You Suite too?" Wendell was now positively gaunt.

"Was there a party going on in that suite? Now I'm

really regretting that I ignored that page." Lanie remarked, half-jokingly.

"Think we're done here for now. I'll wait 'til after the holiday, since he's not going anywhere." He chuckled. "Mom rented a large cabin for us in Northern California. All the Lumquests under the same roof for a week. Better hope nobody brings sharp objects."

"This is Boysie Lumquest, our police chief," the woman explained. "Oh, and I forgot to introduce myself. I'm Lanie Anders Hill. I'm the marketing manager here."

Feather shook Lanie's hand and immediately felt a multitude of voices trying to say their piece. She resisted the opportunity to tell this woman she'd only just met that her dead relatives were talking over one another, each with an important message for Lanie. There was something so familiar about her face, but she couldn't place it.

"Nice to meet you, Lanie. Can you give us an idea what's going on? We came all of this way and now we have to drive back to Charming. It seems like we're owed some kind of explanation."

"I'm not sure of that myself!" Lanie answered, pivoting toward Boysie.

"Murder," Boysie replied matter-of-factly. "We can't be sure what happened yet. It was the darndest thing. Poor fella was wrapped in cranberries strung on twine. Didn't kill him, of course, the blow to the head did that. And he had a gold decoration from this enormous tree in the lobby stuck in his mouth. Quite a sight."

"Oh," a much more subdued Tug replied. "But that doesn't excuse the fact that nobody called us. And now we're stuck spending our Christmas back in Charming."

"What's your name, sir?" Lanie asked.

"So sorry. That was rude of me. Tug Muehler. And this is my girlfriend, Feather." He extended his hand and they shook perfunctorily. Growing up as he had, in a wealthy family, Tug learned first impressions were even more important than how much you had in your bank account.

"Well, Tug, since I learned of this just now, there's nothing I can do. The manager is gone until after Christmas, or I'd make this right."

Feather found it odd that this woman wasn't the least bit swayed by the news of a murder. She considered repeating it, just in case this Lanie person hadn't heard.

Lanie snapped her fingers. "I have a wonderful idea! My husband and I own a home up in the hills above town. We just finished our guest house last month and our plans for Christmas company fell through. Our Sprout, that's what I've taken to calling our daughter, is in the tropics for an extended holiday, so it will just be us and a couple of friends, along with far too much food. Please say you'll join us!"

Feather and Tug exchanged uncertain glances.

Tug was usually open to anything, despite the fact

that he'd grown up in an atmosphere of distrust and competition. Feather, on the other hand, struggled to trust anyone. After her dark times as a child, she had a hard time accepting that some people were inherently kind.

"Maybe just for one night," Feather replied cautiously.

Tug shot her a look of surprise. "Really?"

Feather shrugged. "I don't want to go home. Plus, there are a few things I'd like to research while we're here." She elbowed him.

"No, Feath. Not while we're on vacation," he pleaded.

Feather pivoted to Lanie. "Okay. We'll stay with you. But just for one night."

Chapter Two — Lanie

"Don't you think you're going overboard, just a little, Lanie?" My handsome husband adjusted the Santa hat covering his thick salt-and-pepper hair as he set the boxes of decorations on the counter. "Not that any Christmas with you wouldn't be perfection. I just don't want you to be disappointed."

I kissed him gently on the cheek and squeezed his arm. "How could I be disappointed? I have a beautiful home, the most handsome husband in the world and a perfect daughter. Oh, and a best friend who breaks all the rules. Who cares if my new relatives show up or not?"

I'd been in touch with my father's family, tracking down members who originally shied away from him and his two unstable wives. At first, I was unsure if they would accept me for who I was, and not who the rest of my family turned out to be.

My second cousin, Sylas, said he'd have to think about further contact. To my surprise, the following week, he asked if we could set up a video visit which would include his wife, Tidbit, and young daughter, Eloise. It was as if a light switch had turned on when we saw each other face-to-face. He noticed my resemblance to the rest of the family when I thought I only carried my mother's questionable traits.

He was so enthusiastic, my guard went up, waiting for him to make some unreasonable demand for money. When none came, we began spending hours laughing and getting to know one another without reservation.

Sylas and Tidbit set up their laptop in their bedroom, a cheery flower-themed room, highlighted by a giant, antique dresser. "You must come see it in person, Lanie! It's a part of your story, too!" Sylas insisted.

After months of conversation, I invited them to spend Christmas with our family, over Cosmo's strong objections. Sylas and Tidbit didn't hesitate before saying they would be delighted to join us. Eloise promised to draw me a picture of her home and bring it, when she came, and Tidbit was packing her recipe for Christmas cranberry salad.

Meanwhile, Cos and his friend, Truman, built a lovely guest house on our property—two bedrooms, a gorgeous bathroom, cozy kitchen and living room—with a breathtaking view of the ocean.

I purchased towels and drapes, stocked the fridge with everything they said they liked, and lovingly placed photos of my current family on the mantle. It was the Christmas celebration I'd only dreamt of as a child.

"Mom, we're going to the Bahamas for Christmas. It was a Christmas gift from Obie. Please don't be mad!" My beautiful daughter flashed her expressive eyes at me.

"How could I be mad? You and your boyfriend deserve time away. We'll have plenty to occupy our time, with little Eloise running around. I can't wait to show her our trails and I'm sure Vem will point out every creepy crawly thing. It will be a wonderful Christmas." It was more for myself than her that I uttered those words. Secretly, my heart was breaking.

"If I didn't know any better, I'd think you won't miss me!" she said indignantly.

I took my adult daughter in my arms and held her tight. We'd formed a strong bond in our short time as mother and daughter. There was something about our shared losses that drew us together. When we adopted her, Cos and I were both determined she'd never feel alone again. "No one will replace you, my love." I kissed the top of her head. "I only meant we'll be making memories here. We can both share on New Year's Eve. I'm sure you'll be bored to tears by our stories."

It was during our next rather strange conversation

that Sylas and Tidbit abruptly changed course. Something about broken pipes. I asked if they couldn't give a neighbor the key while they were gone, but they had to go before they answered. Repairs in Arizona must not work the way they did in Oregon.

"Those things happen, Lanie," my deliciously handsome husband said, as he rubbed my tight shoulders. "Don't take it personally."

And yet I did.

There was something about this entire situation that didn't sit right with me.

I asked to video chat with them again the next evening, and though they agreed, it wasn't as heartily as our previous conversations.

Soon after sitting down, there was a knock on the door. Sylas and Tidbit glanced at each other and both excused themselves to answer.

"Do you like my play?" Eloise asked me when they were gone.

"Which one, sweetheart? Is it about lions?"

I knew she had both a fervent imagination and an obsession with stuffed lions.

"No, silly! This one!"

I had no idea what she was talking about, but felt confident her parents would explain when they came back. After several minutes where I could hear arguing in the background, Eloise rubbed her palms together anxiously.

"Do you think you're in danger, Eloise? If you are, I can call someone to help."

She paused for a moment before turning back to the screen. "No, Cousin Lanie. It's the play."

"What do you—"

Tidbit appeared and bent down in front of the camera. "We have to go, Lanie. We'll catch up with you after Christmas."

She shut off the camera and ended the call.

It took me several minutes to digest what had taken place. There was no logical explanation for it, but as Sylas and I had been conversing for several months, I thought he would explain during our next call. The following week I sat, alone, waiting for them for almost an hour.

It was probably better they weren't coming for Christmas. Still, I couldn't shake the feeling that something was really off.

I'll talk to you in January. I'm going to be busy for a while. Cheers!

I shut my laptop, barely giving the email time to send.

When I told Cosmo, he thought Eloise was making up stories. And Sylas didn't want to visit, but couldn't come up with a better excuse than broken pipes. It was all too coincidental for me.

"Lanie? Are you listening? These decorations won't hang themselves."

"Huh? Sorry. My mind is somewhere else."

"What I was saying was that I need to get back to the bakery earlier than usual tomorrow. Someone got us a big contract with the Fallen Branch Resort for holiday baked goods." He winked, turning my insides into goo. "And I'm guessing you'll want to look into the murder at the resort. If I know my wife at all, I'm certain she's feeling the itch to help Boysie."

"Maybe," I replied without conviction. "Are you going to do all of that extra baking on your own? I really will feel bad if our daughter is off on her trip and you can't handle the extra work."

"Shouldn't be a problem. Especially since I've got two different deadlines. The Christmas order is much less than New Year's Eve, and Doris has promised to come in early to help."

"Oh, yes. I almost forgot to tell you. We have guests coming tonight."

Cosmo's muscular arms dropped to his side. "Who? I thought your cousin couldn't make it."

"No, not him. After the holiday rush is over, I may ask Gladys to research Sylas further." Gladys was the town busybody who could uncover information about anyone.

I tapped my bright red nails on the counter, thinking as I tapped. "What I was referring to was that we've got two young guests coming who weren't expecting to be in this circumstance for Christmas. When I was at the Fallen Branch earlier, I ran into this nice young couple. The hotel messed up their reservation, and—"

"Lanie, you didn't..." Cosmo's warning voice fell on deaf ears.

"They were going to have to drive all the way back

to Charming tonight. Do we really want to be responsible if they get in an accident? Wouldn't you feel terrible?"

I already knew the answer. He was one big puddle of *'feelings goo.'*

"I gave them a voucher for the restaurant. As soon as they finish dinner, they're coming over. We've got the guest house all ready to go, and I bought enough food for an army. I think it must be fate."

Cosmo rolled his eyes. "Really? You're going with that?"

"I can't do this all by myself, Cos," I replied cheekily. I picked up a shiny silver ball and hung it on the closest branch of our massive spruce tree.

The doorbell rang.

A little too eagerly, I sprinted over the boxes and to the doorway, almost landing on my rear. One-too-many trips to the emergency room taught me to be more careful, usually.

I opened the door to find the couple, younger than I remembered and much wearier, on my doorstep. The girl had the hardened appearance of someone who'd struggled in life and the young man could've walked off the pages of a magazine. As opposite as me and my husband.

"Mrs. Hill, are you sure this is all right with your husband?" Feather Jones asked timidly.

I felt Cosmo's familiar squeeze of my shoulders as he leaned forward, extending a hand.

"Her husband will be delighted to have guests. I'm

Cosmo Hill, the husband in question. Please, come in. We're going to have a heckuva Christmas together."

Chapter Three — Feather

"They seem like nice people, right?" Feather set Tug's clothes on the top of the dresser, marveling at the sumptuous guest home. It was bigger than their apartment and had a balcony overlooking the cozy living room.

"I guess. I'm uncomfortable staying with some stranger though. Aren't you uncomfortable, Feath?" Tug put his hands on his tapered hips and inspected every room before returning to her side.

"Not really. I've had some interesting communications. Everyone who's come forward has given me glowing reports about our guests. Lanie's got lots of noise surrounding her, but it's nothing urgent, so I've been blocking them out. The spirit world is sometimes like a crowded bar. Both Lanie and Cosmo have been through hell, but they are both survivors. They're good people, Tug."

She pulled him in close and stood on her tiptoes,

nuzzling his neck. "I would tell you if the spirits said something different."

Tug kissed the top of her head and pulled away. "I don't doubt that. It's the fact that you were so quick to say yes that worries me."

Feather sat on the bed and patted the cream-colored bedspread, inviting him to sit. When Tug lowered his thick body beside her, the bed heaved.

"There is something happening at that hotel. From the minute we walked in, I could sense an urgency. Someone there needs my help. I was hoping I could tell you when we got to our room, but..."

His face wrinkled with concern. "What kind of trouble? Are you talking about something besides the murder? Do we need to drive back there tonight?"

"Oh, no. I'm talking about the person who died in our room. Well, what was supposed to be our room."

"Yeah, that." He flopped back against a fluffy pillow and laced his hands together beneath his head. "Shouldn't we leave it to the police guy? We have plenty of cases back in Charming, now that your new agency is open."

Feather leaned back, joining him on the pillow. The act of putting her head down made her realize how sleepy she was. "Kindred Spirits is going well, but no one has come in since December 1st. I think over the holidays, people try to ignore their dead loved ones."

"Go figure," Tug replied as he stroked her arm lightly. "I suppose it's okay for a night or two. But we

CHAOS AND CRANBERRIES

really shouldn't impose on these people longer than that." He leaned over and kissed her. "This isn't my comfort zone, but as you know, I'll do anything for the love of my life."

She snuggled against his chest, relieved that he wasn't upset by her rash decision.

"They asked us to help them decorate the tree. I don't want to be rude," Feather said, through half-closed eyes.

"You can get some sleep and I'll do it, Feath."

"No, we're in this together."

She sat up and stretched, yawning.

"I've always hated stringing cranberries," Lanie remarked, after she'd poked herself for the third time. "My father left when I was four. I'd watched all the Christmas movies and lost myself in the idea of a fantasy Christmas. Damnit!" She stuck her finger in her mouth after poking it again.

"Well, one year I took the money she gave me to buy her booze and bought Christmas decorations," she continued. "I came through the door with a scraggly tree and a box of ornaments, expecting her to yell at me. Instead, she decided it would be more entertaining watching me try to make that thing look like a tree than to get hammered. By the time I'd hung the last of the cranberries and popcorn, the floor was covered in blood and she was laughing so hard she struggled to breathe."

"I don't know that our visitors wanted to hear that story, Lanie," Cosmo cautioned, as he finished his side of the tree and stood back, admiring his work. "You're going to scare them before they've even met our lively holiday guest."

"I'm sorry, sometimes I forget my stories aren't appropriate for everyone."

Cosmo looked at their guests apologetically. "Lanie's family wasn't what you'd call normal."

"And neither was yours," Feather replied solemnly.

"What?" Lanie and Cosmo asked in unison.

"Feather has a gift. She's not trying to be rude or anything!" Tug explained. "She knows how to–"

"You read peoples' minds? I love that!" Lanie replied excitedly. "My friend, Vem, will go crazy when we tell her tomorrow."

"She's crazy all right," Cosmo quipped.

"No, that's not it, Mrs. Hill. Ghosts come to me. When I'm near their living relatives, they tell me everything they think I should know about their families. An aunt of Mr. Hill's told me about his grim early years."

The mood of the room went from joyful to decidedly depressing in a matter of minutes.

"Maybe this was a mistake," Tug said, placing a protective arm around Feather. "There's still plenty of time for us to get home to Charming. It's not that rainy tonight, so I'm sure the roads would be fine."

Lanie squeezed both of their shoulders. "Nonsense. We're all a bit unique here. We don't judge, we celebrate our differences. I'm glad you know about Cosmo's family. It saves us an awkward conversation at dinner."

"And yours, too, Mrs. Hill. I know about your mother's mental illness and your grandmother's–"

Lanie placed her index finger on her lips, pausing the conversation. "That's a hard topic for me." She moved quickly into the kitchen and poured four glasses of eggnog.

"I'm sorry, I didn't mean to upset her," Feather whispered.

"You didn't know," Cosmo replied. "Right? I'm not sure how these things work."

"I guess I should have asked, is everyone okay with almond milk?" Lanie returned from the kitchen carrying a tray filled with foamy glasses sprinkled with nutmeg. "My handsome man there can have tummy troubles after too much dairy." She winked at Cosmo as she offered their guests a drink.

Feather took a sip, marveling at the creaminess. "This is delicious!"

"Homemade. Vem's friends from California send us almonds right off the tree." Lanie smacked her lips after taking a sip. So, tell me, Feather, you arrived at the lodge as Boysie was finishing his preliminary investigation. What did you learn from the newly departed? Or do they have to be gone a certain amount of time before they can communicate with you? I don't know how these things work, but I'm sure Boysie would appreciate it if you could give him some clues about the killer."

"There were so many voices coming from the Fallen Branch Resort from the moment we walked in the door. Everyone wants a chance to say their piece. Some are able to communicate right away, and others can take years, if not centuries before they make their voices heard. If something is happening in our world they disapprove of, or a relative, no matter how distant, is in trouble, that's when they make themselves heard."

She didn't want to explain how she'd heard a voice as they were leaving, that Wendell from the front desk was hiding something dark.

Normally, Feather was uncomfortable sharing this much about her craft with strangers, but there was something so accepting about Lanie and Cosmo she felt her unease melting away.

"If I'm being honest, that was the reason I convinced my boyfriend to stay tonight. I wanted a chance to go back tomorrow and try to learn more."

Lanie's eyes widened. "You're staying more than one night, I hope! Your reservations were for four nights! I won't hear of a minute less!"

"We'll see, Mrs. Hill. We don't want to impose. For all you know, we could be the murderers."

"Tug!" Feather chided. "If they didn't think we were crazy before, they do now!"

"You have your methods of research and so do I."

Lanie walked into another room and returned with a paper she handed to Feather.

"I'm a pretty good judge of character, but I wanted to make sure you were who you said you were. This is basic information I found on you. My friend, Gladys—that's Boysie's mother-in-law—is a master of the dark web search. She was in the middle of preparing to leave for California, but was able to give me a few details."

Feather scanned the page:

Feather Jones—employed at Feather Works Salon, also working as a paranormal detective at Kindred Spirits Detective Agency. Business partner: Gemini Reed.

Currently residing at 511 Indigo Drive, Apartment 32, Charming, Oregon.

Tug Jones—son of Tag Jones Senior, Jones Holdings. Owner of Tug Bars, factory location 1818 Flying High Lane. Former sales associate of Bimbobble health products.

"That's all she could get on short notice. She offered me your financials, and I declined. I just wanted to make sure there were no surprises." Lanie appeared flustered. "Not that there would be. So, I have complete confidence you're decent people. I'd offer you more information about us, but it sounds like you've been able to gather quite a lot from your other world sources."

"Well, now that we're all equally uncomfortable, let's finish these decorations, shall we?" Cosmo asked.

"Cheers, by the way." He lifted his glass in the air and the other three followed suit.

Feather suppressed a yawn and asked, "If it's not too personal, could I ask what happened to your other guests? The ones you built the guest house for?"

Lanie and Cosmo exchanged wary glances.

"I've been accumulating a family, both by genetics and people I love. Recently, I came into contact with a cousin. He and his wife and daughter are wonderful people, and they'd agreed to join us. Something came up at the last minute, though."

"You sound worried, Mrs. Hill," Tug observed.

"Yes, I am. I can't shake the feeling that he might be in trouble. Maybe tomorrow, once you've had some rest, you could ask your spirit friends for help?"

Feather yawned again, this time covering her mouth with the back of her hand. "Of course. Communicating with the dead can leave me a little tired, and ever since I've been here, it's been nonstop. Do you mind if I head to bed?"

"Of course, dear." Lanie patted her back. "We're just delighted you're joining us. You sleep in as long as you like."

"Good night, you two lovebirds!" Cosmo called from his side of the room. "This is going to be a holiday to remember!"

Chapter Four—Lanie

"Today, you'll meet Vem. I need to warn you ahead of time, she's a little out there." I scooped up the last of the chocolate chip pancakes and flopped them on Tug's plate, after he'd inhaled four. It didn't seem important to ask if he wanted more.

He tore into them hungrily and I fought to keep my mouth from dropping on the ground. Cosmo was a healthy eater, but I'd missed out on this stage of his life. I made a mental note to check on the ingredients for our big holiday dinner and make sure I had plenty.

"These are...so good, Mrs.–Lanie," he said between mouthfuls. He nudged Feather. "We should get a skillet for pancakes, just for the weekends."

"I'm sure we'll..."

Her sweet face was frozen in concentration. I noticed the hairs on her arms standing straight up, as if being pulled by a magnetic force. Never actually seeing a paranormal in action before, it was both shocking and intriguing. "Hon, are you okay? Do you need to lie down?" I maneuvered around the island and placed my hands on her shoulders. "Can you hear me?"

"It freaked me out, too," Tug said between bites, "the first time it happened. I almost called 911. I promise you, she's just fine." He shoved another bite of pancakes into his mouth, pouring the last quarter of the bottle of syrup onto the stack.

"Oh," I replied. Piney Falls was full of unusual people, but I'd yet to encounter someone with these particular gifts. I studied her face with fascination. It was taut and discolored. Her eyes were focused but vacant. Her mouth was moving, but no words came out. I couldn't tell if she was with us, or if this gift of hers took her to another world entirely. She got up, as if in a trance, and walked into the other room.

Quickly, I scanned my mind for safe topics to discuss.

"Tug, I don't know how much you've studied our history, but Piney Falls has some very interesting founders."

"Yeah, I've heard some of it. There was a real bad guy, Stanford Aisley. And the women who built a school and hospital, what were their names?"

"Fiona and Faye Scheddy. Remarkable women. Our museum has a room devoted just to them. Unfortunately, it's closed until January. If you're feeling especially energetic, you can hike to the top of the mountain where they're buried. Vem, my best friend and I have been tending their graves. We bought new headstones, and–"

Feather rejoined us looking a little worse for wear.

"Do you need something to drink, hon? Does this experience deplete you?" Most of our volunteer emergency crew was out of town for the holidays, so any emergency care would rest on my shoulders.

"I'm fine, but thank you." She took a drink of her orange juice and I watched with curiosity as her shoulders lowered and her body loosened. I relaxed a little, thankful disaster seemed to be averted.

"It's fascinating, this entire process of yours. Do they ring a mental doorbell, or ask to come in?"

"I wish they were that polite," Feather mused. "I used to get embarrassed when they'd contact me in public. Now, I know that's just a part of who I am. While I'm always free to tell them to bug off, they show up unannounced."

Tug took his plate to the sink and rinsed off the syrup. "So nice of you to make us breakfast. Unexpected guests, and you treat us like royalty."

"I bought ingredients for all of my cousin's favorites. His daughter loves chocolate chip pancakes."

"Eloise," Feather replied. "The entity I just spoke with is concerned about her."

"Oh? Why is that?"

Feather's eyes darted back and forth between me and Tug.

"You can trust me, I promise."

"Eloise doesn't realize what's happening. I wasn't

able to get much more. This woman I spoke with was a bit of a diva." Feather got up and paced, clasping her hands on top of her head. "She said we don't have the right picture, "*dahling*," whatever that means. And then she told me that she was ashamed I didn't know her."

I grinned, thinking of the diva possibilities in my family history. If we had time later on, I'd explain my family roots to her, or at least fill her in on the parts she didn't already know. "Did this spirit say what we should do for Eloise? Or did this person mention Sylas, her father?"

Feather shook her head. "I'm sorry. Sometimes they aren't very helpful."

"Should I call the police in Tucson?"

"They wouldn't believe you, Lanie."

She was right. "After the holidays, I'll try calling Sylas again."

There was too much swirling around in my head right now; too many worries for those I cared for as well as those I'd just met. "We should head out to the resort and see if you can get answers to your questions."

"Something is definitely pulling me there. I..."

She moved quicker now, pacing in a small square back and forth, back and forth.

"What is it, hon?"

Feather stopped abruptly and stared at me. "I feel like there is a connection between your family and the murder at Fallen Branch." Her eyes had fear in them. "I don't want you to think I'm losing my mind. It could just be that I've got too many spirits in my head. They are pretty chatty."

"You know, I'm a bit of an amateur sleuth myself. Piney Falls, while picturesque, seems to draw murderers. As a joke I asked if I should put that on our promotional brochures. The city council encouraged me to do it."

"That's why you were so calm when you learned about the murder," Feather said. "I was wondering."

"What else can you tell us about the murder victim? Did the police chief tell you anything?" Tug asked while loading the dishwasher.

"You don't have to do that," I protested. "You're my guests."

"It's kind of Tug's thing," Feather assured me. "If he doesn't have something to keep him busy, he'll get fidgety."

I shrugged, knowing my Cosmo was much the same. "What I know is the guest's name is–was–Dash something-or-other."

Tug cocked his head to the side. "You're kidding, right?"

"I have to admit, I was skeptical too. I have access to the hotel register online. As the marketing manager for the Fallen Branch Resort, I gather data, like what part of the country our guests are from and how old they are. Last night, after you went to bed, I checked on him. He seems legit."

"The next thing you're going to tell me is that his

home address was the North Pole." Tug smiled broadly. "It's almost like someone wrote this story for a cheesy magazine."

"Let's head over there and we'll be able to ask more questions. Are you ready?" I wiped the few bits of pancakes that Tug hadn't inhaled off the counter and found my keys. As I was reaching for my purse on the hook beside the door, Cosmo breezed in.

"What are you doing home, dear? Aren't you up to your ears in Christmas pastries?"

"We hit a snag, unfortunately."

Cosmo's body language was easy to read. When he was tense, his shoulders practically touched his ears and his nose bunched up in the cutest possible way. He also put his hands in his pockets and paced back and forth.

"Did your other employee mysteriously disappear?"

All three sets of eyes snapped to me. The first two in horror, the last set, rolling.

"No, Lanie. I think I've been baking long enough to make sure that doesn't happen." He pivoted to our guests, hurting my feelings just a little. "What happened though, was a short in the stove wiring. As much as I like to think of myself as a superhero, there's no way I can move the stove by myself. Doris laughed when I asked for her help, and nobody is around today. It's a ghost town, as it always is before Christmas."

"I'm happy to help!" Tug said eagerly.

I couldn't be sure, but I thought I detected a sense of relief on Feather's face.

"As long as it's okay with you, Feath?"

"No problem. Lanie and I have this. I'll fill you in later."

"Are you sure? I don't want to mess up any plans you had for today. There's so much sightseeing to be done here. The cannery museum, Flanagan House, hiking, I could go on and on," Cosmo protested. "You kids probably had an entire week planned out before you got here."

"And yet you didn't offer any suggestions when I asked for your help with the marketing brochure!" I chided him. "Feather and I were going to head back to the Fallen Branch Resort to do a little sleuthing. We're both very curious about the murder."

Cosmo wrapped his arms around me, surprising all three of us. He wasn't one to show much affection around people we didn't know. "My dear Lanie, I know this will fall on deaf ears, but you really should let Boysie handle this. Show Feather the town instead. She might enjoy shopping with you!"

I doubted that very much, but I didn't bother telling my husband. "We've set our minds to this, Cos. If she wants to shop on the way home, I'll be glad to take her by the new outlet mall, or Urica's Gallery."

"It's really fine, Cosmo," Feather reassured him. "I'm not big on shopping. Tug and I didn't have any definite plans. My friend, Gemini, told me the food is great, and we'd love the beach. That was about all. I'm anxious to get back to the Fallen Branch Resort and see if I can help with the investigation."

"Could I make dinner?" Tug offered. "I do most of the cooking for the two of us, so I know my way around the kitchen. I could come home early, and–"

"No, but thanks anyway, Tug. You boys go have fun shoving heavy things around and we'll figure out exactly why someone killed a man named Dash."

Chapter Five — Lanie

My mother used to say I was too curious for my own good. One Saturday, when we were at the mall, I saw a man walking a cat on a leash. My mother was drunk and yelling at anyone who got too close. I was embarrassed to be seen with her, so following the man seemed like a safer option.

It was at Christmas time, the only month our mall reached capacity. When I made it to the discount store that anchored one end, the man and the cat disappeared. I panicked as I glanced around me. At my age, the only thing at eye level were trousers.

At that moment, I was at a crossroads. Should I make a run for it and be free of my crazy mother? Or should I try and find her before she caused a scene?

The huge crowd swelled, propelling me back towards the other end of the mall. The Chester A. Arthur eighth grade band was playing Christmas songs in the center ring and eager parents rushed to watch.

Reluctantly, I followed the mass of feet. When I reached the performance area, to my shock and horror, my mother was directly across from me, her hands running up and down the length of the mall police officer's uniform. He kept inching away and she kept inching toward him.

I was humiliated, knowing she was once again making a fool of herself. And yet, I couldn't take my eyes off of them. If I'd run away, maybe made myself look forlorn and alone in the parking lot, someone would have taken pity on me and dropped me off at the police station. There, I fantasized, they would take pity on a poor, unloved, underfed girl and shower her with all that she'd missed. Instead, I watched with fascination as my mother continued to run her fingers up and down the man's chest.

I'd seen her doting on men before. Somewhere, deep in my memories was the vision of my parents laughing as they held hands in front of the television. She had lots of boyfriends, usually draping herself over them as they sat in front of the television, drinking. It didn't matter what their names were. I knew her affection wasn't enough to keep them around once they couldn't take the other parts of her anymore.

The person in front of me now, this new version of my mother was harsher, more demanding. She smiled as she spoke to the man, dropping her chin and staring up at him with her big, grey eyes. Mother fiddled with the buttons on his coat and I realized this was the way she lured them in. My mother wasn't a maternal figure but a spider, inviting her prey into her web.

"Lanie? Sweetheart, what are you doing here?"

It was our kindly next-door neighbors. They didn't have grandchildren of their own, but they often attended events to cheer on everyone else's.

I glanced at the store directly behind my mother. "I was looking at the pet store."

"Charles, the mother has dressed her up like a harlot again. I'm sure she's lurking around here somewhere."

This was my last opportunity. I could have told them she abandoned me there. Instead, I didn't want to make waves. I really liked our neighbors. They always seemed to know when we didn't have money for food. A casserole would appear on our porch. My mother, never thankful for small kindnesses, would comment, "Haven't they learned I don't like cheese?"

I sucked in my breath. "Mom is talking to a man." I pointed over the head of the very tall trombone player. "She told me I could walk around."

She took my hand and pulled me over to my mother. I steadied myself, prepared for her to make a scene. It wouldn't be unheard of for her to cry and carry on about her missing 'baby,' and how lucky they were to find me.

"I found your daughter," my neighbor said sternly. "She was under the impression it's all right for a six-year-old to wander through a crowd alone."

My mother's eyes grew large. "Oh, did she wander

off?" she asked innocently. "I hadn't noticed." It was an even bigger blow than if she had acted like she was concerned by my absence.

I never forgot that day, nor did I forget the thrill of spying on my mother without her knowledge. My interest in the world around me has never waned.

"Mrs.–Lanie, do you think we can sneak in? Is there a back door?"

Feather's spikey Christmas-red hair leaned against my car window. We'd just pulled up in front of the Fallen Branch Inn and Resort and I wanted to make sure we were on the same page about our expectations.

"Why would we do that? Honey, around here, we're all family. Boysie won't mind if I look at the crime scene. As long as you're with me, you'll be fine."

She viewed me with skepticism but said nothing.

We walked up to the welcome desk, where Wendell was filing his nails. Since I wasn't in charge of employees, I couldn't reprimand him, but I gave him a stern look of disapproval.

He dropped the file when he recognized us. "Mrs. Anders-Hill, wha-wha-what brings you back? I thought you'd be busy preparing for the holiday!"

He jumped off his stool and came around to my side of the counter. "Is there suh-suh-something I can do for you? I think I mentioned my interest in marketing. I majored in marketing at Piney Falls Community College. Well, to be honest, I only took one class. But I really liked it, and someday, I'm going to return!"

"We're going to take a peek at the Fallen For You

Suite. My friend, Feather here, is a sleuth in her own community. She offered to help."

Wendell eyed her up and down, pausing when he reached her combat boots. "Oh, yes. I remember." He pivoted back to me, thankfully. "Officer Holliday is back there now. Suh-suh-seems he came up with new information."

"Thank you, Wendell. We'll talk soon."

We found the elevator and I pushed three for the third floor. After a silence set in, I said, "I know what you're thinking. Wendell is odd. Everyone in Piney Falls is odd in some way. It's what makes us endearing."

"I wasn't thinking that at all. The opposite, actually. There are so many voices, so many spirits around me right now, I'm having a hard time keeping them quiet. I was glad he was nicer today. His Great Aunt Velma would have spewed a lot of hatred if he was rude."

I burst out laughing. "Oh, that's right. He was a bit of a pistol last night. I'm sorry for that. I'll have a talk with his boss after the holidays."

"Please, don't!" Feather begged as the elevator dinged and the doors opened. "I don't want him to get into trouble. I own a salon and I know what it's like to deal with the public all day. Sometimes, you don't have any patience left and you take it out on the wrong people."

"I knew there were many reasons to like you, Feather Jones. We're kindred spirits, you know."

Feather cocked her head to the side. "In what way?"

"Your childhood was a struggle, as was mine. We can't change those things, but we can find others like us and form a bond no memories can break."

"I like that! Back in Charming, I have a friend who says pretty much the same thing. You should come visit. I'll do your hair, free of charge, and you can meet Gemini!"

"When things calm down, Cos and I will make the trip!"

We walked down the hall until we reached double doors with yellow police tape strung across the front. A thin man in a police uniform was standing just beyond the tape.

"I have to warn you, Officer Holliday is no Boysie Lumquest. He's only been on the Tellum police force for a year and he tends to look for the easiest route, even if it's not the best. That's what Boysie says. His assignment during Boysie's absence is more of a punishment than anything. Last month, he wrote parking tickets for every single car on the main street in Tellum, just to fulfill his quota. But don't worry, he's perfectly capable."

Tall and awkward in his stance, his sandy blond hair hung down over his eyes. Not the most professional look for a police officer.

"Lanie! Guess I should have figured you'd be here. This one's a puzzler." He blinked rapidly, something I'd learned meant he wasn't sure of himself.

"The victim was a famous author. Dash Vixen."

"Hmm. Doesn't ring any bells with me."

"The author?" Feather asked. "He was HERE? In Piney Falls?"

We both stared at her. "Who is that? I've never heard of him before."

"He's famous for his horror books. I listen to them on audio when I'm at the gym. They are huge sellers!"

She gazed at me expectantly. She must've assumed that was enough for me to recognize his name. "Sorry, hon. That doesn't tell me anything."

"Well, there's *Jingle Hell*, number one on the horror list for twenty-two weeks. It was the first holiday horror book to make the top one hundred Scared out of My Wits Book List."

Officer Holiday and I both shrugged.

"And then there is *Sleighed By the Fire*," She paused briefly. "Okay, you have to have heard of, *Decked in the Halls*? It's been a top seller in the horror audiobook genre for over five years now."

"Oh, I have heard of that one!"

I hadn't.

Relief crossed her face. "He got a big advance for his next book, *When Santa Screams*. He and the authors in the anthology signed on for the movie version, so the release was delayed until next year. I'm excited for the movie they're making with all six stories." She halted. "I'm babbling, aren't I? If it weren't for these books, I'd quit my workouts after a few minutes."

"You are..."

"Oh, I'm sorry, Officer. This is Feather Jones. She

and her boyfriend, Tug, are our guests for the next few days. Feather, Officer Holliday."

"How d'you do, ma'am?" He tipped his hat, as if we were in the middle of a 1940s movie.

Feather's face became pale and I realized she was about to experience another contact with the deceased. Unlike last time, it passed quickly.

"Is everything all right, hon?"

"There are other authors who died too. They're all connected."

Chapter Six—Feather

Feather always hated telling people about her gift. Most were receptive, but that initial shock was sometimes hard on her ego. It was like they thought she was a freak. Well, she knew she was a freak. She just didn't need reminding.

"Miss...Feather? How could you know that?"

"Elle Vanashelve," Feather replied.

"How could Elle Vanashelve tell you she's dead?" Officer Holiday, on loan from the Tellum police department, squinted and cocked his head to the side, an all-too-familiar sign of disbelief. He leaned toward her in a way that made her terribly uncomfortable.

"Feather has a tremendous gift," Lanie interjected. "That's why I brought her today. She can hear the dead. Don't you think that is an invaluable trait, Officer?" Lanie nudged him encouragingly.

"Oh, I get it. You're referencing the fact that I was on the Wall of Shame at the department." His face was bright red. "Wasn't my fault the mayor didn't appreciate getting a parking ticket."

On the way to the Fallen Branch, another spirit, or maybe the same one, called to her insistently. *There's more than one.*

Once they'd entered the building, the name 'Elle Vanashelve' displayed in big, red letters like a theater marquee in her mind. As they tried convincing the fill-in deputy to let them enter the crime scene, the name and the marquee flashed insistently. She was thankful that Lanie seemed to know this man, and hopefully he wouldn't think she was crazy, too.

A beautiful young woman with copper colored hair and an oblong face stepped away from the maid's cart and joined them. She wore a nametag that read, *"Autumn. Here to help!"*

"That is so cool! You probably talk to famous people all the time! What do you know about–" Autumn removed her phone from her smock pocket and began scrolling.

Feather raised her hand in the air. "No, they have to come to me. It doesn't work if I try to call them. It's almost like you trying to access a celebrity right now. They have to want to see you."

Autumn's face fell as she put her phone back in her pocket. "Oh. I had a complete list of dead musicians and one crazy grandmother I wanted to ask about. I keep them just in case I run into someone like you."

"What about our victim here? Has Dash said

anything?" Officer Holliday leaned in close again and Feather took a step back.

"That's why I needed to return, Officer. When we arrived last night, I sensed an urgent message. I tried asking for more and got nothing. I don't know who it's coming from, since there are lots of lost souls here. If you'd let us in, I might get more information."

"You've probably noticed me angling for a better view." He pointed to his breast pocket, where she could clearly see his badge had a tiny dark hole in the middle. "Just got these Copz Cameras, and the boss wants me to film everything I do. After the mix up with Sheriff's pet pig in Cannon Beach, he doesn't trust me."

"I didn't hear about that, Officer Holliday," Lanie replied in a way that invited a response.

"Well, I've been filling in wherever I can, you know, to make a few extra bucks, and nobody told me that Sheriff Frost had a pig that wanders around town. I found Mittens—that's her name—on the outskirts of town late at night. She didn't have any identification tag, so I thought to myself, 'Now that would make a nice—"

"Oh, Officer! You didn't!" Lanie gasped.

He nodded. "I'm still paying off the cost of a new little pet for the Frost family. Guess you can cut that from my video stream, boss." He took off his cap and rubbed his head. "All that's to say, make sure you're in front of my badge when you're talking, so all that you say is clear. That was the first time I was on the Wall of

Shame. Guys gave me a hard time about that, since no one has been on there three times, and I'm one away."

Something else about this man made Feather very uncomfortable. Maybe it was because she wasn't used to working with law enforcement. Back in Charming, she and Gemini did their own thing.

"Boy, I'm not sure what to do," Officer Holliday continued, his brow furrowed. "What else can you tell me?" He wiggled his fingers by his side with a nervous energy.

Lanie touched her shoulder. "Go on, hon. Do your thing. Show him you mean business," she said encouragingly.

She bit her lip. Lanie didn't understand that the spirits didn't just appear when she asked. They were much fickler than that.

"Your grandfather never told you, but he won a medal for bravery in the war. It's in the chest in your grandmother's basement. I see chaos, too. I don't know what that word means."

He scratched his head, turning his badge away from her.

"See? I told you. Just think what Boysie will say if you solve this murder before he gets back from vacation, and with less work than it would normally take for you." Lanie grinned enthusiastically. "Not only Boysie, but your own police captain. I see a promotion in your future."

Officer Holliday looked at the ground, rubbing his chin.

"Tell you what, I'll give you thirty minutes inside. But if you tell anyone–"

"Scout's honor." Lanie pushed past him and undid the yellow tape. Feather and Autumn followed her inside.

When Officer Holliday looked as though he would protest as the maid passed him, Autumn said, "you don't see stuff like this every day. You can't keep me out."

If Feather were the suspicious type, she would have decided there was an exchange of knowing glances between Officer Holliday and Autumn, but in small towns, it wasn't uncommon for everyone to have a close connection.

A gruesome sight awaited them. A large, dark red stain beside the dresser made it evident where Dash took his last breath. The comforter from the bed was heaped in a pile on the floor, and the trash can was overturned.

"Dash Vixen fought for his life," Lanie observed.

"Why wouldn't an author have a computer with them?" Feather asked, touching the desk lightly with her finger tips. "I thought authors carried that kind of stuff everywhere."

"Officer Lumquest says no computer was found, so we're sure the murderer took it. Must've been something incriminating on that."

Feather baby-stepped to the back of the hotel room, scanning every inch. "Well, Dash knew his attacker. They were friends." She paused. "Scratch that.

They were acquaintances. Dash didn't consider anyone a friend."

Officer Holliday scribbled furiously. "What's this about Elle Vanashelve? She's a famous writer, isn't she?"

Feather nodded, but continued sauntering around the room, pausing to place her hands close to the furniture without actually touching it.

"There's also something about a pizza box. It's got writing on it. I think it may be in the trash." All eyes turned toward Autumn.

"Yeah, I was the only maid who came in this morning. Vonda Mae called in *sick*," she made air quotes and rolled her eyes for emphasis, "with the holiday flu, you know?"

"I know," I replied. As the marketing manager for The World's Best Office Supply Chain, I dealt with that kind of illness frequently.

"Yeah, so Vonda Mae took out the trash yesterday. She'd probably know."

"I'm short on help, this being the holidays and all. Do you suppose you could take another gander inside the trash?"

Autumn's face crinkled into a look of disgust. "Why? You can find someone else to do it, can't you?"

"I'll pay you one hundred dollars," Lanie announced. "That's only if you find a box."

"Are you for real?" Autumn asked, incredulous. "I haven't bought my boyfriend a Christmas present yet!"

Lanie opened her smooth, black leather purse and

pulled out a crisp, one-hundred-dollar bill. She set it on the desk. "This will be waiting for you."

Autumn pushed past them and rushed out the door.

"Feather, would it help you if Officer Holliday and I stepped into the hallway and gave you some space?" Lanie asked.

Feather was grateful her new acquaintance was so understanding. "Oh, yes. That would help a lot!"

"Hmph," the officer grunted. "I'm law enforcement here. You gals come in and want to take over. I didn't invite you to do that."

Lanie put her hand on his back, ushering him outside. "We're not taking over, Officer. You said yourself, you're short on help this time of year. Feather is offering you a tremendous gift. Take it with humility."

The young officer who obviously felt great respect for Lanie, nodded. "Okay, I guess as long as you don't tell my chief that this is how I solve mysteries. I came up here earlier in the week to make sure I understood the lay of the land. He told me to make sure I documented everything I found odd and report back to him." He pointed at Feather. "She's not going in that report."

Their muffled voices continued until they were in the hallway and the door slammed shut. The abruptness of the sound made Feather jump. It was only a few seconds before the hairs on her arms rose.

"Yes, I'm listening. Go ahead."

She closed her eyes, overwhelmed by the crowd of

urgent voices surrounding her. Some wanted messages given to their loved ones. Others were angry about their deaths. Still more wanted revenge. It was hard to decipher which one was Dash.

Candy Canes and stockings. Eggnog and good cheer.

"What?" she replied out loud, annoyed. "I don't do well with riddles."

Fruitcake and elves. Sugar cookies with dark beer.

"You're going to have to help me out. If you want the circumstances of your death made public, you'd better hurry up. Me and my boyfriend are leaving in two days, or maybe even less."

Reluctantly, she opened the desk drawer and pulled out a pad and pen to write down these nonsensical phrases.

"Get it over with!"

Roasted nuts. Yams and glitter.
Find the clue, don't make me bitter.

She bit her lip, trying hard to be patient with this irritating entity.

"Okay, I've written your silly rhyme. I'm not sure if you're toying with me, or if this is serious. Is there anything else you can tell me about the murder? I know you were a very famous man. There had to be many people who were jealous of you. I loved your books, and—"

The pen and paper went flying across the room, slamming into the wall beside the bed. Instantly, her head filled with Christmas carols being sung so loud her head was vibrating.

She slapped her hands over her ears, as if outside pressure would quiet what was coming from within. "Stop! Stop this instant!"

She'd dealt with angry entities before. Once, when she was thirteen, she was visiting her cousin in Portland. It was a sweltering night and they slept with the windows open.

The white, muslin curtains danced daintily in the breeze. That was the last thing she remembered before drifting off to sleep. The next thing she knew, she was being slapped in the face.

Once. Twice. When she opened her eyes, there was no one else there. Feather was certain she was dreaming. She sat up, only to be knocked over and pushed off the bed.

So scared she couldn't speak, she grasped the only thing within reach—a nightstand–and held on tightly. The next morning, she awoke with her head on the bottom shelf of the nightstand. Her fingers were numb, and she couldn't feel her toes.

Her cousin asked if she'd heard the thunderstorm too. Feather nodded. It was their great-grandfather who hated children. He didn't want them in his house. She didn't have the heart to tell her cousin.

That experience was frightening, but not as scary as this one.

"If you can't be nice, I'm leaving. Do you understand me? Dash Vixen does not scare me! I don't care who you were in life, I won't help you!"

Her head filled with the sound of running water. It

was so loud, she put her hands over her ears. Realizing she was holding it in rather than letting it out, she screamed, "Stop!"

When Feather released her ears, the noise stopped instantly. Her curiosity too strong to ignore, she opened the bathroom door, an appropriately squeaky one, and walked inside on her tip toes.

Dash was found on the floor, by the desk. There was no evidence he had fought off his attacker in the bathroom. Still...

She pulled the shower curtain back, expecting a surprise dead body. Instead, the water turned on by itself.

"Did you drown? You must not be Dash, like I thought." She leaned carefully over the side of the tub, her spikey red head as far forward as she could go. At that moment, the water pressure changed and the shower kicked on, soaking her completely.

"For the love of..." Feather jumped up, shaking her wet head and splattering water all over the room. She knew a little something about crime scenes. Nothing should be disturbed until they found every last piece of evidence. Water all over the floor may destroy a key piece.

"Okay. We're done. When you're ready to play nice, I'll come back." She grabbed a towel from the rack above the toilet and dried her hair.

Dash is gone, his soul is still,
Answer this rhyme to find who can kill.

"Lanie! Officer Holliday! Please come in now!" She called anxiously.

Making sure she hadn't missed anything, she closed the bathroom door and stepped out.

"Ma'am, we ask that you don't shower in the crime scene," Officer Holliday admonished her.

Feather finished patting her shirt, drying herself as best she could.

"What did you find? Did Dash show you his death? I've read that happens sometimes," Lanie asked eagerly.

"No, unfortunately. This entity is rather, well for lack of a better term, mean. And it's presence here is strong. It's not Dash."

"So, we're back where we started," Officer Holliday said with disappointment, leaning toward Lanie.

"Not quite. The entity repeated several phrases that I wrote down. I want to speak with them again, when they've learned their manners. Dash's death is connected to Elle's. I know that for sure. I believe Elle died in her bathtub. Christmas lights thrown in the tub to electrocute her."

"And this?" Lanie pointed to her wet head. "I assume you weren't intending on getting wet."

"Nope. This entity guided me into the bathroom and then doused me in the shower. This one's a real jerk." Feather rolled her eyes, hoping Lanie understood she was more upset with the entity than Lanie herself.

"Oh, dear. I have lots to learn about the spirit world. While you experienced that unpleasantness, I did some research. You already knew all of this, but I wanted to make sure I was up to speed. Dash and Elle released a Christmas horror anthology together with four other authors, called *Strung by the Fire*. I learned that besides Dash and Elle, one other person, Ivy Globe, has died. Not a coincidence, I'm sure.?"

"I found your pizza box." Autumn reappeared, wiping her gloved hands on her apron. "Just a random bunch of numbers, written over and over."

She's hiding something.

"And behind your back?" Feather asked, holding her hand out expectantly.

Autumn shook her head, but reluctantly, produced a large book. It was at least five inches tall and eight inches wide. The spine was broken and it was covered in coffee stains, cheese–and blood. The title of the book was *Strung by the Fire.*

"That must be the murder weapon!" Lanie gasped. "Dash Vixen was killed...by his own book!"

"That must be the murder weapon!" Lanie gasped. "Dash Vixen was killed...by his own book!"

Chapter Seven — Lanie

As much as I sometimes hated to admit it, the thought of another mystery to solve really got my juices flowing. I broke it gently to Cos the night before. "Hon, this death at the resort has been really curious. We'd hate to have another serial killer on the loose."

He rolled his eyes. "Christopher Comet was just passing through. He didn't kill anyone."

"But he may have, if the gas station owner hadn't recognized him," I protested. Cos, while being very supportive, was also something of a skeptic. I think that's how he kept himself from worrying about my safety.

"This is really impressive, Lanie."

Feather walked around the massive electronic white board Vem had gifted me recently. I could write on it directly or use my tablet. It was the most practical gift she'd ever given me, next to the herb concoction to cure my athletes foot. Whatever type of animal excrement she'd used really did the trick.

"Yes, it's a fun tool. I took the liberty of writing down the names of all of the authors so we can research each one. I included the stories they contributed to the Christmas horror anthology for reference. The authors still alive are likely in danger. I'd hate for our inaction to lead to their deaths."

Feather nodded and sat down on my cushy office chair, ergonomically correct. It was a parting gift from my old employer, *Work Ahead Office Supplies, the Most Successful Office Supply Chain in the World.*

"Ivy Globe, age twenty-six. Wrote, *Snowily Severed.* Died October twenty-fifth. Impaled on a rooftop ornament that slid off a roof and through her car window."

A shiver ran through my body. That was a horrid way to go. "I forgot to add that when the fire department extracted her, she was surrounded a string of cranberries. Just like Dash."

I scribbled furiously.

"Elle Vanashelve, age forty-two. Wrote, *Red Velvet Death.* Died on November twenty-second in her bathtub, surrounded by Christmas lights. Publicly criticized our most current victim, Dash Vixen about his close relationship with the producer in charge of their upcoming movie, according to *Horror Hound Dog Daily.* I would be suspicious that Dash had Elle murdered. But then, who killed Dash?"

"Lanie, are you noticing a loose pattern? Every

death has taken place around the same day of the month," Feather said. "That means the other three could be in danger on January twenty-second."

I had a bad feeling in the pit of my stomach. Feather was probably correct. Normally it wouldn't be difficult to contact people, but it was the holiday season. People to travel and tracking down the whereabouts of the other authors could take more time than we had.

"We may have to divide and conquer. With the holiday almost upon us, we don't have much time to work. If we each pick—"

"An author, we can save time."

We both jumped, unaware that my best friend had made her entrance.

Today she was decked out in forest green. Her headband, glasses frames and one-piece suit were all in compliment of one another. She'd recently begun using a homemade styling gel that tamed her wild curls from tumbleweed to controlled roller coaster.

"Feather Jones, this is my friend and neighbor, November Bean."

"Ah, a fellow strange namer." Vem shook her hand so vigorously that Feather's head bobbed.

"Nice to meet you," Feather replied shyly.

"Vem, Feather is our guest for the holidays. She and her boyfriend—"

"Were scheduled to stay in the Happy Lover's Suite, but there was a murder in their room. Wendell is in my Moaning for Merriness class. Nothing gets by me."

She stared at Feather intently. I tried placing myself between them, but when Vem was focused on something or someone, her body became immovable. Feather held her ground.

Vem leaned in close—too close—and sniffed. The poor girl's upper lip curled and I could see the terror on her face.

"You smell like...old people." Vem leaned back and pivoted toward me. "Why would she smell like old people?"

"Your grandmother says she knew there would be someone in the family who inherited her great sense of smell. Caffie Bean watches you every day. She's extremely proud."

Vem's mouth dropped open. A silence enveloped the room like no other. I'd never seen her completely speechless in all of our time together. I couldn't decide if I should enjoy it or end it.

"You're... a..."

"I hear the dead. They just pop in and out. I like your grandmother's energy. She's feisty and independent. She also says something about an old family chili recipe."

Vem snapped her fingers. "That's what I was smelling! The room after a pot of Bean's Gassy Gumption Chili! Girlfriend, you really do have the gift! And by the by, it's my ex's grandmother. She always loved me more than him and it drove him nuts. My ex, the toilet paper king was a real jerk, who–"

"That can wait, Vem."

Her horror stories about her ex-husband sometimes ran on for over an hour. My friend would, no doubt have a million questions for poor Feather and we didn't have the time for her to answer each one. "Vem, we need to return to the task at hand. Did you hear all of our conversation? We need to contact these authors right away. I don't want to hear about another death knowing we could have prevented it."

"That's all fine and good, Lanie, but what should I say when I make the call? I know you're going to die?"

"No, just tell your author we're investigating these deaths and want them to know someone might make another attempt on the twenty-third of January."

"How do we find their phone numbers? Famous people like that hide their personal information," Feather asked.

"We could contact Gladys," Vem suggested.

"She's down in California for their big family celebration."

"No worry, Lanie and new little rouge-headed friend. I can do it. I have more money than anyone in this town. If that doesn't buy me someone's privacy, I don't know what will." Vem stood. "What are you waiting for? Follow me."

Feather and I trailed behind her obediently, each removing our shoes before entering her home. Despite her wild appearance, Vem lived an immaculate lifestyle.

Her home was a showpiece of modern art mixed with old movie posters. Two style magazines had done feature pieces on her home and she prided herself on the fact that both photographers got lost trying to find their way out.

We walked upstairs and into a room Vem called her almost-guest room. She opened the closet to display hundreds of jumpsuits of every minute shade of the rainbow. Attached to each suit was a matching headband and a glasses case in a bag looped over the top. Each hangar was labeled above with the name of the exact hue. There were corresponding sneakers underneath each color group.

It was a big enough closet I could have fit my entire kitchen table and dinner guests inside. She parted the hangars, between the Shamrock and Seafoam green and exposed a door.

"Vem! Why haven't you shown me this before?"

November put her hands on her hips defiantly. "If I told you everything about me, Lanie, then there would be no mystery to our relationship. I'd like to keep that vibe going, if you please."

She bent over and took her glasses off, aligning her eye with the keyhole. Immediately, the door buzzed and opened.

We walked into what could only be described as a government intelligence room. It was filled with computers and monitors, each one showing a different city around the world. There was one large screen in the middle that said NOVEMBER INTEL across the front. I had to pinch myself to make sure I wasn't dreaming. This was bizarre, even for her.

She sat down at a computer and typed furiously. In a moment, a computer-generated version of November Bean appeared. It was wearing exactly the same outfit as the real-life version.

"When I sat down, the computer assessed my outfit and made sure the shape of my face was correct. It changes my outfits to correspond with what I'm wearing. And you're probably feeling relieved."

"Why are we relieved?" I asked.

"Because if I had some strange swelling or something else that made me unrecognizable, it would have vaporized you."

She continued typing, oblivious to the seriousness of what she'd just confessed.

"There. I'm in. Tell me the names of the authors we're contacting."

"Okay, but first, I can't get past the fact that you've never shown me all of this equipment before. I wouldn't have to bother Gladys if I'd known I could just come over here."

"Lanie, you don't want to make Gladys feel useless, do you? Let's give the old broad something to keep her busy. And I didn't have all of the equipment until I went to the big auction in California. It cost me a pretty penny, but it's safe to say I could fund an entire espionage operation now."

Feather pulled out her phone, where she'd typed out the names of the authors.

"The first currently living author is Holly Garland, author of *Snowily Severed*."

After typing at the speed of light, putting in all of her top secret codes, she now poked with one finger at the keyboard, stopping and erasing several times. Finally, she had all of the letters typed in.

"I'll find that for you, November Bean," the artificial version of her, wearing a nametag that said, "Gorgeous Bean," announced before disappearing behind an animated door.

"Can I go on the record saying she is a little creepy? Maybe you could change her appearance a little."

"I had a Lanie version, but she was just too bossy."

The A.I. reappeared, carrying a tray with a note on it.

"Please read the information," November commanded.

"Yes, of course. And may I say, you are looking stunning today? Your whole ensemble really works!"

I rolled my eyes. It was all making sense.

"Holly Garland lives at one, one, two, seven Wilmont Drive. Her home phone is—"

"Wait a sec," Feather fumbled with her phone. "I want to write this down."

"No need. She's transferring the number to your phonebook as we speak."

Feather opened her phone and her eyes widened with awe. "That's a little frightening. I have no privacy!"

"Go ahead, Gorgeous. What's the second one?"

"Don Wenow, author of *Possession of the Pine*, I can also pinpoint his location, if you like."

"Yes, I like. Go ahead, you stunning beast."

I chuckled. *Only Vem.*

A map appeared on the screen and it zoomed into the Fallen Branch Resort.

"He's...here? Is he our killer?" I turned to Feather, hoping she had a connection to some spirit offering insight.

"I don't know. When I was there yesterday, I was shoved around by someone powerful. The name 'Don Wenow' doesn't seem to fit."

Feather looked like a young child who had just hurt the feelings of her favorite adult. "It doesn't mean I'm right though."

"Let's go talk to him anyway."

"Lanie, what about our final living author, Nick Chestnut?"

"I've changed my mind. I think we should investigate them one at a time, both living and dead. First, we pay a visit to Don Wenow."

Chapter Eight—Lanie

"Remember, let me do the talking."

I don't know why I wasted my breath. Vem wasn't the type to hold her tongue. Even the time she had laryngitis she croaked responses when I'd asked to be in charge. You couldn't dim that candle, no matter how hard you tried.

"Lanie, I'm always your back up. Don't you know that by now? You're the brains of the operation."

She patted my back before clasping her hands innocently behind her.

I knocked on the door for the second time. We were about to turn and leave when a gruff-looking man wearing only a hotel robe opened the door. His hair, grey, not a salt-and-pepper like Cos's but a flat, dull grey, was parted haphazardly to the side. His face had at least two days' growth and he wreaked of fast food.

"Mr. Wenow? I'm Lanie Anders Hill. This is my

friend, November Bean. Would you mind if we asked you a few questions about your Christmas horror anthology? It's been on the bestseller list for six months and still going strong. As soon as I'd heard you were here, I suggested to Vem–November–that we come and speak with you. She's got a local paper called Bean's Happenings and she'd love to run a column on you."

That was much more than I'd intended to say. I was waiting for Vem to interrupt, and when she didn't I carried on, ad-libbing as I went.

He stared at us with intense, beady brown eyes.

"Yeah, I suppose." Don ran his fingers through his greasy hair. "Do you want to do it here?"

I shuddered at the thought of doing an interview with this man clothed only in his robe. "We'd happily buy you a coffee or a drink at the bar, Shall we say, ten minutes?"

He shrugged. "Whatever."

The door shut as abruptly as it had opened.

"Do you think he'll show?" Vem asked.

"Hard to say. I wasn't going to sit in his room, so if we missed an opportunity, it wasn't meant to be."

Right now I regretted my decision to leave Feather at home. I'd suggested a walk in the woods to clear her head but right now, I needed her ability to leverage people with information about their past.

We took the elevator to the first floor and walked down a long corridor, until we reached the pool area, where a tiki bar stood. It was decorated in festive

Christmas lights with stockings, each with the name of an employee, hanging above the booth.

Charlie, the most recent hire, was delegated to holiday duty. "Hi, Mrs. Hill," he called in his half-lower register, half-higher state of speech.

"Hi, Charlie. We're expecting a guest named Don Wenow. When he arrives, can you tell him we're waiting in the restaurant?"

"Sure thing, Mrs. Hill."

We found comfortable chairs and sat down after ordering two coffees. It was always a little scary ordering fully-caffeinated coffee with November. She was full of energy, no matter what time of day or night. The addition of caffeine sometimes made her speech so quick no one could understand her.

"Are you sure you don't want decaf, Vem? I think it's when you're at your sharpest," I suggested.

"No, that will not work on me this morning. I know you don't like my aura when I'm fully energized, but you may need it today."

She slurped down one cup and ordered another. I swallowed hard. "I wonder if he'll show. We may need to find a different angle."

"Sorry I'm late, ladies. My agent called. There's an offer to buy my story."

Don pulled out a chair and sat down beside me, smelling like a pine tree, a considerable improvement over our first meeting.

"That's exciting, Mr. Wenow."

"Please, call me Don. He scooted close to the table and his hands brushed mine.

"I'm Lanie Anders Hill. This is–"

"November Bean. Reporter, Yoga Instructor, Master Moaner, and Lanie's right hand. Well, I suppose I'm her left hand too. I'm multi-dexterous that way."

I was relieved when she stopped to take a breath.

"Don, who is buying your book?"

"It's a company that only produces horror films. They're called Brain Gravy Pictures. I'm sure you've heard of them. They just released–"

"The Beast that ate Beech Street. It grossed just over seven million last week. Of course, it was much smaller than their opening weekend, but they've made their investment back and hope to make a sequel. I did my homework, Lanie."

I studied Vem for warning signs. Her eyes were displaying surprise, a hint that soon she would hit her over-caffeinated stride.

"You must be thrilled. Is this your first offer?"

The server came over and he waved her off. "I only drink when I'm writing," he explained to us. "Coffee or booze, it doesn't matter. No, this is a new book Our anthology movie is coming out next Christmas. It's going to be a huge success, judging by the number of books we've sold." He paused and looked at us expectantly.

"Wow," I replied with little enthusiasm.

"Dash Vixen, one of the other authors in the anthology, has been stubborn about signing on. He doesn't want any one of us to have success unless he's sure he has more. Last month, I had a company contact me about making Fruitcake Murders into a movie, and when Dash got wind of it, he told them, falsely, that I'd already signed with someone else. The man is intolerable."

"Why would he do that?"

Don shrugged. "That's the way Dash operates. He's only here for himself. If he gets a whiff that someone else might find more success, he's immediately got to squash it. That was the main reason I hesitated before signing on for the anthology. His reputation precedes him."

Vem hopped up from the table and did two sets of fifteen squats. I hoped Don wouldn't ask her why.

"Why did you sign on for the anthology if Dash is so disagreeable?"

"The publisher was quite persuasive, you might say." He smiled in a way that made me a little queasy.

"So, Dash killed the new movie deal for you," I continued, trying to divert his attention away from her. "What about everyone else? Poor Ivy? And Elle? Did he interfere with their deals? And what about Strung by the Fire?

"Ivy didn't want the Christmas anthology turned into a movie. She never really explained why, just that she didn't want to deal with Brain Gravy. I'm not sure why she eventually changed her mind. Elle was a prima donna, so everything with her took extra work. And

Nick, he's interesting. He was very enthusiastic about the entire project, and then, abruptly, he dropped out of sight."

"What do you mean, 'dropped out of sight?'"

"Exactly what I said. The man came to our author dinner party and three weeks later, he was in the wind. The owner of Brain Gravy knew him before, apparently. He said Nick was like that. We authors are a curious bunch. Some are quite outgoing. Others can be downright odd. I'm glad I don't fall into either category. And I need to correct you. The movie is in preproduction. Brain Gravy's lawyers are trying to find a way to work around Dash."

"Were you surprised by Ivy and Elle's deaths?'

Don raised an eyebrow and leaned in far too close. "I thought you wanted to interview me? Your friend is doing laps around the pool and you haven't asked one question about my writing process. What's really going on here?"

I glanced over at Vem, who was eliciting hoots and hollers from the kids in the pool as she jogged by them. Each round, she bent down and gave them a high five as she passed them. At least she was occupied.

"Dash was murdered yesterday. Right here, in this hotel. Our police chief is out of town over the holidays and I've helped him before, so I offered to check out hotel guests." I studied him carefully, but if he had prior knowledge of Dash's death, he was doing a good job of hiding it.

I took a long sip of my coffee, hoping Vem's loud

activities didn't interfere with our conversation. "It surprised me when I learned you were staying here too. It is quite the coincidence, you'll have to admit."

He placed his hairy hand on the table, our pinkies touching. If I removed mine, he may take it as a sign I'm not strong enough to withstand his silly games. I left my hand and stared him straight in the eye.

"Why are you here at the same time as Dash, Mr. Wenow?"

A creepy smile crept over his face. "You fashion yourself an amateur detective? Isn't that lovely. I may have to include you in my next book. Let's see, how shall I kill you? A knife to the sternum? Or perhaps a bullet right between those glistening eyes?"

"We're in public, Mr. Wenow. There are cameras everywhere. You would never be that sloppy. Your sleazy attempt at distracting me isn't going to work. Why are you here?"

He pulled his hand back and placed it in his lap. I'd never felt like I needed a shower more.

"Yes, I was here to see Dash. We have group chats online every week. Well, what's left of the group. Elle and Ivy are dead, and Nick's in the wind. At the last one, Dash mentioned he'd be here for the holidays. He has a relative in the area. I followed him."

"Because he'd threatened you somehow?"

"Because I didn't tell you the whole story about our contract. We never thought the book would be such a success. Most of us were struggling authors before the anthology came out, so when we signed off on a movie deal, we agreed to a contract that in the event of our deaths, all rights to our stories would revert to Brain Gravy Studios. That meant they would have complete control over a sequel, or whatever else they wanted to do with it. Dash refused."

"So, you did see him?"

Vem was now forming a conga line with several soppy swimmers. She was singing a heavy metal song she'd recently found online and they were following suit. If I wasn't in the middle of such a serious conversation, it would be amusing entertainment.

"Yes, I did. I took him out for dinner. In the middle of the most perfect steak I've ever seen in my life, he got up and threw the table over. He was drunk, or maybe just being Dash. He said he would not put up with our tactics anymore. Then he stormed out."

"When did you have dinner with Dash?"

"The night before last. I've been in my room ever since, working on my next novel. If you're insinuating that I was somehow involved, I can assure you, I had nothing to do with his death."

"I don't believe I mentioned how he died. Why would you assume he was murdered?"

He stood abruptly. "This farce of an interview is over." Don walked over to the side of the pool, where November was rapping Christmas carols, and shoved her hard.

Chapter Nine — Lanie

"Well, I never. The nerve of that man, giving me a shove without so much as a, 'You're looking especially festive, Ms. Bean.' I thought holiday spirit was implied today. Isn't it implied, Lanie?"

"I can help you clean up the—whatever it is—in the ladies' room," I replied, keeping my voice at an even tone. Don, feeling offended or maybe getting the clue that I wasn't interested in him, walked over to Vem and attempted to push her into the pool. He had no idea what kind of physical strength she possessed, and instead of knocking her in the pool, he caused poor Charlie to lose his balance and spill a cranberry cocktail on Vem's jumpsuit.

He wasn't getting away this easily.

When Vem had removed the stain as best she could —thankfully today was a red-themed day, she met me outside of the restroom.

"Can't even tell!" I said in my cheeriest tone.

"Hmph. I've got a mind to tell that hairy has-been off. You'll wait for me, Lanie?"

For once, I agreed with her. "I believe we should go back to his room. He thinks because we're women he can push as around—literally."

Vem smiled with satisfaction. "Great! I'll go into the cleaning closet and find something sharp."

"No, we won't be needing weapons of that kind. We've got words that are better weaponry."

She stared at me, puzzled.

When we reached his door, I knocked, timidly at first and then with force. The more I thought about his behavior, the angrier I became. I would knock all night, if that was what it took.

Finally, the door flew open. "What!"

Don Wenow was wearing a men's swimsuit that came up to just below his armpits. On his head, a bright blue swimming cap covered his dreadful hair entirely and he held purple goggles in his hand.

"Before you go to the pool, we need to talk."

He shifted his weight to one foot and crossed his arms. "And what makes you think I'll say any more to you, lady? I've chewed up assistants half your age and spat them on the ground without a thought."

Ignoring his attempt to belittle me, I cleared my throat. "First, you owe my friend an apology. I don't care who you are, you have no right to—"

"I'm sorry I tried to push this crazed woman in the pool," he replied, making a brushing motion and not even glancing at Vem. "Is that all? "Did your assistants know you'd been hacking into their emails?"

His face became as pale as his chest. "I have no idea what you're talking about." He attempted to close the door, but Vem's quick reflexes were too much for him. She lodged her foot firmly between the door and his puffy body.

"We're not leaving until we have a real discussion, Mr. Wenow. We could stay here all night, order room service and charge it to you, whatever it takes," Vem said. "And you're not strong enough to take me down. Words or bodily." She smiled at me with satisfaction. "Isn't that right, Lanie?"

"Absolutely, Vem. Are you going to let us in, or do we need to stand here, making a scene all evening? At the very least, you owe my friend a heartfelt apology for your rude behavior."

Reluctantly, Don held the door open and we walked inside. When it clicked shut, he placed one hand on his hip. "Now you're going to tell me about your hocus pocus."

"I will do that. But first, I need to know everything about Elle Vanashelve's husband. Don't leave anything out, or I'll be forced to share with your agent that you erased emails from prospective clients last week."

"Brooks? I barely know him." He flipped his hand dismissively.

"That's how we're playing this game? While I was waiting for you to answer the door, I sent a text to my friend, Feather. She's been able to uncover some interesting information about you, Don. Including the fact that you've been hacking your agent's email as well. She's happy to call him, if I give her the word."

Feather and her abilities were proving to be priceless to our investigation.

"All right, all right. I get it. You're some kind of mind reader. I've seen your type before, though they are usually not as good as you. It's an old party trick and I've used it a hundred times in my books."

Don sat down on the edge of the bed.

"Elle and I met when we were young writers. We'd both just finished our first novels and met at a conference. She was exquisite in everything she did—hair, makeup, decorating, writing. We decided to keep in touch, which we did for almost a decade. I'd never met anyone with her panache. And then at the writer's conference, I met Brooks. I was smitten."

Vem gasped dramatically. "I've heard this story before. My ex, the toilet paper king, had the same kind of roving eye."

"Vem," I warned, shooting her a look of caution.

"Elle came from money. She financed Brain Gravy and all ten of their films. Brooks was grateful, but he didn't love her."

"Are you telling me her husband killed her? For her money?"

"Gracious, child. Where did you get that idea? Brooks could never kill another living soul. He was planning to end things with her after he signed all of us from *Strung by the Fire* to a picture deal. Some of the authors, like Dash, were being greedy. He was holding out for more money because, well, because he was Dash. He wasn't any more talented than the rest of us."

"Brooks was waiting until the contracts were signed to...run away with you?"

Don sighed. "That was my dream. But he never said that directly. He made it seem like he was more interested in Elle's assistant, Trudy Seasons. I always thought it was a ruse. Then, after Elle's unfortunate death, he quit communicating with me."

"She died in the bathtub, right?"

Don nodded. "Christmas lights electrocuted her, unfortunately. Poor dear. Shall I continue my story, or are you going to lead this conversation?"

"Go ahead, please."

"We met in the bar that night at the writer's conference. Sir Nicolas' Grog, if I recall. He was drunk, we were all drunk. He pitched this idea to us to create horror stories all based in some way a maniacal lumber yard owner from the turn of last century.. He said it was guaranteed to be a hit, if we'd agree to base our stories on this historical figure. No one would be dim enough to turn that down."

Chapter Ten — Feather

"I'm surprised to hear from you," The deep, smooth-as-butter voice of her mentor, Jayden Ko purred into the phone. "Last I knew, you and Tug were on a romantic holiday. Did that fall through?"

Feather chuckled to herself. Jayden was gifted with not one, but two talents. She spoke to the dead and also had the ability to read the minds of the living. "The moment you picked up the phone, you knew that, Jayden."

"Yes, I did." Jayden sighed. "Sometimes I play along, just because I want to partake in normal conversation."

Jayden Ko wore cat suits and exquisite wigs. She was a stunning wonder who always turned heads when she walked down the street. Where some would have hidden their true selves under the cover of darkness, Jayden proudly displayed her style.

"In all of our phone calls, you've never mentioned that before," Feather replied. "I've always admired your ability to stand out in a crowd without feeling out of place. I wish I was better at embracing my...uniqueness."

"It will come. If we figured out our personal puzzle right away, there'd be no reason to get up every day." Jayden chuckled, a deep throaty laugh that always caught Feather off guard. "So, why don't you tell me, from your perspective, why you called me today? Tired of decking the halls and all that?"

"Well, you already know there was a murder in the room we were supposed to occupy. Then this nice lady invited us to stay at her home. It's massive, and–"

"Feather Jones! The reason you called, please! I have my own holiday activities!"

"Yes, sorry." Feather reset herself, somewhat flustered. "Last night, when we were checking in to the resort, I heard many voices. It's on the grounds of a former cult, a place where lots of pain and suffering happened, so I wasn't surprised. But nowhere in that sea of voices did I hear a murder victim. Today, I wanted to check out the room where the murder occurred, and I was pushed up against a wall by an entity."

"That's unusual. For you, anyway. Your connections are polite in nature, even if their message is harsh."

"Right? It was the strongest entity I'd ever encountered. No matter what I said, it would not leave. It kept whispering nonsensical rhymes. And Jayden, I'm positive it wasn't Dash—that's the murder victim. Maybe not even the person who hit him over the head with a book."

Jayden was silent. Feather knew she was trying to reach Dash herself.

"He was killed by a...book? That's a new one."

Feather didn't reply, hoping to give her the silence she needed to concentrate.

"Hmm. Give me a minute. I'm going to set the phone down and see what I can find out for you."

Feather waited patiently with complete confidence in Jayden's ability to suss out the truth.

After five minutes that felt like an hour, Jayden returned. "Okay, I'm seeing a cloudy picture. Dash is very sure of himself. He's told the front desk he's not to be bothered by fans. When he opens the door, he invites this person inside. Does he know them? I'm not sure. But he's at ease, so when they hit him over the head, it comes as a complete surprise."

"Is that all?"

There was no way she'd be able to solve this in one day if Jayden didn't offer more information.

"No, unfortunately. The person who hit Dash was under some kind of control. An evil presence."

"Are you telling me that this person was in a...trance?"

"Not a trance, but without the urging of this entity, the murder never would have happened. It's the same entity that attacked you. And Feather, there's more than one person under this entity's spell."

"Oh boy. That sounds complicated, more so than anything I've dealt with before."

"Whatever evil forces are there with you have blocked me from seeing more. This one is extremely dangerous, Feather. To you and your entire party."

It hadn't occurred to her that Lanie and Cosmo might be in harm's way. "What can I do?"

"I want you to carry a weapon on you at all times. Bear spray, a knife, whatever is available to you."

"Am I going to encounter a murderous bear?" Feather joked. "No wonder Dash doesn't want you to see his murderer. He's embarrassed he let a wild animal into his room."

"Human spirits of this magnitude are far more dangerous than nature."

"Wouldn't it be easier if you told me what those were?"

She could hear Jayden tapping her nails on her glass desktop. "You know me as the answer to all of your questions. Unfortunately, today those are lacking. I can't see your future, nor can I see the person or persons who wish to harm you. Instead, I have a vision of your sense of being extracted from your body, and then, darkness. It makes me feel like I'm suffocating."

This wasn't the first time Jayden had foretold an unpleasant encounter, but it was certainly the most graphic.

"Can you at least tell me what day, or where I'll be?"

"All I know is that the darkness is almost upon you."

"Well, THAT sounds ominous." As much as Feather tried to make light of her situation, she was scared.

"It is, I'm afraid. And to answer the question forming in your head, yes this entity is a danger because of your gift." Jayden sighed. "But also, because of your gift, you have the ability to protect others from it."

"Thank you, Jayden. I wish we could solve this right now."

"I have confidence that you will eventually. Please, please watch out. I've got to run, love. We'll talk soon."

The phone went silent.

So many thoughts swirled around in her head. How was she going to protect everyone, all at once? Lanie, Cosmo, November, and Cosmo's friend Truman were too many people to keep track of, let alone her beloved Tug.

Chapter Eleven — Lanie

"Any luck with your mentor?"

"Not really."

Feather's gaze fell to the floor. I couldn't tell if she was sad or didn't want to share the results of her conversation. Either way, I wanted to wrap my arms around her and soothe her troubled heart.

"Thanks for finding me. I'm not used to walking in the woods."

"No problem, hon. Vem put a tracking device on my phone for just that reason. I can connect us, if you like?"

Her cheeks burned. It was embarrassing. "Yes, please." She handed her phone to Lanie, who spent a few minutes tapping buttons.

"There. All set. You can find me and I can find you. Just tap on the Lanie Locator on your home screen."

Feather glanced at the app, still feeling ashamed. It

was her generation, not Lanie's that was supposed to have all of the technological acuity.

"Vem! Could you join us in here, please? I found information on one of the dead authors. Maybe we all should read it."

I wiggled the mouse to keep it active. "You know, Feather, I'm so glad you're helping us, but you don't have to feel obligated. You and your boyfriend were supposed to be relaxing and we've put you both to work."

This young woman with the vibrant, red hair and combat boots struck me as someone who, like me, hadn't been mothered properly. I wanted to take her in my arms and hug her until the hurt was gone.

"Oh, it's fine, Lanie, really." She crossed one leg over the other and smiled. "We can always come back later in the year. It took me a long time before I made peace with my gift. When I did, I realized how much it could help people. Now that I have the opportunity to do that, it feels good."

I wasn't convinced that anything felt good for the poor girl right now.

I clucked my tongue sympathetically. "It must've been a lonely childhood with your gift. I looked like a famous person, so my mother forced me to perform at our mall every weekend. I was different and I hadn't asked to be."

Vem bounced into the room, jelly dripping from her hands.

"You know I did just have the rugs cleaned?"

It never ceased to amaze me how her home remained immaculate. She was the messiest person I knew.

"Yes, you mentioned that. 'Five hundred dollars is far too much.'" Vem's voice rose to a level that was too high to be mine, but I knew that was her intent. "It's robbery, that's what it is!"

Feather giggled in the corner, quickly covering her mouth with her hand. It was good to see her letting loose, even if it was just a little.

"Sorry. It caught me off guard."

"That's all right, hon. She teases me all the time. I've gotten used to it." I gave Vem a stern look and returned to the computer.

"This article is about Ivy Globe's death. She was a cute little thing." I moved the mouse over to a picture of the young author. With a tuft of cotton-white hair over her dark brows, she appeared about the same age as Feather. Her eyes were bright and full of life, and she had a smattering of freckles dusting her small nose.

Vem stood uncomfortably close and read aloud:

Ivy Merrilee Globe was a prolific author, completing seventy-nine books in her twenty-six years of life. Her most recent, Snowily Severed, was a short story featured in the massively popular Christmas horror anthology, Strung by the Fire.

She recently signed a contract with Brain Gravy Pictures to turn her short story into a movie.

Driving home from physical therapy, she stopped for children crossing three blocks from her home, when her neighbor's sleigh ornament slid off the roof of their home and through her car windshield, impaling her. Ivy herself couldn't have written such a dramatic end.

Ivy leaves behind three brothers and a cat named Ice.

"She didn't die on the twenty-second like the other two. Find the date of the Frosty attack, Lanie," Vem urged.

I typed in the information and when the page came up, our mood was somber. "Ivy was attacked on the twenty-second by the Frosty wannabe. They intended to kill her that day, and when it didn't work, they came back to finish the job."

"Poor Ivy," Vem lamented.

My phone rang and I jumped up to answer. Even though we'd been together for several years, I was always expecting his call.

"Babe?"

"Mrs. Hill? This is the Tucson police department."

My heart sunk. That was never good news, unless it was Boysie, calling to tell me he'd finished making my beef jerky.

"I'm afraid I've got some bad news. Do you have a relative named Sylas Hill?"

"Yes," I whispered.

"I'm sorry to inform you, Sylas and his wife, Tidbit were found dead today in a burning car outside of town."

"Oh no!" Shock and sadness filled me. I'd been so excited to finally have a relative who wasn't involved in crime or garden-variety crazy. "And what about Eloise? Their daughter?"

"We didn't know about that. There was no sign there was a child when we found the bodies. They were wrapped neatly in flame retardant Christmas wrap, their identification sitting on top. Oh, and there was a string of cranberries wrapped around each body. Someone spent some time staging this scene before setting it all on fire."

"That's just...awful."

I blinked away tears.

"Your address and phone number were sitting on the kitchen counter of their home, along with a single laptop and a box of crackers. Other than that, the place was cleaned out. Not a spec of furniture or clothing. Figured you'd know what was going on."

"I'm afraid I'm just as confused as you are. It sounds like they died before the car was set on fire. Do you have any idea what happened?"

"Preliminary results tell us they were bludgeoned with a large object." He chuckled. "Maybe a phone book?"

It couldn't be the same murder weapon used to kill Dash, could it?

"Will you let me know when you find Eloise? I'm worried about her."

"I will. We did a thorough scan of Sylas's email. No sign of this Eloise, but we found an unsent email to you."

Though I've never been superstitious, the last few

years taught me to pay attention when my body felt strange. I took a relaxing breath, trying to let go all the tension that had built up inside me but it was no use.

"Go ahead, officer. Read it to me."

"Dear Lanie, I'm surprised to hear from you. I knew of your existence, but that was all. Can you give me some time to think on this? It's not that I don't trust what you're saying, but I'd like to talk it over with my wife. Is that okay? All my best, Sylas."

When I'd contacted Sylas, he wrote back almost instantly with an enthusiastic, "Let's get together!" He must've had a change of heart. It was my mother's side, more than my father's, known for their impulsiveness.

"You'll let me know when you find Eloise?" I asked through my emotions.

"We sure will. And I'm sorry again for your loss, ma'am."

I felt a familiar hot breath on my neck and pivoted quickly, before Vem could frighten me.

"You know the cousin I've been talking about on our walks?"

"The one who told you he was coming for Christmas and then bailed?" Vem pushed her glasses up her nose. "Jerk."

"Well, that jerk is dead, alongside his wife. And Vem, here's the strange thing: they were wrapped in Christmas wrap. Doesn't that sound peculiar, given our most recent investigation?"

Vem slapped her leg. "I'll be an elf's uncle. That's insane!"

She leaned in closer and hugged me, her thick curls falling into my face. "I'm sorry, sister-friend. You've been so excited about this relationship."

"Thank you, Vem." No matter how strange her actions, she was always there when things got rough. "I suppose it wasn't meant to be. Besides, I've got a family here. All of you are the best." I wrapped my arms around her waist, hugging her tightly.

When she was done with emotion for today, she jumped back abruptly. "So, what happens now? I do own an armored tank. It's sitting in a storage facility in California, but we could fly in and drive it over to Arizona. It might make for a nice holiday diversion."

I smiled, thankful for her Vem-ness. "No, but I appreciate the offer. And after Christmas, we need to discuss this tank, and whatever else you purchased at this auction. I want to know about where you've got it stored and why you felt the need to purchase it." I took a deep breath and focused myself. "Two days until Christmas, so we have to work quickly. Everything will shut down and people will scatter, so we need to make as many contacts as possible."

"Right-o." Vem saluted me.

Chapter Twelve—Feather

Her last case involved a deceased grandmother who didn't approve of her granddaughter's intended spouse. Grandma was breaking glass objects around the house, only when her granddaughter's fiancé was present. Her unsuspecting granddaughter cut her foot more than once when she walked into a room.

Feather went into the home twice. The first time, she spoke with the grandmother and asked her to leave nicely. The grandmother was adamant she wasn't going anywhere.

The second time, she returned with stern words and a promise to bring in Jayden and others more powerful than herself to remove grandma, whether she wanted to go or not.

Grandma left, or at least, remained silent. The woman and her fiancé married, and Grandma promised Feather would pay for her interference.

One day, as she was driving down the street, Feather looked down for a moment and when her eyes returned to the road, there was an old lady walking across. She slammed on her breaks, nearly careening into a tree. When she got out, there was no one in sight.

It was a powerful reminder of what the spirit world could do. Until yesterday, she thought messing with her mind was the limit of their capabilities.

She picked up her phone and dialed the number November's creepy computer had transferred to her contact list.

"Miss Garland's personal assistant, can I help you?"

"Oh, I, uh..." It never entered her mind that someone else would answer the phone.

"I'm a friend of Miss Garland's. I'm actually Dash Vixen's personal assistant. He wanted me to call and ask her about—"

"She isn't signing with his production company. Dash can ask everyone he knows to call, and it won't happen."

"Excuse me? I think you've got me confused with—"

"You're Dash Vixen's assistant, at least his assistant this week. Last week it was someone named Tiffany, and the week before it was Mandy. He wants you to convince Miss Garland to sign over her rights to *Wonderland of the Damned* to him. It's not happening. Not with you, not with anyone. She's planning to sign with Brain Gravy."

"Okay, I get that. I wanted to ask her about—wait, did you say he has a new assistant every week?"

"Oh, doll. You're being played. I'm sure he's asked nicely if you'd stay late after work to discuss his favorite wines. Don't do it! He has cameras all over his place. He has this weird fetish where he gets off watching a woman drink wine and then he posts the videos online. That's why Mandy left. She confronted him and he refused to apologize or take them down."

"That's a little creepy."

"Honey, you don't know the half of it. Dash can't keep his hands or his thoughts to himself. He thinks because he's come into all of this money, he's untouchable. Well, I'm here to tell you—"

"What money? He's mentioned nothing to me."

The voice on the other end chuckled. "You really are that green?"

Feather said nothing. One lesson she'd learned from the spirit world, the more space you give them, the more they will inform.

"Dash was given a big bonus to get all of the authors on board for the movie. When he discovered his big bonus was really the same money everyone else was receiving, he decided he'd form his own production company. He refused to give back his advance, telling the other authors that Brain Gravy owed him that money for the privilege of working with him. Dash tried convincing the others to renege on their contracts too and join his new venture. He has no idea how much clout and money that takes. Anyway, Dash, being Dash, thought it was in the bag. Only, when he contacted Ivy, his wine photos had already victimized her. He posted them to a seedy online site and other creeps like Dash were emailing her all the time. She turned him down flat."

"When did this happen?"

"I can't really say. Maybe this summer?"

"Did Elle Vanashelve have the same reaction?"

"That one is even juicier. Elle and Dash had a brief fling. Not only did he have photos of her drinking wine, but he took them while she was in his bed. You can see how she wouldn't want that getting out."

"So, Dash was going to blackmail her into signing with his production company?"

"That's what her assistant said. But Elle died, rather recently, I think. All of her rights reverted to the publishing company, Dead on the Chimney Publications. Well, all except her anthology. Those rights went to Brain Gravy. It was in the contract."

"Let me guess, Dash wanted a piece of the action?"

"Something like that. The police questioned him regarding her death, but they never could pin anything on him. You should watch your back, honey."

"Dash is dead," Feather blurted. "There's no reason for me to worry."

"Oh," the assistant said with little enthusiasm. "What happened?"

"We really don't know all the details yet. You don't think—no, probably not."

"That my boss is responsible? I doubt it. She's away in the Caribbean."

"One more question, do you know the whereabouts of Nick Chestnut?"

"Nick is such a nice guy. He seemed excited about the prospect of their own production company, at least in the beginning. Then one day, he showed up at Holly's office looking like he was scared for his life. He said he wouldn't be signing anything, and that he was going out of the country for a while to get some rest. No one has heard from him since."

After the conversation with Holly Garland's assistant, Feather followed the voices of the living into the spacious den area, where Lanie and Vem were relaxing with a cup of hot cocoa.

"Dash has had a series of assistants who all left abruptly," she exclaimed before she'd fully entered the room. "According to Holly Garland's assistant, they've left because he's very difficult. Also, Dash had a fetish where he liked to watch women drinking wine and, well, he was just a big creep."

"I wasn't expecting that." Lanie replied.

When she'd explained everything, Lanie asked, "Why did it take so long for Dash to die? With so many enemies, he should have been the first one the killer found."

"I wish I knew. Do you mind if I walk around in the forest? To clear my head? Sometimes it takes a good dose of fresh air to get my thoughts together."

"Not at all, dear. Just stay on the path so you don't get lost."

"Do you really think that's safe, Lanie?" November asked with concern. "There's a lot of creatures roaming around out there, and you're just about the size for a good bite."

"She'll be fine, Vem. Keep your phone with you at all times, Feather. You call us if you need anything, okay?"

As Feather meandered down the forest path, she could hear the sounds of cars whizzing by on the highway and a sea lion bellowing to make his presence known.

This time when the hairs rose on her arms, she knew it wasn't from the breeze. She'd worked up a sweat and it would take more than a wisp of wind to calm it.

"Who are you?"

You can't see my face. Not until I'm ready.

"That's fine. I don't need to see you, but I need more information if you want my help. Are you connected to Lanie?"

Yes. We share a bond.

"I see." Feather had learned that any kind of emotion on her part could cause the spirit to leave before they'd finished their conversation, so she did her best to remain matter-of-fact.

"If you're here with Lanie, you must care deeply for her."

She's a part of me.

"Are you a relative?"

No.

"Now you've got me confused. Did you die here in Piney Falls?"

Stop them before they kill again.

"Who? A man or a woman?"

Either.

Feather's anger welled up inside her. She took a deep breath to calm herself. Spirits often spoke in riddles, but usually they tried just a little to get their message across. This one seemed to be playing games with her, though not in a violent way. "You may have died here or may not, and you have a connection to Lanie, but you aren't related. Did I get that right?"

Yes.

She continued on, relieved her only shoe-of-choice was the one comfortable enough to traipse through the woods.

"Is there someone else I can talk to? Someone who isn't afraid to show me who they are?"

She heard only the sound of rustling leaves for the next hundred yards. As Feather was about to turn around, a voice whispered in her ear, and she felt a sudden peace.

Chapter Thirteen—Lanie

"Slow down, hon. Tell me one thing at a time."

Lanie put one hand on Feather's chest, where the young woman's heart was beating so hard and fast her fingers bounced rhythmically up and down.

"I spoke with a spirit in the woods. Whoever it is, had a connection to this land. They said they wanted to help."

"Who was it?" Vem asked. "Did they smell like garlic?" Vem's phone buzzed, and she stepped out on the patio to answer it.

"They wouldn't say," Feather replied. "But they showed me a scene from an event that happened recently." She shook her head. It was the first time she'd experienced this, and she was fascinated.

"Dash was attending a party at Holly Garland's home. Dash excused himself, presumably using the bathroom. Instead, he went upstairs and leaned over the railing, videoing all the women in the room as they drank their beverages. He later posted to a fetish group that made the rounds on the internet. Holly was furious when she found out. Dash edited the video to look like she'd been a willing participant. She told her assistant to go through all of her books—there are over fifty—and write down every method of murder. She wanted to choose just the right one."

"Well. That is interesting, isn't it?" Lanie leaned back in her chair, staring up at the skylights in their gorgeous main room. "If Holly was our killer, she certainly didn't think things through. When the lab results come back on the anthology, there will no doubt be a link to whomever was holding it. With that many books published, wouldn't she come up with something more creative?"

Feather leaned forward in her chair, causing her legs to make a squeaking sound against the leather. "I thought of something, Lanie. Doesn't the resort have cameras? Shouldn't we be asking them for evidence?"

Lanie smiled and Feather could feel her insides warming up. Lanie had a gift too. She had the ability to make strangers feel like they'd known her all their lives.

"That's a good idea, Feather. Unfortunately, the cameras haven't worked since the place opened. Management has had two different companies try to fix the problem, but no one can seem to get it functional. There isn't a good explanation."

I'm not ready for you to see me.

Feather blinked rapidly. "Did I mention that the

spirit has a connection to you? I don't want to scare you."

"Hon, you have no idea how crazy life is here. If all of the mysteries in this little community haven't scared me off by now, nothing will. Go ahead."

"There's an entity that spends part of its time in the woods and part of its time at the resort. It's... someone connected to you."

Lanie tapped her fingers on the armrest. "I have a pretty intense past. I can only imagine who–"

"I don't get a sense you've met. It could be a relative who wants to keep their distance." Feather closed her eyes tightly.

When the time is right, love.

Feather shook her head. "This spirit is stubborn. I'm not sure when, or ever, we'll know who it is. I'm sorry."

The door swung open, and November Bean entered in a swirl of energy, nodding to Feather before gazing at Lanie.

"I have some big news!"

Vem plopped down on the floor beside Lanie's chair, sitting with her legs bent backward. Feather used to sit that way as a child, but as she'd grown, her legs didn't move that direction. In fact, no adult Feather had ever encountered had that kind of flexibility.

"Feather says there's an entity splitting its time between our woods and the resort."

"Did you tell her?" November asked, oblivious to Lanie's revelation.

"I was just about to."

Defying all laws of nature, November Bean bounced up and down on her already-stretched thighs. It took everything in Feather not to stare.

"You look like you have feathers stuck in your mouth, Feather," November said, ending with a giggle.

"I...uh..." Feather found the words caught in her throat as she tried to process the gymnastic feat she'd just witnessed. "I spoke with Holly Garland's assistant. She said Dash went through several assistants and had a fetish for watching women drink wine."

"Vintnomagaly. I've heard of it." November sniffed with authority. "They did a whole series on those nuts on my favorite podcast, *Strangely True.*"

"It's frustrating that we haven't been able to rule anyone out. The more we dig, the more enemies and potential murderers we're finding."

"Maybe we've been looking at this all wrong, Lanie." Feather stood and walked around the furniture. She found she did her best thinking when she was moving. "We know all the authors had a motive to kill Dash. But we don't know exactly why the other two were killed first. Do you think they threatened to out Dash for his fetish? We need to dive deeper into the circumstances around their murders and see if Dash was there." She paused. "As long as that isn't treading on Officer Holliday's territory."

Vem and Lanie looked at each other and laughed in unison. "He's completely out of his league," Lanie explained. "His chief has had him on parking meter duty and he's anxious to prove himself so he's not on the Wall of Shame again. He'll welcome any help. And of course, Boysie won't be back until after Christmas."

Feather's face almost matched her hair. "Charming is a small town, but when we solve mysteries there, we have to make sure we don't step on the officers' toes. That's why I was asking."

"We get it, hon. Things work differently in every city."

"I'm going to do some research on the death of Elle Vanashelve. But first, I'm going make us some lunch. Vem, are you staying?"

Feather had a feeling November never turned down a free meal. She was incredibly fit, but also, from what she'd witnessed, a voracious eater.

"I'll make sandwiches, Lanie. Unless you already ate up the squid ink egg salad I brought over last night." She sprung up from her odd sitting position and bounded to the refrigerator, throwing both doors open.

"Yes, we finished that off. Cosmo couldn't help himself." She shook her head emphatically at Feather, mouthing, *"It was terrible! We threw it away!"*

"I've got some soup I can heat up, and some fresh bread from the bakery."

"Can I do anything to help?" Feather asked.

"You can call those boys and see what's going on."

Feather hadn't thought about Tug since they'd left this morning. Here they were, in a strange town with people they'd never met before, and she didn't worry once for his safety.

She pulled her phone out of her pocket. "Tug? Is everything okay? I haven't heard from you."

She could hear the sounds of men talking and things clanking in the background.

"Everything is fine, babe. We pulled the stove away from the wall and found more problems. Cosmo called an emergency electrician, but we have to repair the flooring while the oven is out. He said it was lucky we showed up when we did. He needed an extra pair of hands."

Feather felt an immediate sense of relief. "Oh good! I was worried you were bored." Now that she heard his voice, she missed experiencing these new people without him.

"How are things there? Have you caught the killer yet?"

She knew he was kidding, but it still stung a little that he didn't always take her second profession seriously. "No, we're still figuring out the details. Will you and Cosmo be here for lunch?"

"Cosmo said I could have anything I wanted from the display. He closed the bakery for the day, so I have a whole lot to choose from!"

"See you tonight, I guess."

"Don't sound so glum, babe."

"I'm just a little disappointed that we planned this romantic getaway, and the only thing we've done is get away from each other."

When she rejoined the two women, Lanie asked, "What was it you wanted to tell us, Vem?"

"I spoke with Nick's assistant, Belle Wringer. Nice gal. She said he's currently on safari in Africa. Left the country abruptly, needing a breather or some such thing. Those author types are all a little off."

Chapter Fourteen—Lanie

"H'lo? Who is this? I don't recognize the number." The voice was gruff, older than I expected with a sister as young as Ivy.

After fortifying ourselves with vegetable soup and rye bread, we returned to my office to call Ivy Globe's brother. He was listed as next-of-kin in her obituary.

"Mr. Globe? My name is Lanie Anders Hill. My partners, November Bean and Feather Jones, and I have been investigating a murder and we think it might be connected to your sister's death."

"Oh really?" He sounded skeptical. "After all of this time, you think it's what, a serial killer?"

"No, we're not ready to make those kinds of assumptions. We know your sister was part of a Christmas horror anthology. Did she mention having problems with anyone in the group?"

"Yeah, every single one. They were all a bunch of

big-headed idiots, if you ask me. Ivy was making more money than all of 'em put together, but they treated her like she was lucky to be in the group because of her age. I told her she never should have signed the contract."

"Why did she?" Feather asked. "Sign the contract, I mean."

We could hear the sound of his hand placed over the phone. "I had to move to another room. I don't want my wife to be upset by what I'm about to tell you."

The three of us leaned in closer to the speaker.

"Go ahead, Mr. Globe."

"Dash Vixen invited her over to discuss the book early on. She told him flat out she didn't want to do it, but he wouldn't take no for an answer. I'm sure he realized her huge following would bring lots of readers. One evening, he invited all of the authors to dinner. Ivy went reluctantly and he got her drunk on wine."

I tried imagining my own daughter forced into a situation with a lecherous man like Dash. A chill rushed down my spine.

"He took pictures of her, almost passed out, with a wine glass in her hand. Nasty man. A few days later, he sent the pictures to her, explaining he was planning to blackmail her. Said he'd release the video on the internet, complete with his disgusting noises in the background. She had a fan base of teenagers. There was no way she wanted that out in public."

"That sicko was a vintnomagal-o-file," Vem said. "We know all about it. Did he torture the poor girl?"

"In a manner of speaking, yes. She was forced to work with him when she wanted to run in the opposite direction."

"Ivy must've been so uncomfortable. I replied sympathetically.

"That's not all of it. After their book was published to rave reviews, all six of them got together to celebrate. It was supposed to be a relaxed evening of cocktails and hors d'oeuvres. Ivy didn't know any of them, outside of their names. My sister kept her head down and spent her days at the computer. She didn't socialize."

"Boy, I can relate," November interjected. "As I hone my moaning craft, there's always someone trying to interrupt me. If it's not Lanie, asking for a cup of sugar, it's the hunter down the lane asking for extra ground moose dung. A girl can't get a decent day's work in!"

I shook my head. "That's not entirely true, Vem. Please continue, Mr. Globe."

"Well, Dash sprung it on them that he'd been approached by a production company called Brain Gravy Pictures to make their anthology into a movie. Ivy wasn't interested. She'd already been blackmailed into writing the darn story in the first place. She told him no and excused herself."

Even though they were listening on a speaker, the room filled with tension. Feather's pulse quickened for the second time in a few minutes.

"Elle Vanashelve followed Ivy into the restroom. She shoved her into the hand dryer, causing a nerve in Ivy's back to seize. Elle didn't care. She told Ivy in no uncertain terms that they were signing this movie contract with Brain Gravy, no matter what. If Ivy didn't comply, she'd make sure someone came after her."

"When you say, 'come after,' Mr. Globe, what exactly do you mean?" Lanie asked pointedly.

"She had people who would take her down, end her career by posting negative reviews of her books, that sort of thing. You probably know that Dash was going to back out of the deal because he wanted to start his own production company. It wasn't Dash, it was Elle who caused her the most grief."

"Oh, that's a relief," November replied. "I thought you were going to say Elle threatened to kill her."

"That, too. She told Ivy she had no problem hiring someone to do the deed. That's what Elle said—*do the deed*. Even if Elle didn't kill her, she contributed to Ivy's death. On the night she was impaled in her car, my dear Ivy was coming home from physical therapy. She was going for help with the injury Elle had caused her that night in the bathroom."

The three women sat in thought after the conversation ended.

"Lanie? What wheels are turning in your head?"

November pivoted toward Feather. "She gets like this when she's got a good idea. It's odd, but we've all come to accept her strange behaviors."

"The timing of this whole thing is weird. Right before Christmas, just like Sylas's death." Tears filled my eyes, the feelings I'd been trying to avoid, and Feather patted my back uncomfortably.

"This must be a terrible blow to you, Lanie. I'm sorry."

"It really is. I'd invested a lot of myself into his little family. Time and time again, I've been disappointed by my relatives. I don't know why I thought this experience would be different."

November handed her a handkerchief she'd pulled out of her jumpsuit. To Feather's shock, Lanie didn't blink twice before blowing her nose in the suspect piece of cloth.

"Would you like me to see if I can contact your cousin and his wife?"

Relief washed over me. I couldn't believe what good fortune we found when Feather and Tug showed up at the Fallen Branch Resort. "Would you? Feather, I'd be so grateful."

Chapter Fifteen—Feather

She found her way to the woods for the second time that day. Feather Jones didn't mind nature, she enjoyed it as a matter of fact. What she didn't like was this powerful entity she'd encountered, and the probability that it would show up again when she least expected it.

Feather took in the comforting scent of wet pine and slowed her gait. She closed her eyes and breathed in and out. Even if she couldn't enjoy it with Tug, it was nice to experience this.

As she made her way through the tall pine trees, a cool, salty breeze drifted in from the ocean. The hairs on her arms rose, and for once, she wasn't certain it came from a spirit.

"Is anyone there?" she asked out loud. "Ivy? Is that you? You were the one who showed me the scene with Dash, right? I want to talk to you and Sylas, if he's there with you."

When no one, living or dead responded, she continued on. Maybe it was a relative of someone else who died in Piney Falls. It wasn't uncommon for the spirits to find an open channel like hers and try to transmit a message.

The leaves rustled, this time very definitely. Feather stopped and held her breath. When nothing happened, she put her hands on her hips and yelled, "You're going to make yourself known, or you're going to leave! I've got things to straighten out today, and I don't have time to play games."

She felt something poking her, and as she whipped around, caught a shadow out of the corner of her eye, darting behind a tree. "I don't run, and I don't have a sense of humor."

At this point, she had two options. One, she could block out all voices and just take a nice, leisurely stroll, or two, stay until whoever this was made themselves known.

"This is ridiculous! I'm going inside." Feather pivoted abruptly and shooed away the unseen irritant.

This time, she found herself directly in front of a partially formed entity. It was a stern man wearing clothing from the early 1900s. His hands sat on either side of his broad hips and even though she couldn't make out his face, he gave off the aura of a spirit with an ax to grind.

"Who are you, and why are we doing this dance?"

I want to see if you have any mental acuity. Most women don't.

His voice came through garbled, as though they were talking on a phone with a bad connection.

"Why does that matter to you?"

The entity darted to her right side and then behind her. Feather's head moved so fast she thought she might be sick.

Those with simple minds bend to my will.

"And those who don't?"

You'll see. I'll be watching you, Feather Jones. I'll be watching.

She stopped abruptly, though her head continued to spin. "I refuse to allow you space in my mind, whoever you are!"

This time she was poked in the back so hard she lost her balance and fell forward. Feather could feel something trying to force her mouth open, but she held her jaw firm.

Leaves beat against her closed mouth trying to enter. They hit with such force they scratched her neck. They began swirling around her body, stirring up dirt and forcing her to close her eyes. He was trying to shut her up.

You can't stop me. No one can.

She resisted the urge to break down in frustration. He could sense weakness. But she had no idea what to do next. He filled her head with stories of his conquests and never-ending words.

Just as suddenly as it began, the leaf storm ended. She could feel sunlight on her face. When she looked up, she saw the shape of someone or something.

I'm here to help you, lass.

Chapter Sixteen—Lanie

I pulled her in close, hoping the warmth of my body and my heart would comfort her. "When you're ready, you can tell us. For now, just put your head on my shoulder and breathe."

We sat together in the wooden rocker, the one our good friend Truman carved out of a tree with a story to tell. It nearly missed his house when lightning struck in the middle of the night last August. Always the good sport, he decided it was a gift to receive more wood to carve without the arduous task of chopping it down himself.

I'd never given birth to children of my own, but felt so much gratitude to be a mother to my adopted daughter. My job as marketing manager at The World's Best Office Supply Chain kept me busy enough that I tended to think of that as my baby. If I was being honest, as I was these days, it was a nice diversion, so I didn't have to think about relationships and children.

Today as I sat rocking this young woman and stroking her wild red hair, a sadness overtook me. Cosmo and I would have made beautiful babies.

Vem brought one of her topical remedies and covered all the scratches on Feather. Out of all of her homemade medicines, this one had the desired effect.

"It's all right. You're safe now. Vem is a master of karate."

"Kar-ah-tay, Lanie." Vem corrected me. "And I'm also actually quite good at Jiu jitsu. I teach self-defense classes, and–"

I knitted my brows and shook my head, and miraculously, she clammed up.

Feather's breathing was returning to normal, her chest rising rhythmically against my body. She sat up and smiled at me and for the first time, I noticed a small dimple on the right side of her face.

"Are you feeling better now?"

She nodded.

"Do you want to tell us what happened?"

Feather slid off my lap and stood, the blanket Vem had tucked around her falling to the ground.

"I was walking through the woods, trying to reach your cousin. I knew someone was there, but it didn't feel like one of your relations. This one was dark, evil —a man from the early nineteen hundreds. He started poking me and laughing."

"Sounds like a jokester. Why did that scare you?" Vem asked. "You're a professional with these types of things, right?"

Feather took a deep breath and moved a few steps over to the large picture window, presumably to get away from Vem's piercing gaze. It was raining fiercely now and the windows I'd sprayed with fake snow had an extra layer of depth, with rain drops running down the outside.

"I could feel him before I heard him. That's when I know it's a powerful entity. I smelled...his breath. Tobacco mixed with some kind of alcohol. He shoved me down."

The lights flickered and I wondered if we were in a bad dream.

"As I was on the ground, fighting to breathe, he said he'd seen everything. He'd been here since the town began. Not Piney Falls, not Flanagan."

"Aisley Lumber Township?" I asked, incredulous. "It was a wild time here. The place was full of brothels and gambling establishments. It could be any number of people."

I went down the list of criminals I'd uncovered when I first came to town. They were too numerous to speculate which one might be terrorizing this poor girl.

"A movie of his life played while I was subjected to his torture. He ran a lumber mill, and everyone was in debt to him in some way. He was pure evil."

"Stanford Aisley? I can't believe it." I leaned back in my chair. "No, that came out wrong. It isn't that I don't believe you, it's that, after all this time, I'm shocked he's even around. Never a peep out of him until today."

"He's been here. He tells me there has been a lot of turmoil in town. More than once, Mr. Aisley has been the cause. He has the ability to get into people's heads, those with weaker minds. He said he enjoys creating chaos."

Vem sprang out of her chair, causing me to jump. You would think after all this time, I would be used to her motions, but I was never prepared.

"You know what? That makes sense," she said excitedly. "So many murders here don't have a logical explanation. Ooh. This gets my juices flowing. I'm going to pull up all of our old cases, Lanie."

"You're forgetting that tomorrow is Christmas Eve, and we've got a murder right in front of us. We need to get this in hand before Feather leaves." I turned toward her. "I don't suppose we could talk you in to staying a few more days?"

Her face was drawn and tight. I wasn't sure if I had said something wrong, or if she was embarrassed.

"I'm...not sure. Tug and I came here for a romantic Christmas getaway. He wasn't happy I agreed to stay, at least not initially. Not that you haven't been a wonderful host, Lanie. But you have to admit, this is all a little strange."

I burst out laughing. "I'm sorry, but the woman who runs from dead people in the woods thinks this is strange?"

A smile crept over Feather's face and her brow relaxed. "I guess you're right. Well, I don't have to go back to work until next week. Tug is his own boss, so if it's okay with him, we'll stay a few more days. As long as you don't mind hosting us?"

"Mind? I'd love it!"

Vem put her hands on her hips. "Good grief, you two. This kind of mushy behavior should stay behind closed doors. I'd like to get back to the matter at hand. You said Stanford Aisley has been in the minds of some locals. Do you think it has something to do with Dash Vixen's death?"

"He never mentioned that, but it's possible. Though it doesn't explain the other two deaths."

"What happens now, Feather? Should we track down his relatives and see what they know?" I asked.

Years ago, on the anniversary of Stanford Aisley's death, there was a gathering of Aisleys. The picture from the paper was hanging in the Piney Falls Museum, right beside the photo of Mrs. Bonitam, State Fair Marionberry Pie Champ, four years in a row. The only reason she didn't win a fifth, according to local lore, was that she added blueberries when she ran out of marionberries.

"That may help," Feather began. "But what really frightened me was his strength. The harder I fought, the more he worked against me."

She brought her fingers up to her face, where we could see a thick layer of dirt under each of her nails.

"You only made it back here because of sheer determination! You were out there over an hour. How did you finally get free from his grip?"

"I think I may have passed out or he knocked me

out," Feather's mouth quivered. "When I opened my eyes, I had a sense someone else had saved me. I was experiencing a peace, exactly the opposite of what I'd been feeling earlier."

"You must have a guardian angel watching out for you. Do you have any ideas who that might be?" I asked.

"Oh, I've got a hundred ideas in my mind," November interrupted. "There's Nochturn, and Myles, and then Bar–"

"It was the same spirit I encountered before, the one who knew Lanie."

Over my career I'd made many enemies. Too many to count. I was ruthless as a businesswoman, leaving many ruined lives in my wake. I regretted that now. It was hard to imagine someone who thought fondly enough of me to save Feather, at least some one long gone.

Vem's eyes grew wide. "What does that mean? Some kind of shape shifter? A vampire? You know they can travel anywhere they want, Lanie."

"Mr. Aisley has the strength of ten spirits. He may be causing chaos that we haven't even uncovered yet."

"According to her brother, Ivy was threatened by not one, but two authors from the anthology," I reminded them, as I poured another hot chocolate for Feather. "I wonder if they were under the influence of some kind of evil spirit?"

"Normally, I would say no, but with Stanford, I believe anything is possible." Feather placed her arms around her middle, hugging herself tightly. "I've never been this afraid before."

"There is some angle we're missing." I took another sip of my cocoa, reminding myself it was my third cup and that was two over my limit for today.

"You know what I'm thinking?" November gestured wildly with her arms. "Let's say I'm Ivy." She flipped her curly hair behind her back. "I'm Ivy. I write books and talk down to those who can't," she said in a falsetto voice.

"Vem," I replied between giggles, "we don't know she was rude. Just because she was good at what she did, doesn't mean she wasn't humble."

Vem closed her eyes and put her fingers to her temples. "I'm in character, Lanie. Please don't interrupt." She opened her eyes wide and moved in front of Feather.

"I'm Stanford Aisley," She grumbled in her lowest octave. "I've come to make life miserable for this cute little gal. I'm going to write my own story about her death and use her as an act-tor in his movie."

All three of us giggled.

She made a whooshing motion with her arms, starting at the left side of her body and moving to the right. Her legs were positioned in a wide stance, a slight bend at the knees, and she had a dramatic look on her face. November Bean was in the moment, and I loved it. "Aaand scene." Vem placed one hand at her waist and the other behind her as she bowed, causing both Feather and I to stand and applaud.

"You know, that's a good thought, Vem. Have you read any of this anthology, Feather? Maybe there is a clue in their writing?"

"I can download it tonight," Feather replied. "I'm a pretty fast reader. I think you mentioned you were too, Ms. Bean?"

"First of all," November stuck a very long pointer finger in the air. "You don't need to call me 'Ms. Bean.' That's for people who I don't like and the garbage man who doesn't appreciate my recycling methods."

Before she got to two, I interjected. "We need to go to the Fallen Branch Resort and talk to Don Wenow again. I know I said I wanted to research Ivy, but the more I think about it, the more I want to talk to a living being. I'm convinced the anthology and Stanford Aisley are connected. He's a disagreeable man, but he's our only lead right now."

"Lanie, would you mind if I stayed here again? This has been too much excitement for one day."

"You go ahead, hon. Have a nice nap. Vem and I will take it from here."

Chapter Seventeen — Feather

She heard the sound of a buzz saw in the background before Tug moved somewhere quiet.

"Must be a big project there. Bigger than you expected."

She didn't want to frighten him with the events of today. Just seeing the physical effects on her body would worry Tug enough.

"Once we pulled the stove out, there were all kinds of electrical issues. Cosmo has orders that have to go out tomorrow, so he called everyone he knew with experience. Some guy he didn't even know showed up. He said he used to run his own bakery in Tellum and heard there was a problem. Cos is a great guy, Feath. He's desperate for help over the next few days and wants me to stay and chip in. I said I'd have to talk to you first."

She breathed a sigh of relief.

"Are you mad? Cause I can tell him—"

"No! Not mad at all. You are the best baker I know. It's a great idea to help him. I think Lanie is glad I'm here to help her too. It's not the trip we'd planned, but—"

"It's the one we needed," Tug finished. They were always talking about how things came their way when they needed them to, not necessarily when they planned them. She was glad he couldn't see her smiling. "I'll stop worrying about it now."

"Oh, Cosmo said to tell Lanie we would be here late, and not to hold dinner for us. We're at a bakery, so it's not like we'll starve."

"Will do. And Tug?"

"Hmm?"

"I love you. I can't think of a better way to spend our romantic Christmas getaway."

"Love you too, Feath."

She heard her stomach growling and decided to help herself to some chicken salad, taking care to sniff it first. She didn't want to partake in November's squid ink salad by mistake.

As she was scooping the last chunk on her bread, she felt the hairs on her arms rising.

"Really? Now?" Part of her was still traumatized from what happened earlier. She didn't have the energy, mental or physical, for another encounter with Stanford Aisley.

Swallowing hard she put the knife down and turned around. There was a strong scent in the room she hadn't smelled before. A floral scent of some kind. Was it lavender?

"Hello? Are you the spirit who helped me earlier?"

A cool breeze swept through the kitchen, even though the doors and windows were shut. The air pushed her toward the large glass patio doors, where she could see the pathway she'd taken earlier. Shoving aside the warning bells in her head, she said out loud, "Okay. I get you. I'll meet you in the woods."

Lanie and November,

Needed to stretch my legs. Back soon. Feather

She crossed that out. There was no way they would understand why Feather would even consider stepping foot on that pathway again. She didn't really understand it herself.

Hi, guys,

I'm tracking down a lead. Back soon.

Feather

It was funny, these entities had all of eternity but seemed impatient if they had to wait.

Quickly, she found her way to the spot she'd been before, when she'd met Stanford Aisley and nearly died at his hand. "I'm not afraid," Feather said out loud, just as much for her benefit as for the evil entity. "No fear at all," she repeated. Closing her eyes, she pictured a warm, yellow light. Mixed in with the mild, mid-winter scent of pine, she smelled the lavender scent once more. This time, she heard the rustling of leaves and swooshing clothing.

When she opened her eyes, she was shocked to see

a fully formed apparition. Never before in all of her life, had she seen a ghost with so much detail.

A small woman, about her height, who was wearing a black mourning dress buttoned up to her collar gazed at Feather with curiosity. The black lace down the front of her dress made her appear well-to-do for a woman of the early twentieth century. Her brown curls were piled high on her head, and she had a piercing stare, one that would have been unsettling had she not been surrounded by such calm and warmth.

I'm Fiona Scheddy. This is my land you're on here, lass.

"Lanie told me about you, Fiona," Feather replied, trying not to sound as eager as she felt. Who knew what would scare away someone like this. In addition to Fiona's ability to appear as a living being, her Scottish brogue was lyrical, almost joyful in its rhythm. "She said you were a great lady. Powerful. I know it, too, because you saved me earlier."

Oh, if that were entirely true, I'd not still be wandering these woods.

She stared at the thick forest beyond Feather wistfully.

"You saved me today. Thank you!" She couldn't help the tears forming in her eyes.

You mustn't feel bad. Much as he's tried, Stanford has never been able to do much in these woods. He's all huff and puff.

"Do you know about the deaths? The authors? Oh, and Lanie's cousin?"

That's a mouthful, id'n it? Fiona laughed softly, giving Feather the impression that in her lifetime, she was embarrassed to do so.

"And Stanford Aisley? Do you know he's been in people's heads?"

The expression on Fiona's face became somber. *That I do, lass. That I do.*

"I'm sure he's too powerful for you to get rid of him, but could you help me?"

Who says he's too powerful for me? she replied indignantly. *I'm the one who put a stop to his dirty dealings in life. Nobody else. I'm here to help you, just as I did earlier. But you have to know that someone close to you is in grave danger. I can't help you with that one, only warn you.*

"Who is that, Fiona? My Tug?"

Feather had a sudden urge to call him and warn him to stay somewhere safe until she got there.

No, not your lad right now. It's Lanie.

Chapter Eighteen—Lanie

"Elle Vanashelve wrote *Death in Red Velvet*. I read the reviews. It sounded like your average Santa-bites-it-hacker-slasher."

"Mm-hmm," I was trying to listen to Vem while formulating questions in my mind for Don. Something about these murders didn't add up for me. If it was truly some kind of possession, then why did it take so long? Over one hundred years had passed since the Aisleys lived here. It seemed so random.

When I first arrived and uncovered the true story of Piney Falls, the local paper did a series on the Aisleys. It even won some kind of award. Why didn't that upset Stanford Aisley the way some fictional stories did?

"I read through the whole thing. Pure drivel, Lanie. I could write a better story while standing on my head. Did I tell you I started doing that every night? It really helps to watch the news that way. Puts things into perspective. Anyway, the shine on the black boots really threw me..."

The other thing that was bothering me was that both Dash and Don were staying at the Fallen Branch at the same time. I didn't buy Don's surprise, that he was unaware Dash was dead. There had to be something more. Maybe we could interview Dash's relatives and find out why they didn't want him around for Christmas.

"Right, Lanie?"

"Huh?"

I hated when she caught me drifting off. A lecture would follow.

"Are you thinking about your grocery list again? You've got a caterer coming for Christmas Eve. Remember how you promised we'd have all the Thanksgiving goodness I missed when I was in California for the military auction?"

"Yes, I remember." I found it a little ridiculous that she would spend her money on those kinds of things. She had no use for them here in Piney Falls. But Vem had more money than everyone in town put together, so my worries would fall on deaf ears.

"There's no reason your attention shouldn't be focused on the engrossing conversation right here in this car," she continued.

"You caught me, Vem. I've got errands to run all next week. I really should make a verbal list, like you said."

"Not verbal, Lanie. HERbal. It's a product I

created using crushed ivy, nutmeg and wild chicory. You won't forget a thing if you start taking it twice a day. But what I was saying before you so rudely left me was that Elle Vanashelve mentioned in an interview that she was fascinated by the story of Stanford Aisley. She went to the little town where he grew up and researched his family, in hopes of writing a story about them some day. Do you know he was born on Christmas Day?"

I slammed on the breaks, causing Vem to grab her door handle. "What? He was born on Christmas?"

"Fudge and cookies, Lanie! Are you trying to kill us?"

"Sorry, Vem. I was shocked is all. That can't be a coincidence."

"We'll do some research at the library when we're done at the resort. I'm sure we can—"

"Closed, Lanie." Vem turned her body with the ease of a rubber band. "Everything here shuts down on Christmas Eve's Eve, everything. I can't even get a decent toothbrush."

We pulled into the parking lot, where large rivers of water raced across.

"I'll drop you at the front door and then go park. I don't want to be responsible for any more of you getting soaked."

After she got out of the car, I felt my phone buzzing in my pocket.

"Hello? It's good to hear your voice, hon!"

I hadn't let myself feel the loss of missing

Christmas with my daughter. She and her boyfriend planned an exotic getaway, one they both deserved. It was her right to do something of her choosing.

"You won't believe what's happening here. There was a mur–" I stopped myself just in time. There was no reason to pull her into this story. "Your dad is working hard on Christmas baking, and I've been chauffeuring a guest around town. She and her boyfriend were here for a nice getaway, like yours. The resort lost their reservations, so I invited them to stay with us. You'd really like Feather and Tug. We'll have to invite them back this summer. Oh, and my cousin and his wife couldn't make it. Next year."

Tears welled up in my eyes as she described swimming with dolphins and drinking exotic drinks from a pineapple. I couldn't help myself.

"It all sounds wonderful, sweetie. I'm so glad you called, because I've been thinking about you. Yes, Dad and I love you too. Have fun!"

I was relieved, for once, that the rain would make a mess of my makeup. No one would assume I cried hard after I hung up, missing our holiday together.

I scurried past the front desk, but not quickly enough. Wendell hopped off his stool. "Mrs. Anders Hill! What a pleasant surprise!"

When I rejoined Vem, she was standing at Don Wenow's door doing jumping jacks.

"Geez, Lanie. You look like you took a header in the parking lot. Are all of your parts still there?"

"Fine, Vem."

Don opened the door abruptly. Upon seeing us, he sighed. "Is there no peace and good will for me?"

He wore a tiny swimsuit, one that was much too small for his oversized body. He wore a pale-yellow swim cap on his head, adorned with a pair of lightning-blue goggles.

"Don, I had a few more questions. Do you know anyone by the name of Sylas Anders?"

"Who? I don't think so. You can ask my assistant. In fact, you should call her for anything further." Don tried slamming the door, but I put my foot in to prevent it.

"It's either us, or the police. Boysie is legendary across three counties for his interrogations. They can go on for days."

"Days and days, until your rear is the same shape as that chair," Vem embellished, using her hands to create the shape for emphasis. "I've heard stories of prisoners who come out with the silhouette of a plastic chair.."

I frowned at her but continued.

"We've recently been made aware that the three authors who died had researched Stanford Aisley. What can you tell us about that?"

He studied my face. "All right. Come in. But only for fifteen minutes. I like to keep to a routine, even when I'm on vacation."

The Fallen Branch Resort pool was Olympic-sized. The local high school used it for swim meets and parents booked their children's birthday parties there. It was a destination all in itself and I couldn't blame him for wanting to take advantage of that again. I did want to mention his skin wasn't going to react kindly to so many dips in the pool, but I refrained.

"You're wondering about Stanford Aisley. We were at a bar, drinking when Elle's husband suggested we write stories about Stanford. More than suggest, he was adamant. He said we'd be wealthy beyond our wildest dreams."

Vem made a wrapping motion with her hand. "Get on with it. We know this part all ready."

"But why Stanford?" I asked.

He clucked his tongue. "She said her husband, Brooks was a history buff. He'd been studying the history of coastal towns and came up with the story of Stanford Aisley and his manipulations. He was fascinated."

I tried to glance around the room while he was talking, just in case he had anything telling just sitting around. It was surprisingly neat.

"We were on our fifth drink when Brooks suggested we connect for a Christmas anthology and make Stanford Aisley the centerpiece. He didn't want it obvious that Stanford was the focus. We all agreed and signed a contract the next day. The process was almost identical when we were approached about the movie, only this time, Dash refused to sign the contract. Later on I heard something about him starting his own studio. When we had dinner the other night, he bragged that the other authors wanted to sign on with him, but were too afraid of Elle's husband and their expensive lawyers. I knew that was ludicrous."

"Why should we believe you now, Don? You have so many versions of the truth, I don't know which one to choose."."

Vem leaned in and sniffed his shoulder. "I smell something. Can't tell if it's deceit, or too much garlic."

"When we'd agreed to write the books, Elle was excited about it," he continued. I'd struck a nerve.

"But when it came time to sign on for the movie, she was hesitant. Maybe Dash sensed that and didn't want to put his work in a bad place. At least we can hope Dash was concerned for something besides his ego and his wallet."

"I'm curious about something, Don. What was the big attraction to Stanford Aisley? He's not a well-known historical figure. How would Elle's husband even know about him?"

"Elle's husband came to Piney Falls before the conference. He was searching for his roots. His great-grandfather was the illegitimate son of Stanford Aisley. His name is Brooks Stanford Carol."

Chapter Nineteen — Feather

When she returned from the woods, she'd called Lanie, just to make sure she was all right. Fiona's dire warning scared Feather. Maybe it was the fact that she and Stanford displayed more power than any entities she'd encountered before. The other option, the one that concerned her most, was that Lanie would be injured and Feather didn't do enough to stop it.

"We're on our way home, sweetie. In the meantime, there's a nice tub in the guesthouse bathroom and plenty of bath salts. Go give yourself a soak and then you'll sleep like a baby."

No one had ever taken care of her like this before. Her parents barely knew she existed, and she'd been on her own since she was eighteen. Part of her wanted to be wary of Lanie's kindness, but she knew better. This woman was genuine.

Soaking in a big tub did sound wonderful. Their

small apartment only had a shower. She grabbed her headphones and turned on the water. A scented salt called Nighttime and Nutmeg sat on the edge of the tub, so she poured it in liberally and prepared for her bath.

Feather stepped in and placed her earbuds in her ears, listening to the sounds of her favorite band, Tumor, as she closed her eyes. Immediately, her entire body relaxed, and she felt as though her stresses were melting away.

The next thing she knew, she felt ice cold water sloshing against her chin. Feather bolted upright. How long had she been in the water?

Glancing around the room, she could see the candles melted down to stubs as though they'd been burning for days. Had she really slept that long?

Carefully, she stepped out of the large tub and found her robe. "Tug? Are you here? I didn't mean to–"

As she rounded the corner towards the guest house kitchen, she was met by a sharp, cold draft of air. She pulled her robe around her body tightly. When the hairs on her arms rose, she realized this was no run-of-the-mill draft.

"Who are you?"

You know.

"Mr. Aisley? What do you want? Unless you're here to tell me about Dash's murder, I'm not interested in anything you have to say."

There were three.

"Yes, I know. We've already come to that conclusion. Do you know anything else, or are you just here to see me naked?" He was the type of spirit who might be motivated by embarrassment.

She doesn't know anything. She's just a dream.

"Do you mean Fiona? I don't think she's a dream at all. Tell me what you want or leave. I don't have time for you or your games."

The breeze whipped around her body again, reminding her that this particular entity possessed strength beyond any she'd dealt with before.

My powers are too much for you girl, admit it.

She squeezed her eyes closed, willing the scene to leave her, but when she opened them again, she was in the middle of a rapid current rushing through her room.

A dog paddled frantically to the edge of the room, where a desk sat against the wall. She hung on tightly while she thought about what to do next. The desk pulled away from the wall, and with it, Feather's grip was lost.

Stop interfering. You're insignificant and you'll never stop me.

"Mr. Aisley? You can end this now. Let's right your wrongs by giving this community some peace during the holidays!" She made small circles with her arms, trying to keep her head above water. She'd never learned how to swim, but Tug told her you just had to keep moving.

This time when the breeze came up, the French

doors burst wide open, allowing a river of rain to flow inside. Feather grabbed a desk drawer floating by, trying to stay upright and fighting to see if the entity was showing its face.

The entire time, her mind was filled with worry. How would she explain this to Lanie, who had been so kind to her? This cottage would need major renovations after so much water. And what about Tug? Would he be upset her attention to ghosts brought havoc to this kind couple's home?

The water was rushing in at a brisk pace and showed no signs of slowing. Not just from the doors, but from the windows. Feather looked down to find her robe floating as the water rose above her knees. She tried to hoist her body on top of the desk, but her hands were too slippery.

As the water reached her mouth, she fought to swim her way to the French doors. If she could make it that far, at least the water level would even out. After several minutes, struggling just to stay in place, she realized her efforts were futile. Stanford Aisley would claim another victim. This was the end. She would never see Tug again, nor would he understand how hard she fought to live for him.

Wake up, lass. You can save yourself.

Gasping for breath, she opened her eyes. She was in the bathtub and her head was wet. The candles were still burning and the air was still. The water was still warm. She'd been fighting for her life inside a nightmare, one created by Stanford Aisley.

Chapter Twenty — Feather

She pulled her thick, pink sweater over her head and zipped up her jeans. There would be no sleeping now.

The rich smells of Italian cooking met her nostrils. Taking a deep breath, she walked into Lanie's kitchen.

"...and if you mix a little tree bark with chocolate, it makes it taste like..."

They both looked up when Feather entered the room.

"How was your nap, hon? We didn't want to wake you when we got home, so we've been as quiet as possible."

"It was...enlightening." She placed her hand at her throat, comforted by the feel of her pulse and the life that came with it. The scratches from earlier were already less angry. "Oh, Tug called. He said they'd be late for dinner. And that Cosmo loves you very much."

Lanie cocked her head to the side. "My sweet man. What did I ever do to deserve him?"

She was proud that she'd embellished; Cosmo seemed like the type of guy who would say that, had he been around during their conversation.

Help yourself to a little pre-dinner snack. It's a dip my daughter makes..." Lanie's voice trailed off.

She bit her lip.

"Just to tide us over," Vem finished for her, gesturing for Feather to sit.

Feather pulled out a stool and seated herself at the kitchen island with Lanie and Vem following her lead. They munched on carrots and crackers heaped with dip as a fire crackled in the living room fireplace.

"I saw the person who saved me from Stanford," she said between bites. "Her name is Fiona Scheddy."

Lanie and Vem dropped their forks in unison.

"THE Fiona Scheddy?" Lanie asked, incredulous. "It's hard to imagine. What was she like? Did she tell you about her family? Or the cannery? You had the great privilege to see a local celebrity!"

Vem bounced up and down. "This is so cool! Tell us more!"

"Well," Feather began, aware that the message wasn't a pleasant one. "She had this wonderful Scottish accent. And she was dressed like she walked out of a fashion magazine from her era."

Lanie raised an eyebrow. "And?"

"And, she said you are in grave danger, Lanie."

Feather reached over impulsively and hugged Lanie. "I'm so worried for you!"

Lanie returned the hug and stroked her hair. "There's no need to worry about me, hon. I've got you and your strong boyfriend, and my Cos, and of course—"

"November Bean! Super woman!" She curled her arm to show off her impressive biceps.

"While you were making dinner, I had one of Cosmo's energy drinks from the garage. Didn't want to poop out early."

"The point we're making, Feather, is that there is absolutely no reason to worry about me. I'm sure Fiona has heard my concerns about my cousin, and the fact that I'm missing my daughter. It's emotion, that's all."

Feather was no more convinced of Lanie's safety than she was that November Bean would be sleeping tonight. As a guest and someone who thought highly of her, she decided the best thing she could do was ease her mind. "And me, Lanie. I won't let you out of my sight until the moment we leave."

"Good! Then it's settled." Lanie stood and placed her napkin on the counter, staring down at the empty dishes. "I made some chocolate-peanut butter crispy treats for Eloise. Would you all like some? If the boys will be late, we've got some time to digest before dinner."

"Just four or five." November patted her flat stomach. "I'm a little full."

"I don't eat sweets. I'm kind of an oddity," Feather replied.

"Boy, I'll say," November remarked, as Lanie sat the entire plate down in front of her.

"Thank you for your help earlier. That's quite the connection—Stanford Aisley and Elle Vanashelve's husband, Brooks. If I hadn't been able to message with you, we would never have had the leverage to get information from Don Wenow."

The back door opened, and Cosmo and Tug appeared. Feather ran to Tug and jumped in his muscular arms, kissing him hard on the lips.

Cosmo glanced at Lanie, pointing to the young couple. "Are you seeing this? Why don't I get the jumping thing?"

Lanie smiled and sauntered over to Cosmo, kissing him gently. "Because we're old and our parts don't move like that," she quipped.

When Tug eased Feather down, he whispered in her ear, "Is everything okay? Not that I didn't enjoy that."

"We need to talk later. I'm just glad to see you, babe." She took his hand and led him into the kitchen. With her other hand, she pulled the edges of her sweater up as high as they would go, hoping Tug wouldn't notice the few scratches on her cheeks.

"Tell me what's going on," he urged.

"Creepy stuff. The only way to fix it is to stay until its done."

"I figured. Cosmo needs my help too. With this

mechanical problem, it's really set him back for holiday baking. He's got parties clear up until New Year's Eve."

He stared at her plaintively. "I don't suppose you could—"

"Cancel my holiday appointments? It's a busy time of year at the salon." She purposely avoided his gaze, knowing he would be disappointed. "But we're needed here, and I can reschedule everyone with another stylist. But just until New Year's Eve. Then we really have to get back to our regularly scheduled jobs!"

Tug grabbed her and pulled her in close. "Thanks, Feath. I knew you would understand. I just wouldn't feel right, leaving this poor guy with all of those orders and no one to help. His daughter is coming back on New Year's Day. If we can stay until then, I'd feel a lot better about it."

"Of course. We should have this murder investigation wrapped up in a day or two, and then we can do some sightseeing. You don't mind, do you?"

Tug's face changed. "You've got scratches all over your cheeks, Feath. Are you sure there's nothing you forgot to tell me?"

"Feather? Tug? Grub's getting cold!" Cosmo called.

"Later I'll tell you. I promise."

Holding hands, they joined the others, where a virtual feast awaited them. In a big tureen were meatballs covered in a brilliant rich, red sauce. Next to them sat a large bowl of thick-cut pasta, clearly homemade, or Cosmo-made. A festive salad with dried cranberries and chopped hazelnuts sat beside a long basket of garlic bread.

"This looks amazing!" Tug pulled out a chair for Feather by the fireplace where Lanie and Cosmo had added extra seating to their small dining table.

"We'll use the formal dining room tomorrow night for Christmas Eve. Cos and I save it for special occasions." Lanie glanced at her husband lovingly. "Though every night with you is a special occasion, my love." She poured glasses of Sassy Lasses Piney for Pinot for each of them and sat down.

November gestured with her finger towards her throat. "Blech. You two are nauseating." She pulled the huge pasta bowl in front of her. "I might only choke down two helpings tonight. Unless there is dessert. Is there dessert, Lanie?"

"Your favorite, Vem!"

"How did I miss that?"

"What is your favorite, November?" Feather asked. The more time she spent around November Bean, the more she enjoyed her eccentricities.

November leaned across the table, narrowly missing the sauce with her curly hair. "Girlfriend, this one," she gestured toward Lanie, "makes the best cheesecake. It takes two days and has a crust of dark chocolate and other madness. You'll have to–oh, that's right, you don't eat dessert." She shrugged. "All the more for the rest of us."

"Lanie, I could use help like this guy all the time.

Not only is he built like a Roman statue, but he's not afraid of hard work."

Feather squeezed Tug's knee, pleased with this report, but not surprised. "Tug's been developing his own line of protein bars."

"Oh, really?" Cosmo raised an eyebrow. "You never mentioned that. Tell me more!"

Tug, flushed with pride, squeezed Feather's hand back. "They're in the development stage. I decided to use as little sugar as possible, so they're sweetened naturally. I've got six flavors so far."

"You know, I've been thinking about adding a little something to the check-out area. A display stand of your bars might be just what we need."

"Really? That would be great!"

"O'course I'd need to taste them first, just to make sure they don't taste like something Bean over here would make." Cosmo gestured with his thumb at their next-door-neighbor.

November lowered her fork, revealing ear-to-ear red sauce and a compliment of two napkins tucked into the front of her shirt. "Say what you will, Cosmo Hill, but you loved my brownies."

"Cos," Lanie cautioned, before he had a chance to answer. "Be kind. We have guests tonight, and we don't want them to think we're rude."

Cosmo wiped his face with his napkin and smiled at his wife. "You don't have to worry, Lanie. I'm as polite as they come."

"Thanks, dear."

"I was just gonna say, the only reason I liked those brownies was because she put something funky in the frosting. My head wasn't right for almost a week afterward."

"So, let's discuss what we're doing tomorrow, everyone," Lanie replied quickly. "Feather, November and I are going to Tellum to interview Dash's mother. What else we do depends on how long that takes. I need to be here when the caterers come tomorrow afternoon."

She pivoted toward Feather. "I feel the need to explain—usually my daughter makes our holiday feast. She's a fabulous chef, along with being a world-class baker. Since she's gone this year, I knew I couldn't do her recipes justice. I hired professionals to come in and help. I'm glad I did now, because that gives us extra time to investigate."

"Feather and I can go to Tellum without you, Lanie," November offered, slurping a large noodle off her plate. "That way, we don't have to be back at a certain time. You can stick around and make sure everything goes smoothly. I'd hate to have Christmas Eve dinner without all of my favorites."

"That would be much appreciated, Vem. And what about you guys? Cos, how is everything going?"

Cosmo threw his napkin on his plate and laced his hands together on either side of his head. "That was wonderful, Lanie. I think we'll be busy up until the very last minute. We missed out on valuable hours trying to figure out this oven issue. If Tug weren't here helping, I'd be a mess right now."

"I can come help, if you like?" Lanie offered. Feather noticed her nose twitching, a sign she wasn't entirely enthusiastic about making this offer. Lanie glanced over at Feather.

"You're watching me for signs, aren't you?" she asked.

"What? No, I—"

"It's perfectly fine. I do the same. Everyone has a 'tell,' or something they do to signify they aren't being truthful. It comes in handy when you're investigating crimes, doesn't it?"

"By this conversation, am I to surmise that you aren't interested in joining us tomorrow?" Cosmo asked, winking at Feather.

"To be honest, I'd like to stay here, ladies. You know how I like things to be perfect for our holiday dinners." She glanced at Vem. "It's a childhood throwback, I'm afraid."

"That's fine, really. Tug and I can handle the orders. He's offered to stay for the week and help out. Things are going to go smoothly, Lanie."

She rose and began collecting dishes. "Coffee with your dessert?" she asked. "For everyone but Vem, that is."

Chapter Twenty-One— Lanie

I never enjoyed Christmas as a child. Early in November, my mother taunted me with thick catalogs filled with toys. "Pick what you like, Lanie," she would say. Every single time, I fell for it. I dog-eared the pages, even took the time to write a description of each item on the back of a newspaper ad, the only kind of paper we had in the house.

When I showed her what I chose, she would nod her approval. "Those are good options, but Santa has the final say."

Christmas Eve I barely slept. I envisioned waking to a bushy green pine that filled our tiny living room. My eyes would struggle to adjust to the bright string of lights and baubles. Surrounding the tree would be many large boxes, wrapped in different colors of foil. Each one containing a gift I'd chosen from the magazine, each more exciting than the last.

One year, I chose a *Call Me Patty* doll from the

magazine. She had a little string coming out of her neck and when you pulled it, she would say, "My name is Patty. What's yours?" Her long platinum blonde hair was shiny and came with its own brush. Three outfits were included—everyday overalls, flannel pajamas, and a dress for all the parties she attended.

I circled that page with my pen several times and put a star beside it, the way my teacher did when she thought I was using words far beyond my years in completing my homework assignments.

That Christmas morning, I crept quietly into the living room. My mother's negative demeanor wasn't invited. I wanted to enjoy this without her complaints. How I'd convinced myself so assuredly is still a mystery. There were no previous experiences to lead me to believe this Christmas would be different. No promises of a big Christmas dinner or long-lost relatives coming to visit.

Nonetheless, my joyful heart hit the ground with a giant thud when I saw nothing out of the ordinary in our living room. Several crunched up packages of cigarettes and food wrappers from Piggy Pork's, my mother's current favorite drive-thru.

That was it.

Still unable to accept my fate, I opened the refrigerator, hoping to at least find a surprise dessert. It was empty, other than a six-pack of cheap beer and a carton of milk of questionable origin.

I flopped down at the kitchen table, my emotions dulled by years of practice. It was a way I had of protecting myself from the world my mother created for us. Even at my tender age, I knew she couldn't help it. Her mind didn't work like mine, or anyone else's.

Getting up this morning, I was cautiously optimistic. Christmas Eve with my family-of-choice, which this year included Feather and Tug, would be something to behold.

I made a breakfast of French toast with blueberry compote, chicken-apple breakfast sausage, and toast from our bakery bread. I slid a note under the door of our guests and then set a covered tray of my creation, including coffee, outside.

When you feel better about yourself, you have more to give others. Happily, I bounced to my home, where I had a list of things to prepare for tonight's Christmas Eve dinner. Each guest would find a little gift at their place setting, wrapped in different colors of foil. In addition, I asked a chocolatier who was new to our downtown area to make chocolates with each of our initials. When I explained to her that our guest list had changed, she happily made corrections.

The caterer would be arriving at four, but that gave me plenty of time to return to the Fallen Branch Resort and question Don again. I was certain that one more interview would give us more to go on.

I was pouring myself another cup of coffee when I heard the door rattle and I rushed to let them in.

"Good morning! I hope you slept well. Merry Christmas Eve!"

Feather was bright-eyed and seemingly refreshed, as

was Tug. He was carrying the tray of breakfast dishes, which, to my sheer delight, were completely empty. They enjoyed my cooking.

"I'm so sorry, Mrs. Hill. We slept in later than we'd planned. We're normally early risers, either to go to the gym or get ready for work. All of that lifting and moving things at the bakery with Cosmo yesterday wore me out." He glanced lovingly at Feather. "I'm sure she was just being nice and letting me sleep in."

Feather nodded to me, and I returned the favor. "Thank you so much for that lovely breakfast! We didn't expect you to treat us like royalty."

"I'm glad to see you're both feeling well today. You came here for a nice getaway and it was spoiled. Whatever I can do to make that up to you, I will."

Tug placed his hand on his chest. "I grew up in a well-to-do family. We were more about business transactions than familial relationships. The only people who were nice to our family were paid to do so. I guess that's why it's so hard for me to believe there are good people like you and your husband, Mrs. Hill."

My mind drifted back to those Christmas mornings of childhood. Alone, or wishing I was alone. I didn't believe kind people existed either. I squeezed his chiseled arm. "Thank you, Tug."

"You look like you're going somewhere," Feather observed, pointing to my purse sitting on the table.

"I thought I would re-interview Don today. Your revelations yesterday led me to believe he's hiding something more. I'm sure the man is sick of us by now, but time is of the essence."

Tug's head snapped to the side. "What revelations? You never mentioned anything."

"I didn't want to upset you, and I was too exhausted to go through it all. There's an entity from the town's origins who has been playing inside the heads of residents. We're thinking he might be encouraging some of the locals to do things they wouldn't otherwise do."

"But isn't Don one of the authors? He doesn't live here, right?"

"Feather had a heart-to-heart with a local spirit," I interjected. "He made it seem as though many people were under his control Isn't that what you said?"

"Yes, I'm pretty positive." She looked up at her boyfriend. "This Mr. Aisley is a strong entity, Tug. The strongest I've ever encountered. I'm afraid he's easily taken control of suggestive minds and won't stop now."

Tug studied Feather's face for a moment before raising his brows. "Those scratches on your face and your chest..."

I was shocked they hadn't discussed this the night before.

"Feather was so brave, Tug. She fought him off."

"This is getting too dangerous." He reached out, gently taking her face in his hands and scrutinized every scratch. "No, I think we need to leave. Today."

I couldn't say that I blamed him. Cos would feel the same way.

"We need to stay," Feather replied firmly. "If we don't get to the bottom of this now, this entity could very well follow us home and it will never end."

When he appeared doubtful, she continued, "You're always saying there's no case I can't solve. Let me prove it."

I wanted to add something supportive, but I didn't know which side needed it more.

"What kind of a man would I be if I didn't stand behind my words?" Tug said. "We'll stay, for now." He kissed the top of her head. "But you've got to be completely transparent with me from now on. We made a deal to have each other's backs and I can't do that if I don't know you need me."

My mind drifted back to those Christmas mornings of childhood. Alone, or wishing I was alone. I didn't know there were people like Tug, who kept their promises. I didn't know about the Feathers of the world, good, kind people who would do what they could for others, no matter the risk to their own personal safety. I smiled warmly. "Thank you, Tug."

Chapter Twenty-Two —
Feather

"You stay put, Lanie! I love cleaning up the kitchen!" Tug insisted, taking the dishes from her hands.

"Are you sure, Tug? Cosmo said he was coming back to pick you up soon."

"I'll be done by then," he called, already making clanking noises.

Lanie put her hands behind her head and leaned back in her chair. "I could get used to this," she said with a contented smile. "Christmas Eve with new friends and old. What could be better?"

There was a loud clunk from the kitchen and then a thud. Lanie and Feather exchanged horrified glances before rushing to the kitchen to see what was happening.

On the tile floor they found two broken syrup-coated dishes. The dishwasher door was open, and Tug was on all fours, his body heaving as he tried to expel something lodged in his throat.

His face was crimson. Taking turns, one fist then the other, he attempted to dislodge whatever was blocking his airway.

Feather bent down to help him, but some invisible force prevented her from touching him.

She tried again and again, banging her body against the unseen wall that had formed around her best friend. Feather refused to give up as the life was draining from his eyes.

Lanie joined in, banging her body against it, but she couldn't penetrate the invisible wall.

A Christmas tree-green arm reached in from out of nowhere and punched Tug in the gut, causing cranberries to shoot across the room and landing on Lanie's cream-colored blouse.

Tug immediately fell to the floor, gasping for air. Whatever held Feather back was gone as well, and she bent down by his side, cradling his head.

"Babe, are you all right? What happened?"

"I...don't know," he whispered. "I was loading the dishwasher and saw these cranberries rolling around on the counter. Something told me to try one, so I did. It was like it was magnetic. Six more practically jumped in my mouth and they lodged in my throat so quickly I didn't have a chance to call for help."

"Oh, Tug." Feather caressed his head in her lap. "This has to be the doing of Stanford Aisley! That's the little game he plays."

"There were cranberries strung around Dash's body too. It can't be coincidence, can it?" Lanie asked, incredulous. "How did he do that?"

"Is anyone going to address the elephant in the room?"

They all glanced up at November Bean, who had reached in and saved Tug at the last minute.

"Thank you Ms.—November. I don't know how you did it, but thank you."

November placed her hands on her tiny hips and smiled with satisfaction. "Something told me I was needed here. Not that I wasn't coming anyway, but I was waiting for the crushed dandelions to dry on my patio lighting first. Call it a premonition or just November Bean, communing with the spirits."

Feather had a suspicion it was Fiona Scheddy, but now wasn't the time to get into that.

"I'd ask what that means, but then you'd tell me," Lanie replied dryly.

Tug had managed to regain his composure, now in the sitting position. His eyes were still red and watery, but his breathing had returned to normal.

"Do you think he's been directing people to murder?" Lanie still appeared skeptical. "Not that I don't believe it, but why here? Why now?"

"I have an idea about that." November went over to the front door and picked up a large item she'd dropped when she hurried in. It was the Christmas anthology, though not the one used to kill Dash.

"Last night I started some light reading. *When*

Santa Screams, that's the worst of this ream of paper." She let it thunk on Lanie's table, causing our coffee cups to shake.

"No offense, Feather, but normally I wouldn't use this to clean my little squirrels' behinds."

Feather wanted to ask why she was doing that in the first place, but decided it was best to leave it alone.

"I found the reference to Stanford Aisley, after forcing myself through every single page." Vem put her fingers up to her temples and began to rub them. "It was awful. Just awful. The story was about a man who is possessed by the spirit of Santa. He kills everyone in his lumber mill by stabbing them with an ink pen and then wraps them up in cranberries, meant to be strung on the tree."

For the first time today, Feather examined the wonder that was November Bean. In addition to her Christmas-tree-green jumpsuit and glasses frames, she was sporting dangling Christmas tree earrings. They were adorned with tiny lights that blinked on and off.

"Vem, I'm impressed! You've upped your detective skills. Good job, friend!" Lanie rubbed her friend's arm supportively, but November pulled away.

"You didn't trust me?" The hurt in her voice was obvious. "Maybe it's because you skipped last month's Moan-giving class, where we all shared our strengths. I had to use the abbreviated list because several people seemed to have the urge to use the bathroom at once."

Lanie wrapped her arms around her friend's green shoulders. "And you should know by now that I trust you implicitly. At this special time of year, I have to remember you are one of the best gifts I've ever had. Your friendship is what I waited my entire life for."

November seemed satisfied with that response, so she continued. "After cleansing my palette with a nice eggnog and sugar cookie, I began *Snowily Severed* by Ivy Globe. It was much better. I can't believe she agreed to have her work in the same book as Dash. It was a step down. Her story is about a logging company from nineteen hundred. The owner of the company, Giles MacNub kills six employees, putting each through the lumber chopper-thingy." She made a chopping motion for emphasis.

"I can go into detail if you want."

"No, that's okay!" Feather and Lanie said in unison.

November shrugged. "Suit yourselves. The gist of that story was that Giles was evil and he ruined Christmas for the surviving employees. The first murder, however, happened when a wooden cutout one of them was making slid off the hill and impaled its creator."

"That's odd. Strangely similar to Ivy's death."

"But how do we know she was talking about Stanford Aisley? Maybe she's got a great imagination?"

"Oh, my red-haired friend, I thought of that too." November 'booped' Feather on the nose, causing her to jump back in surprise.

"It's just what she does," Lanie apologized, by way of explanation.

"At the end of the story, there are notes."

November picked up the large book and licked her finger, turning the pages until she found the right one. "And I quote, 'The character of Giles MacNub is based on the real-life lumber mill owner, Stanford Aisley. His large empire existed in what is now Piney Falls, Oregon.'" She looked up at everyone proudly. "You see?"

"Now we need to read the other two stories. I'll get on that tonight," Lanie said.

"You forgot about my speed-reading skills, Lanie. I can read a four-hundred-page book in two hours." She smiled with satisfaction. "Which made getting through this drivel quite easy."

"And?" Lanie asked impatiently. "What did you find?"

"Elle Vanashelve's story, *Red Velvet Death*, was about a woman who refuses to marry the most powerful man in town. She is taking her bath, once a month, I'd imagine," Vem squeezed her nostrils together to emphasize her point. "And she was electrocuted by an electric toaster thrown in the tub. One of the earliest models."

"Now we're all waiting to hear about Dash's story. Did the Stanford character really kill him with his novel?" Lanie asked.

November shook her head. "No, that ridiculous story ended when the main character was poisoned. Of course, all three bodies had strings of cranberries placed around them."

Tug cleared his throat, causing everyone in the

room to turn. Feather, having left his side to hear the story, walked back and helped him up. "Are you feeling better, babe?"

"Not really." He rubbed his throat. "I mean, I can breathe and all, but after hearing about this creepy goon, I'm really concerned for our safety. The force it took to lodge those cranberries in my windpipe was, well, superhuman. I know what I just said, but maybe he's too much for us. If he followed us home, at least we'd have your paranormal group to help fight him."

It wasn't like Tug to walk away from a challenge.

"He's here for a reason, Tug. Give me one more day, and then I promise, if I don't have a way to defeat him, we'll go. With all of us fighting him together, he doesn't stand a chance."

Chapter Twenty-Three — Lanie

"I say we stick to our original plan," I said, waving to Autumn as she walked by, pushing the cleaning cart.

"Hi, Mrs. Anders Hill!" she replied, waving eagerly.

It didn't seem fair that most of the staff had the next twenty-four-hours off, but Autumn still had to come in and do her job. I made a mental note to ask if she was receiving holiday pay. If not, I would supplement for her.

I watched with regret as Vem and Feather drove off together earlier. They were going to meet Dash's mother in Tellum and see if she had any insight into her son's behavior.

I hated missing out on their sleuthing today, but I needed to satisfy myself that we'd gotten everything we needed from Don Wenow. In addition to that, the caterer insisted that I was home when she came. She had a new employee and didn't want to chance it in case something broke in my absence.

"Vem, please remember to keep your questions short. That gives your interviewee plenty of space to answer."

"Lanie, I'm offended. You know I've been publishing Bean's Happenings for almost a year. It wouldn't be the smash hit in the newspaper world that it's become if I didn't understand the art of the interview."

"You're right, of course."

"Where are you, anyway? The background noise doesn't sound like your kitchen."

Vem always knew.

"Oh, I decided to make a quick trip to the Fallen Branch Resort." My eyes darted back and forth. Ever since they left, I'd had a sense of unease. I couldn't put my finger on it, but something seemed off. "With Cos and Tug working hard on the baked goods for Christmas dinner here, I wanted to make sure there were no surprises.

I prided myself on my instincts when I worked for Work Ahead Office Supplies, The Largest Office Supply Chain in the World, as their marketing manager. One time I pulled an ad for mesh trash cans at the eleventh hour. My boss and just about everyone else questioned whether I knew what I was doing.

At my last convention, I'd slept with the marketing manager of our competitor. Greg Floyd from Pens, Pads and Parchment, Oh My! He accidentally told me about all of the products they were planning to discount in order to compete with us.

The next day, I was relieved to see the trashcans we'd initially put on sale were sixty percent off at Greg's store.

I wasn't always so wise about other things in life, unfortunately.

"Feather, let your truth burst from your bust," November whispered, and then louder into the phone, "I'm going to use the ladies' room. You know how I have that weird thing, where my brain tells me halfway to Tellum that I have to go? We're at that spot. You can talk to Feather now."

When I'd heard the door close, I asked, "What is it, Feather?"

"Lanie, your relatives tell me that Sylas is alive but in trouble. I didn't want to upset you, especially today, but—"

"He's alive? How can that be?"

"Eloise is safe," her words were measured. "We do need to find her soon, though."

Between the holiday and trying to solve this mystery, I didn't see how we were going to do that. But it was a little girl, my relative, and her life was much more important than a giant turkey and sides.

"Where do we start, Feather?"

"We start with—"

"I'm back, Jacquelines! It's time to get on the road!"

"We can talk more about that tonight. Drive safely,

you two! Don't forget, dinner starts promptly at seven."

"Don't go anywhere else alone, Lanie!" Feather blurted out.

"No need to worry, love. I'm just fine."

There were muffled noises, most likely Vem explaining her superior protection methods.

"We'll be back in a few hours, and I won't let you out of my sight."

My appearance at the front desk really threw Wendell.

"Ma-ma-Mrs. Ha-ha-hill! What are you doing here? Don't you have to be home for your caterer?"

"I'm amazed by your ability to remember mundane things, Wendell. I'll be home in plenty of time for the caterers. How are you on this fine Christmas Eve?"

He seemed more flustered than usual, shuffling papers around. I placed a hand firmly over his.

"Stop. Wendell, it's me. You can tell me what's bothering you."

Wendell refused to meet my gaze, which hurt my heart. We'd started working at the resort at the same time and had built up a good rapport, at least that's what I thought.

"No, it's nothing. I have ca-ca-company coming this evening is all." He tapped a finger against his skull. "Too much to think about."

"You're only human, Wendell. Do what you can and try to enjoy the evening." I tilted my head so that I could see his eyes. "Right?"

He nodded without looking up.

"Now, I'm here about Don Wenow. Is he in the pool swimming?"

"Na-na-no, he checked out this morning."

"Oh, really? I wanted to talk to him. Do you have a phone number on file?"

"Fa-fa-forgot to get it," he said, turning away from me. "I'm ba-ba-busy today, no time to chat."

I shoved the hurt I was feeling to the side.

"Well, Merry Christmas, Wendell! Have a wonderful holiday with your family!"

I walked inside and dropped my purse on Cosmo's recliner. Instead of staying put, I heard a thunk as it hit the wood floor. To my surprise, there was a package sitting in the chair, wrapped in shiny gold foil and a beautiful red bow.

Cosmo was always doing wonderful things like this. He was the most thoughtful human I'd ever encountered. This year, he insisted over and over that all he wanted from me was my undying love.

Following my instincts, I found something wrappable instead. In the closet of the guest home, where Feather and Tug were staying, was a beautiful, navy blue fishing pole with hip waders and a hat displaying his bakery logo.

We would laugh about it later, how he always

talked about fishing but never took days off to actually do it.

I picked up the box and shook it. It made a lovely rattle, or rather a side-to-side thunk. I knew I should place it under the tree with the other gifts I'd wrapped. *Should.* But I was here alone, and I didn't want to risk a disappointed face in front of my love or our guests. Cosmo studied my face like an FBI agent in an interview every time I opened a gift. If he saw the slightest twinge or blink, he declared his gift a failure. No, opening it now was a sound decision.

Carefully, I slid a kitchen knife under the paper and began dissecting my gift as carefully as possible. If I took my time, I wouldn't tear anything and I could rewrap easily. After an arduous thirty-five minutes, the paper was off. Once more, I paused, glancing at the box.

After my childhood disappointments, Cosmo promised each year would be better than the last, and if I didn't like what he gave me, I could return it. Never, ever would I return a present from him.

Slowly, I lifted the lid, smiling in anticipation of this year's delight.

Inside was a copy of the horror Christmas anthology, a string of Christmas lights, cranberries on twine, and a piece of a Rudolph rooftop ornament, covered in blood. It was a reference to all the murders so far—Dash's death by hardback and cranberries, Elle's electrocution in the tub, and Ivy's impalement on a rooftop ornament that came crashing through her car windshield.

Sitting on top of these disturbing items was a card in a festive red envelope. Despite the terror in the box, my curiosity got the better of me and had to open it.

Dear, Sweet Lanie,
Tik Tok, Tik Tok.
Your time is drawing near.
Enjoy your Christmas, my dear.

Chapter Twenty-Four — Feather

"And that's when I said, wait just a doggone minute. You can't tell ME how to moan. I do it for a living!"

November Bean was on her third story about various people in Piney Falls who took classes from her. The first two involved people she said were plotting against her. This one was the dog catcher, who was a slug in a previous life. Or so she thought.

"Are we almost there?" Feather asked politely. "I'd hate to be late for Lanie's big dinner."

"Yep. Funny you would ask, we're at the city limits of Tellum right here." She gestured to a friendly brick sign surrounding the words, "Hiya, Folks! You're in Tellum!"

The endless strip malls reminded Feather of Portland. The idea of each one containing five or more stores with twice as many employees overwhelmed her small town, simple life mind.

"It's slightly bigger than Piney Falls, but we all believe it's a matter of extra livestock. You never know what they count these days."

Feather surveyed the town as they drove down the pine tree-lined street. It was quaint, though the buildings didn't have the pizazz of Piney Falls, nor the clean look of Charming. All that they passed were in need of a good paint job.

"Here we are. Thirteen-thirteen Marionberry Lane."

November stopped the car in front of a tiny, dark purple home. A circular sign stuck in the front yard read, *'Madame Mystery, Palm Readings.'*

"The last time someone tried reading my palm, she ended up in the hospital with a nervous breakdown," November commented as she exited the car.

Feather paused, as the hairs on her arms rose. Strangely enough, the feeling passed quickly.

"What's the hold up?" November mouthed through the closed door. She placed her hands on either side of her head and stared in the window.

"Sorry, I had to center myself. My brain needs a beat to catch up."

"Each goddess to her own," November replied, shrugging her shoulders with indifference.

Whoever you are, you'll have to wait.

She exited the car, and forced the corners of her mouth into a smile. "Do we know what we're going to ask her? Lanie's taken charge of that everywhere else we've been."

November placed a hand on her chest. "Of course we do! I taught her everything she knows about investigations. On the way home, I'll tell you about the time we searched a winery for signs of a killer. It was me who—"

The door opened before they even knocked. A woman wearing a long, purple gown opened it slowly. Her tight, grey curls peeked out from underneath a dark purple velvet hat. She took time to gaze at each woman with contempt.

"You said thirty minutes on the phone. I've got customers coming soon."

"Well, actually it was my friend, Lanie, who spoke with you. And it takes thirty-two minutes to drive here. We're early, if you're going to be technical."

The woman snorted in disapproval as November pushed past her and into the cozy space. "Ooh! This is cute. I believe my realtor might call it, *'a charming space for your pet.'*"

Feather put her hand over her mouth, embarrassed by her new friend.

"Don't worry, dear. I knew exactly what I was getting in to," Madame Mystery whispered in Feather's ear as she gently nudged her inside.

The dark blue ceiling of her living room had bright, gold stars hanging down from fishing line. They were painted with a fluorescent paint that made them more impressive in the dim light. Three green velvet couches lined the room, and in the center, a small desk held a crystal ball.

November homed in on the crystal ball. She bent down so that the ball was at eye level and placed her glasses as close to it as she could. Feather stood opposite of her where she could view the eyes of November Bean in great detail. She stifled a laugh.

"Can you see Mars from here?" November asked.

"Maybe. I've never tried. Why don't you take a seat, Ms. Bean. I've got twenty-nine minutes until my next customer." Madam Mystery seated herself on a chair behind the desk, her numerous bracelets jangling as she adjusted her hat.

Feather rested on one of the green couches and November, not surprisingly, flopped down inches from her on the same couch.

"We're sorry about the death of your son, Madame," Feather began, unsure of how to address her.

"You can call me Phyllis. And thank you. My Dash was my world, at least for his childhood. He grew into an insufferable jerk. I blame his father for that. What?"

Feather and November exchanged glances. "We didn't say anything."

"No, not you. It was Lazlo. He's my helper."

They surveyed the room for an assistant. Upon finding no one else, November continued the conversation, as if what just happened was completely normal. Feather, meanwhile, continued eyeing the room for any clues about Dash. She was shocked when she discovered a large velvet painting on one wall. It was Dash draped across a chair with a string of cranberries surrounding him.

"I can relate. I have a son with the same source of jerkiness. Not the beef kind. My ex is the Toilet Paper King, so—"

"Phyllis," Feather interrupted quickly, to avoid another sticky situation, "when was the last time you spoke with Dash?"

"It was clear back at Thanksgiving. He promised to spend that day with me, but like always, he flaked out. I should have known," she sighed.

"Why would you know? He was your son, wasn't that expected of him?" Feather asked. Though her own parents hadn't spent a holiday with her since she was seventeen, she always assumed it was different for everyone else.

"No, like I said, Dash wasn't the same person I used to know. He wanted to be an airline pilot growing up, just like his grandfather. Then his Daddy, Dashiell Senior, showed up. He abandoned us when Dash was three and I was kind of hoping he would never return. When he did, he brought a new wife with him. She was interested in raising a son, so they bought my Dashie a shiny blue bike in exchange for his coming to live with them. I couldn't compete."

"I couldn't help but notice, you have a painting of your son hanging there," Feather gestured to the creepy velvet painting. "What is the significance of the cranberries?"

She turned around and stared, as if she had

forgotten it was even there. "Oh, that. Dash had a thing for cranberries. He said they were part of his brand. I thought the painting was ridiculous, but I don't have to repaint that wall as long as it's hanging there."

Phyllis brought both hands to her temples, producing a beautifully melodic sound as her bracelets clanged against one another.

"I'm getting something. Do you have the sight, child? That's what Lazlo says. He's impressed by you."

November cleared her throat. "Why, yes, I'm very good at reading people."

"Not you, the girl. Feather Jones, can you speak to the dead?"

Feather had underestimated Phyllis's gift, or whatever it was. "Um, sure. I do, I mean."

"My spirits tell me you've just recently begun to use your skills. Lazlo says you've helped many already and that you have a good heart."

Anyone could come up with that, she thought. And Tug set up a web page for her, so it wasn't exactly a secret.

"You don't seem terribly broken up about your son's unfortunate interpretation of having the book thrown at him," November observed.

"No, I don't, do I? His promises included visiting me once a month, writing me into his stories and the best one, buying me a new home with the proceeds from his novels. None of that happened. We didn't have a good relationship, so I'm not sure what you think you'll gain by asking me about him."

November shifted one leg up underneath her body, forcing Feather to inch away.

"In his defense, Phyllis, he probably didn't make enough to buy you a house. His stories are pure—"

The ring.

"Phyllis, did he give you a ring? Was that his only gift to you?" Feather asked.

Her dark, penciled-on eyebrows rose, before she broke into a wide grin. "Yes, you are correct. It's wonderful having a fellow empath in the room. There are three of us in Tellum. One is a complete quack and the other one looks at me strictly as competition, so we never speak. At least on purpose."

She rose and disappeared into the kitchen. When she returned, she was carrying a tiny, worn black box. "Last Christmas, out of the blue, Dash sent me this ring. There was a note accompanying it that said when he sold his first book, *Scared the Dickins out of Dudley,* he remembered his promise to buy me something nice. It had an emerald, a ruby, and a diamond. With all of his other lies, I determined none of them were actually real stones. I don't know why I kept it, or why he sent it. He'd never made any such promise."

She handed the box to Feather, who examined it carefully. She opened the case to find a stunning ring, real or not. Feather pulled it out of the box and then dug her pinky finger into the small slit where the ring sat.

"Don't do that!" November hissed. "If you ruin the box, she'll expect us to buy her a new one. I'm loaded, but I want to spend my money on fun stuff. Not ring boxes."

Feather curled her pinky around a small piece of paper and pulled it to the surface, where she was able to retrieve it with her other fingers.

Phyllis leaned forward, examining the paper. "I've never seen that before. Did your spirit friends tell you about that?"

"Sort of. I don't always get clear messages."

"You will, eventually. Keep working on it. If you can impress Lazlo, you're on your way to great things."

"What does it say?" November asked impatiently. "We've got a roasted turkey calling our names, remember."

Feather uncurled the little paper. "It's a number. Forty-seven-eleven."

"That's it? What a disappointment!"

She tried blocking out November Bean.

I'm here. Talk to me, Feather implored the spirit.
She's on my side.

Feather's eyes popped open. "What did he promise you?"

"I don't know what you're talking about," Phyllis replied, clearly confused.

"You've been hearing an entity. He promised you something you wanted, and in exchange, you did something in the human world for him."

Phyllis's breath quickened. "I...you need to go. My next appointment will be here any minute."

Feather stood and leaned across the table, poking Phyllis in the chest. "It was Stanford Aisley. You summoned him once before, and that's why he's able to control so many."

She could barely contain her contempt. To think someone purporting to talk to the dead was making deals with an evil entity made her blood boil. "He promised you he'd bring your son to your next séance. In return, you agreed to...Phyllis, you agreed to destroy Dash's next book? Why?"

"Stanford promised that in return for my help, he would come to all of my readings. My business has gone up fifty percent since he's been in attendance." She poked a ringed finger into Feather's chest. "He's not happy with you, and Stanford is very powerful." Phyllis replied tersely. "You'd better leave now, if you know what's good for you."

"I'm not going anywhere until you tell me what was so important about that book," Feather replied with quiet resolve. Stanford had been attempting to contact her in the car, she realized now. He wanted complete control.

November placed herself in front of Phyllis menacingly. "I know all the moves, lady." She cracked her knuckles and sneered at her.

Phyllis stepped around her so she and Feather would be face-to-face. "That was the deal I made with Stanford. Well, one of them. Don Wenow was in on it too. He said once he got Dash's computer, he'd rewrite the story and make me the main character. I needed to help Don and Stanford by getting the computer."

"How would you do that if you and Dash haven't spoken?"

"Well, I wasn't entirely honest with you," she replied sheepishly. "I invited Dash to spend Christmas with me. Don and I planned it out ahead of time. As soon as Dash arrived in town, I called him and said I'd like to meet him for drinks. Don broke into Dash's room and took the computer. That was a few hours before Dash's death."

"Did Don Wenow kill Dash?" November asked. "Unless he pushed Dash in the pool, I doubt Don had the gumption to kill anything that wasn't grilled first."

"No, he just wanted the computer. He swore to me he didn't hurt my boy."

"Oh, wait." November pulled her phone out of her pocket. "Tell me your phone number, Phyllis."

She recited the number and November proudly showed the picture she'd taken at the crime scene. "He wrote your number on the pizza box, over and over. It was like he was in a trance."

"Not a trance," Feather replied. "Under the control of Stanford Aisley."

Chapter Twenty-Five—
Lanie

I stared at the box I'd just unwrapped, my body paralyzed with fear. The fact that it contained a reference to the deaths of all three authors—a copy of the horror Christmas anthology, a string of Christmas lights, cranberries on twine, and a piece of a Rudolph rooftop ornament, covered in blood was unsettling enough. But to include a threat to me—why?

I read it out loud, again.

Dear, Sweet Lanie,
Tik Tok, Tik Tok.
Your time is drawing near.
Enjoy your Christmas, my dear.

Were we getting too close?

When the doorbell rang, I jumped out of my skin. Logically, I knew the caterer was arriving, but the threat contained in this package was so unnerving, my brain wasn't ready to move back into holiday mode.

I looked through the peephole, twice, assuring myself that Bev's Catering was truly run by a master in the kitchen and not an evil murderess.

When I opened the door, she knitted her newly dyed black brows together and glared at me. "What's wrong, doll? Are you sick? If so, I'm afraid I'll have to leave everything by the door. I can't risk being ill when I have three grandkids to care for."

"Oh, no, it's—I'm fine." I put my hand on my forehead and paced the foyer. *Should we go ahead with Christmas? What if I were endangering my guests?*

"Guess I didn't need your front door code after all. You mentioned you might be gone when I arrived. Better change that thing right away. You never know who might get ahold of my phone and steal all of your Christmas goodies."

"Thanks, Bev. I'll get on that," I answered absently.

"Lanie? I'm going to unload now. Unless you've got something else to tell me. You know, some of the folks think I'm their drive-up shrink. Last week, I was serving steak and potatoes for fifty. That little gal has way too many relatives she doesn't like. I'm not so sure she didn't poison one of them after I left."

Bev had prepared all of this wonderful food. What was I going to do? Tell her to throw it away? No, it was going to be up to me to make the holiday as happy as possible.

"I'll open the garage door and you can come in that way. Thank you, Bev. When you catered the city council luncheon, everyone raved about your sides. I know my guests will do the same."

Bev's face creased with delight. "That sure is nice to hear, doll. I threw in one of my specialties for free. You hadn't ordered it, but my cranberry salad is always a hit. I always order extra cranberries, so I can string some for the tree."

The blood drained from my face. "What did you say?"

"My cran-berry sal-ad!" She mouthed.

It was pure coincidence. Nothing to worry about. *You're being paranoid, Lanie.*

"Thank you, Bev." I pivoted quickly and went to the garage. When I lifted the door, she had two assistants waiting patiently with our roasted turkey, mashed potatoes, green bean salad, and pies. Of course, the completely innocent, *no-connection-to-a-creepy-gift* cranberries were included too.

"Got me a new helper. Name's Autumn. She'll be here any minute. She's going to complete the set up so I can get along to my next job."

The poor girl, not only was she working one job over the holidays, but now two. I made a mental note to talk to Cos about hiring her. He believed in paying his employees a fair wage. "That's fine, Bev. I'm happy for the expert help of anyone."

"Yeah, she had some fancy credentials from a cooking school I never heard of. Figured that was good enough for my holiday rush."

"Can you let her in when she comes? There's some...wrapping I need to do in my bedroom."

She nodded.

While they did their magic in my kitchen, I carefully moved the box to my bedroom, where I could examine it in better lighting. The first thing I noticed was that the box itself had a peculiar smell. Almost like a perfume, or an essential oil... Yes, that was it. An orange oil with some mint mixed in. I removed the string of Christmas lights first. There was no way of knowing if these were the very same lights thrown in the bathtub with Elle Vanashelve.

"You're being ridiculous, Lanie. There's no way someone could remove them from the evidence box. Even Boysie Lumquest would refuse that request."

I set them to the side, planning to find a manufacturer and possible distributor later.

The next thing I removed was a piece of a Rudolph roof ornament covered in blood. Very quickly, I realized it was theatrical blood. *It was fake.* Very convincing, but fake. The ornament looked familiar. Did someone in town have one on their roof? That would be easy to figure out. Piney Falls wasn't that big. I could drive down every street in an hour.

I knew for a fact that the copy of the Christmas anthology used to kill Dash was in the evidence locker. Boysie made a point of telling me before he started his mini vacation.

The heavy book's pages were wavy, as though they'd been dunked in water. There was definitely real blood on the back cover though. As if someone had used it to slap Dash across the face. I thought back to the crime scene report:

Subject was lying on his back with a deep contusion on the left side of his face. Three broken fingers, as if subject were trying to shield his face from the attacker.

That attack—this book—didn't kill him. It could have injured him, but something else did him in.

The last thing in the box was a string of cranberries on twine, like those found around Dash's body.

"The murderer hit him with the book, dazed him and then used another unknown method to kill him. The string of cranberries was there to show us said killer had a sense of humor." Although the autopsy report wasn't in, I hadn't heard any mention of another method used to facilitate Dash's demise.

There was a knock on my door, and I jumped up too quickly, spilling the contents of the package on the ground. Stumbling as I tried to find my footing, I stepped on the cranberries, squirting the red juice all over our expensive white rug.

"Damn!" I hopped over to the door and opened it.

A pretty, copper-haired young lady with cream-colored skin and expressive brown eyes glanced at me sheepishly. The hallways of the Fallen Branch Resort were dim, due to the use of energy-saving lights. I hadn't really observed her in daylight until now. She was stunning.

"I'm sorry to bother you, Mrs. Hill. It's just that your phone has been ringing for the past five minutes.

We thought it might be urgent." She tried to glance behind me to see what I was doing, but I leaned sideways and blocked her view.

I took the phone from her hands. "Autumn, you're working two jobs over Christmas! You poor thing, you must be exhausted."

She nodded uncomfortably.

"You're not disturbing me," I continued. "Thanks for letting me know." I closed the door before she had a chance to reply.

Unknown caller.
Unknown caller.
Unknown caller.

The phone rang again, with the same caller I.D.
"Hello?"

I heard heavy breathing. In order to keep us safe, our daughter insisted on installing apps on our phones that, in case of emergency, would download all of our calls and messages to the other two family member's phones. I didn't want them to know about this and think I couldn't handle this sleazy attempt to threaten me.

"If you're trying to scare me, it's not working. Your blood is fake, your game is fake. It's Christmas, you know, the holiday when we all spread good cheer? Go find something to do to celebrate."

"Cousin Lanie?"

It was sweet little Eloise.

"Hon, where are you? Everyone is worried about you!"

"I want to visit! Can we come now? You promised presents."

How could they do this to a little kid?

"Eloise, can I talk to your new friends? So we can set up a time for you to come over?"

I heard whispering, negotiating.

"You received my gift, I assume?"

It was the mechanical sound of someone using a device to disguise their voice.

"What would I have that you want? Whatever issue you had with my cousin Sylas, that doesn't have anything to do with Eloise. She's just a child! Bring her to me and I won't call the police."

"You're in no position to make demands, Mrs. Hill. I hold all the cards."

"So, what is the point of this?"

"You have something we want."

"What—the fake murder weapons? Your fake blood was a nice touch, but not impressive."

"Those are real. Please feel free to verify their authenticity when we're done here. You have something else much more valuable."

"And that is..."

"You'll find out soon enough."

None of this was making any sense.

"When?"

"Everything, and everyone, in Piney Falls has a connection, Vem."

It was my own voice, from a conversation with

Feather the day before. We were in the car, MY car. They'd been recording our every word.

"You're not going to hurt my friend," I replied firmly. "If you return Eloise to her family without harming a hair on her head, I'll pay whatever it is you want."

"You'll be hearing from us again soon. How nice it will be to meet, face-to-face!"

They hung up.

Now I understood. None of us were safe. They were watching. Everywhere.

Chapter Twenty-Six — Feather

They were greeted by the comforting smells of holiday food as they entered Lanie's home.

"Friend! We're here!" November called, flopping her purse on the floor and kicking her shoes off.

She turned to view Feather's stunned face and remarked, "Lanie loves it when I do that. Makes her feel like I'm staying for a while."

It was hard to imagine that, Feather thought. She kept her combat boots snug on her feet and walked toward the kitchen, where three people were busily preparing their dinner.

There was a large bowl on the edge of the counter with the words, "leave your phone here during dinner, please," written on the side.

Steam rose from the stove and a perfectly browned turkey rested on the countertop. Not wanting to intrude, she continued moving until she reached the formal dining room, where she was greeted by a magnificent sight.

A deep burgundy-colored tablecloth was topped by cream-colored, gold-rimmed China plates.

Two gold-rimmed glasses sat at the top of each place setting, one for wine and one for water. The silverware was a matching gold, as were the napkin rings, each holding a cream-colored napkin.

The most impressive part of the decor were the centerpieces. Along the long, square table, tall, cream-colored hydrangeas in slender glass vases were surrounded by seasonal greenery. It was the most magnificent thing Feather had ever seen in her twenty-four years of existence.

She pulled out her phone and quickly snapped pictures to show her co-workers back at the shop. They would never believe she dined in such elegance if she didn't have visual proof.

The back door opened, and she heard male voices.

"Tug? Where are you?"

They met in the hallway, and he embraced her tightly, kissing her first on the forehead and then on the lips.

She melted into his touch. The taste of his lips was like touching home base. He was what kept her grounded.

"I missed you, babe!" She breathed.

"You won't believe my day!" They said in unison, dissolving in delicious laughter.

"Beauty first," Tug encouraged.

"We met Dash's mother. They weren't close, but she had a painting of him wrapped in cranberries. She's made a deal with a spirit, and she thinks the spirit will bring Dash back."

"That's crazy! You don't think his mother..." Tug's voice trailed off.

Feather shook her head. "No, but she's definitely a suspicious character." She studied his face for any signs of distress from his experiences. "Tell me about your day."

"We worked in this old bakery all day, making breads, muffins, cakes, and pies. It was exhausting and exhilarating. I loved every minute!"

His cheeks were flushed and there was a shine in his eyes she hadn't seen in a long time.

"We were meant to be here, Tug. We're both needed."

He looked at her warily. "I feel like there's more you aren't telling me."

"Tonight, we're going to get in that big bathtub together and I'll give you a play-by-play." She rubbed his solid bicep. "I'll talk until you start to nod off."

"You're having fun too." He grinned. "I can't wait."

"I'll go shower before dinner. Something tells me it's not going to be like the takeout we'd planned." He planted one more kiss on her cheek before leaving.

The last attribute to be added to the table, the tall, cream-colored candles, sparkled off the gold of each component of the table. Feather wanted to take more pictures of the dramatic Christmas scene, but with everyone there, she felt silly. They probably ate like this all the time.

The wine glasses were filled with a dark red wine of some kind. She wasn't much of a wine drinker and worried she might make a face if it didn't taste good. It would be better if she took a drink first so it wouldn't be a surprise, either way.

Glancing around to make sure no one was watching, she took a little sip out of the glass sitting beside a gold name card, surprised by the light, fruity taste.

"Pinot Noir," a voice said. She pivoted to find one of the caterers wiping her hands on a dish cloth. "It's a versatile wine that goes with everything. Good, right?"

"Please don't tell Lanie that I snuck a drink! I wanted to make sure I knew what it tasted like. No surprises, you know."

The woman put her finger to her lips and winked. Now she realized she'd seen this woman before, at the Fallen Branch Resort.

Feather was grateful Tug insisted she pack something somewhat dressy. "We're staying in a nice place, Feath. We should be prepared for whatever."

Feather found a green-and-black plaid wool skirt at the store next to theirs. The owner refused to sell it to her unless she also included a black, cashmere sweater.

Feather politely declined such an expensive gift, but the shop owner wouldn't hear of it. Feather Works Salon was a good neighbor to her. The only condition was that Feather wear the ensemble once for her so she could see it.

Tug, wearing his dressiest pair of khakis and a pink-and-white striped shirt, pulled Feather's chair out for her. "We clean up pretty nice, don't we, babe?" He quipped. Smelling of expensive soap, and dressed in the outfit he wore on their first date, he was the most attractive man she'd ever seen.

Beside Feather was a place card that read, "Truman Coolidge." She didn't have to wait long to see this mystery guest.

An older man wearing red-and-green-striped overalls and a tie containing all the president's names placed one hand on her shoulder and the other in front of her. "Truman Coolidge. Presidential expert and best friend of Cosmo Hill."

"Nice to meet you!"

Feather felt a quick rush of air and heard a very official-sounding voice say, *"He's done a fine job of representing us, dare I say?"*

She pushed it away, as she'd learned to do when she wasn't in the mood for spirits to interfere with the living world.

November Bean had gone home to change into a jumpsuit adorned with tiny reindeer, matching glasses frames, and headband, too. She had bells that jingled on her sneakers, which she hadn't removed, and something brown and shiny around her neck. Lanie warned Feather privately not to ask about it.

Cosmo sat across the table from November. A handsome man the age of her father, he had a ruggedness about him and stunning blue eyes. There was something extremely appealing about his obvious devotion to his wife.

Lanie came in last, and she was a sight to behold. Her honey-blonde hair was pulled back with a diamond-encrusted silver barrette. She was wearing a black-floral dress with intricate embroidery and a delicate tulle overlay.

Her full lips were covered in a rich, red lipstick. It was like someone Feather saw in the black-and-white movies her mother watched. She never paid much attention, but she remembered, in passing, a beautiful woman who seemed to appear in just about every movie of the era. Tulip something-or-other.

There was an audible gasp in the room when she entered. Cosmo rose and took her hand, kissing it lightly. "There is nothing that brightens a room more than my beautiful wife."

She gazed at him with adoration and blew him a kiss. It made Feather warm inside, witnessing such devotion between two people.

Cosmo pulled the chair out for his wife, and she sat, her cheeks flushed from the candlelight. She winked at Feather.

"Before we begin, I'd like to say a few words," Lanie began. "We're missing a few familiar faces this year. But thanks to fate, we've acquired a few more." She nodded toward Feather and Tug.

"Don't know what I'd have done without you today, buddy," Cosmo said, raising his wine glass to his new friend.

"Any friend of Cosmo's is a friend of mine. In the words of Woodrow Wilson, 'Friendship is the only cement that will hold the world together.' If it's good enough for a president, then it's good enough for Truman." He lifted his glass as well. "And I'll add some gratitude for good people in general. Got myself a new neighbor whose been leaving nasty notes in my mailbox. Seems he doesn't appreciate my midnight fireworks to mark presidential birthdays. Yesterday, my firework launcher disappeared. The nice one Lanie ordered for me from her supply place. Got a good idea where it went."

"I'm grateful you shared your home with us," Tug said, continuing the conversation. "Feather and me, well, we've had some rough Christmases. Thank you." Tug raised his glass.

Nervous energy boiling up inside her, Feather bumped her glass nearly knocking it over. "I'm so glad I can help you solve these cases. Lanie and Cosmo, you are the most amazing people I've ever met." Feather lifted her glass.

November cleared her throat in a deliberate manner.

"And November," Feather added quickly. "I've never met anyone quite like you."

The appetizers of ham wrapped dates, brie and honey on a hearty cracker, and cherry-filled miniature pastries were served, then the turkey and sides. Finally, it was time for pies.

"Autumn, our little helper, seems to have disappeared," Lanie observed, standing. "No matter. How many for marionberry, how many for pumpkin, or for a complete change of course, what about cheesecake?

When every hand went up for all options, they all dissolved into laughter. "Does this make up for your turkey-less Thanksgiving, Vem?"

November smiled with satisfaction. "It was worth the wait, Lanie."

She took a count and disappeared into the kitchen.

"Do you need any help, Lanie?" Feather called.

"No, just enjoy. And don't let Vem convince you it's time for a digestive moan."

"I can't even muster an objection," November replied, patting her distended belly. "Did I ever tell you about the time, in California, when the toilet paper king rented out an entire hotel for Christmas? It was just like a horror movie. The halls were empty, and when we went down for dinner, they had twins, dressed exactly alike, serving us. I can't tell you how many therapy sessions it took to get over–"

There was a loud, piercing scream, and then a muffled, "Cos! Help me!"

He jumped up from the table, followed by the others. They ran to the kitchen, where both pies sat, face-down on the floor. The door to the garage was wide open and a raccoon sat just out of reach.

Immediately, every phone began buzzing in the giant bowl in the kitchen, causing it to vibrate off the counter.

"You're all celebrating like no one is dead," a computer-generated voice said when Cosmo found his phone and answered.

"Who is this? What did you do to my wife? If you harm a hair on her head, I'll–"

"Oh, didn't Lanie tell you about our plans? She's going to miss out on dessert."

Chapter Twenty-Seven — Feather

"Lanie?" Cosmo called, becoming more frantic each round he made, going upstairs, downstairs, and outside. "Lanie?" His voice became weaker "Babe?"

Feather and Tug immediately ran outside, watching helplessly as a white Bev's Catering van peeled out of the driveway.

"Did you get the plate number?" Tug asked.

"It was too dark."

Feather called to any spirits in the area willing to speak. "Now you're quiet?" She snapped in frustration.

They went back inside, where Cosmo was pulling things out of cupboards in a frenzy. The pile of boxes and cans accumulating as this strong man fell apart caused a lump to form in Feather's throat.

Meanwhile, November Bean stood in the living room, howling.

Truman Coolidge walked from room to room, tapping on the walls, and announcing, "Solid!" as he moved to the next one. Each of her loved ones were dealing with this shocking development in their own way.

When she had a chance to regain her composure, Feather studied Tug's face. It was tight and drawn, and she could tell he was sinking into himself, his own way of dealing with stressful situations. She squeezed his hand, hoping to bring him back. "We'll find her, babe," she whispered supportively.

When Cosmo realized they were standing there, he rushed to Feather and began shaking her.

"Tell me everything! Who would do this? One of the authors?"

Tug, forced out of his trance-like state by Feather's impending danger, gently removed Cosmo's hand. "We don't know, Mr. Hill. Feather is as upset as you are. Right, Feath?"

She nodded, not at all sure that she hadn't caused this somehow. "Lanie's missing cousin called. The little girl? She was in trouble. She didn't want to tell you because it was a special day. I'm guessing that whoever took Eloise also took Lanie."

"Bean?" Cosmo hollered in an irritated voice. "Come in here! Now!"

November, hands on hips, entered the formal dining room with irritation written all over her face. "What? I'm calling to the moon for answers! Unless you have a better idea?"

"Tell me about the phone call from Eloise. What did she say?"

"I don't know anything about that."

Cosmo grabbed her arm as she was about to turn away. "You're not leaving until you tell me everything."

"Unhand me, you beast!" She spat.

"November doesn't know anything. Lanie told me in confidence," Feather said apprehensively, concerned he might focus on her again. "She was going to tell you all tomorrow."

Cosmo let go of November and moved away from her, rubbing the back of his neck.

"Why would my best friend keep something like this from me?" November asked.

"She didn't want to spoil Christmas for anyone. What can we do now? Should someone contact Officer Holliday?"

"We're going to call up everyone in town and divide into search parties." They pivoted in unison to see Truman Coolidge, holding his phone in one hand and an old phone book in the other. "And someone is going over to Bev's Catering first thing."

As Cosmo opened his mouth, Truman continued, "Not Cosmo. You'll be too emotional. If we want Bev to talk, we have to be firm but calm."

"Tug and I can go," Feather offered.

"It's a holiday, buddy. Doubt anyone wants to interrupt their nice dinner," Cosmo said rocking back and forth with his hands in his pockets.

Truman moved further into the room and set his

phone on the beautiful table that was still littered with remnants of their fine meal.

"We'll see about that. Your wife has lots of support in this town. They'll want to bring her home."

"I can lead a search party, Truman. With my superior nose and unmatchable detective skills, my group will find my best friend before Santa makes his appearance."

Cosmo stormed over in front of November once again. Feather held her breath, fearing what might come next. Lanie mentioned there was a contentious relationship between the two, but she'd never said why.

November's bottom lip quivered, out of fear or defiance or both. When Cosmo was directly in front of her, he threw his arms around her. To Feather's shock, Cosmo rested his head on November's shoulder and began to sob.

At first, she seemed taken aback and stared helplessly at the other partygoers. As soon as she realized what was happening, November patted Cosmo's head uncomfortably.

"Shh. That's okay, Cosmo. We'll find our Lanie.

Tug's lip quivered, too, and Feather noticed a tear running down his cheek.

Feather wasn't comfortable with that kind of vulnerability in herself. She began gathering the rest of the plates and took them to the kitchen. She set them in the sink, dropping a large dollop of mashed potatoes on the way.

There was a towel with a crocheted top hanging on

the refrigerator handle, and when she went to grab it, she paused to view the pictures displayed. Happy faces, several framed in magnets that read, *"Family"* and *"The best things in life."*

For a moment, she felt anger. No, it was jealousy. She deserved a mother like that, someone who loved unconditionally and covered every available surface with her pictures. Instead, she'd found herself saddled with a family who didn't appreciate her gifts and rarely contacted her.

An overwhelming tide of emotion rolled over her and she, too, began to cry.

"Feath? Are you okay?" It was Tug, her champion, as usual.

She cleaned up the mess and then stood, wiping her eyes on the backs of her hands before smiling up at him.

"I was in the middle of a real nice pity party. Leave it to you to interrupt, reminding me that I have no reason to attend in the first place."

Puzzled, he pulled her in close. "I don't understand. I just wanted to check on you."

"I'm fine. It's Cosmo who needs the help. I'm going to wash these up. I don't want any evidence of our celebration to further upset Cosmo. Poor guy."

Tug kissed the top of her head. "You're amazing, you know that? You ran in here to cry alone. My sweet Feather, always thinking of others."

She blushed. "Something like that."

Feather watched as he walked away before

returning to the task at hand. When all the dishes were washed, dried, and set upon the counter, she tidied up everything the caterers had missed.

Placing her hands on her hips, she surveyed the large space for anything she'd missed. It was spotless. With a measure of satisfaction, she hung the towel on the refrigerator handle and prepared to turn out the light.

The hairs on her arms rose.

Don't give up, lass. She needs you.

"Is that all, Fiona? Couldn't you help us a little more?"

"Feath?" Tug asked. He had his coat on, and he held hers out. "We need to go. Cosmo gave me directions to the caterer. He wants us to get there ASAP."

"Right."

Fiona would have to wait.

They rode down the winding mountain in silence. No amount of cheerful banter would change this dreadful situation.

"Did Cosmo call the police? I know Officer Lumquest is out of town, but whoever is on duty should be able to help, right?"

"I heard November on the phone with them as we were walking out," Feather replied. "If it's Officer Holliday, he won't be much help. He's barely capable of the basics. His only concern is staying off the Wall of Shame, and he's not too worried about public safety."

She tapped her toe nervously, making a clicking sound on the floorboard. They approached Piney Falls and the lights of the city shown in the car. Feather realized she'd left her boots untied. Bending down to tie the first one, she noticed worms crawling out of the eyelets. The worms were bloody, covering her boots in an eerie red trail.

I can control you, too.

Feather sat up abruptly. She was relieved to see Tug immersed in the Christmas music playing on the radio. He hadn't noticed anything. She glanced down again, only to find her shoes tied and the disturbing vision was gone.

"I know you're not real. Your silly games don't scare me." She closed her eyes, concentrating on a visualization game she played. In it, the entities were shorter than her and transparent. Only the strength of her mind could make them move. Feather pictured Stanford Aisley, a stubby man in old-fashioned clothing and a top hat, feeling the wrath of her power. She pushed until he was gone, blown away in the wind.

Stop! You're hurting me!

Feather's eyes snapped open, and she grabbed Tug's arm.

"What is it, babe?"

"I heard Lanie's voice. I'm really worried!"

Chapter Twenty-Eight — Lanie

I awoke to excruciating pain in my scalp. I tried to reach up and touch it, but my hands were bound. Glancing around, I realized I wasn't in my beautiful home, celebrating Christmas Eve with loved ones any more. This place was dark and damp and smelled of mold.

The last thing I remembered was placing cheesecake on a plate for Vem. We'd discussed the appropriate dessert for Christmas, and since she missed Thanksgiving, she insisted on a cheesecake topped with chocolate chips. It was her favorite.

"Hello?" I called. No answer.

I wiggled my hands, trying to free them with no luck. In the process, I realized I had scrapes on both of my arms that were bleeding. My beautiful dress, the one I'd bought with my earnings as the marketing manager for the Fallen Branch Resort, was ripped and most likely ruined.

I had no concept of how much time had passed. Was it Christmas Day? New Years? Or was it still the evening they'd taken me?

The more alert I became, the more I felt concern for my circumstance. There were no sounds at all, not even traffic whizzing by, which meant we weren't close to Piney Falls. Now I understood the term, "silence is deafening." It was hard to tell whether if the problem was my hearing, or if the room was soundproof.

Taking a page from November Bean's colorful book, I closed my eyes and breathed in deeply through my nostrils. There was still a slight hint of saltiness. The ocean was nearby. At least I hadn't been carted away to lands unknown by some crazy drug lord. The familiar scents of bakery goods and fresh seafood weren't there. I wasn't in town, but still at the coast.

"Don't lose it yet, Lanie," I uttered bravely. "You can channel your mother tomorrow."

It struck me that if it was, in fact, still Christmas Eve, I had a chance to get back to my family before Christmas Day and our family-of-choice's celebration. Vem would wear her obnoxiously bright gold ornament jumpsuit and put a bow on her head. Cosmo would sing off-key, making up his own Christmas carols while Truman told the stories of presidential Christmases.

I thought about our first Christmas as a couple. I found what I thought was appropriate for a rugged man like him out of a fancy catalogue leftover from my days in Chicago. It was a thick, navy sweater covered in snowmen, the thing ads convinced me ruggedly handsome men were wearing.

Dutifully, he pulled it over his head and declared it the best gift he'd ever received. His sister, Cedar told me later that Cosmo hated sweaters because they made him feel like he was being constricted. A throwback to his time in the cult when his every move was documented.

The next week, I gathered all of our offerings for the local food and clothing bank for the needy. When he noticed I'd included his sweater, he grabbed my arm. "You're not taking this, Lanie."

"But...you hate wearing sweaters. Cedar told me so. I was only thinking of myself, and not your needs." I fought back tears, once again only thinking of myself.

"That would be the case if some random stranger gave me the sweater." He dropped it and wrapped both of his muscular arms around my waist. "But this particular sweater came from the woman I'm going to marry. Every time I wear it, I'll think about the first and only woman I've ever loved."

We kissed passionately, and I knew from that day on that our futures were forever intertwined.

Until now.

I struggled to loosen the restraints on my hands, using superhuman strength only available to me because of the vision of that beautiful face in my mind.

If I was restrained like this, they weren't planning to kill me right away. I had time to figure out how to escape. I glanced around again, this time, without emotion. There was always a crack or crevice.

"You can see, Lanie. That means light is getting in somewhere."

Wiggling my feet, I realized with relief that my legs weren't bound. I rolled to my side, tasting the dirt from the floor on my lips. Now was the time Vemcersize, the exercise routine we'd been doing together once a week, was really going to pay off.

"Knee to chest, Lanie. Flab isn't fab, lift, lift, lift!' I recited, hoping to channel her enthusiasm as I used my newly-acquired ab muscles to reach a sitting position.

I could hear the sound of someone walking down a hallway, their shoes clapping against the flooring.

"Hello? Please, talk to me! I just want to know where I am!"

The steps paused.

"I'm begging you. Just a few words is all I'm asking."

The footsteps continued until they reached my door. I heard keys unlocking it and a dark figure appeared. It was a man, slightly shorter than Cosmo. His face was covered with a mask like I'd seen in bank robberies from the movies.

"Can you loosen these just a little? My arms are going numb." I wiggled my arms in an exaggerated manner.

He stooped down and loosened whatever was being used to restrain me. I took I deep breath, trying to memorize his scent. It was an essential oil. Orange, maybe. It was the same scent I'd smelled in the package I opened earlier. *Good Lanie!*

My arms actually did feel better once the restraints were loosened.

"I don't suppose you're going to tell me why I'm here? On Christmas Eve? Whatever it is, couldn't we discuss it face-to-face? I've kept secrets before. I'm happy to help you, as long as I can see you."

He stood, immobile. At least he wasn't leaving.

"I...could use water too. Do you suppose I could go to the restroom and get a drink? Women my age have a constant need for both."

The masked stranger turned and walked away.

"Please don't leave me! I'll do whatever you want!" I called with desperation. At least he'd left the door open.

I scooched over, listening to the sound of my delicate dress tearing with each scooch. When I reached the doorway, I peeked my head outside and looked to the left. It was a long hallway. It was definitely a commercial building, not someone's basement. I looked to the right and my eyes were met by the legs of my captor.

"I'm sorry, you just scared me when you left. I was looking for—"

He grabbed one of my arms, causing me to wince with pain. The brute pulled me to my feet and drug me into the dimly-lit corridor. I looked down and saw my beautiful ruby-colored heels were gone. Vem and I scoured every store within fifty miles of Piney Falls trying to find them.

We stopped when we reached a doorway with no door. Inside was a toilet and a sink. He shoved me inside.

"Can I have some privacy? I'm a little shy, if you know what I mean."

He moved slightly to the side. At least he wouldn't be staring directly at me.

I stepped back out. "Oh, and I need a free hand, to, you know."

Without giving him the chance to think about it, I turned my back towards him and he loosened my restraints, which I now realized were zip ties. I pulled one hand out, grateful for the freedom to do so. Now I understood how people could bond with their captors. I almost loved this man as much as my husband right now.

When I returned to the bathroom, I turned on the light. The reflection greeting me was horrifying. My hair was knotted in several places on my head. I had a fat lip and three long scratches on my right cheek.

I didn't want to see what was left of my dress, so I kept my gaze above my chin. Summoning Herculean strength, I fought back tears.

Using the cup he'd placed in the bathroom and drank several glasses of water, knowing it would cause a return trip to the bathroom later.

"Okay, I'm ready to return to my tomb," I said, half

joking. If this was the way it ended, it had been a good run.

Instead of leading me back, he took my arm and we continued in the opposite direction from my cell.

"Where are we going? I didn't mean to upset you!"

We reached a winding staircase and I stared up pensively. Was this going to lead to my death? He pushed me until I began to climb the steps. My arms and legs ached with each new move. If I were home, Cosmo would rub Vem's secret oils on my sore parts and tell me I was beautiful, no matter how much I felt otherwise.

On the landing, he shoved me again, this time toward a shiny blue door. Christmas music blared from behind it. I turned to question my guard, but he had disappeared.

"Come in, Lanie! I've been waiting!"

Chapter Twenty-Nine—
Feather

"Lanie? Are you out here?" Feather called into the dead of the mid-winter forest. She knew better than to expect a response. Whoever took Lanie wasn't about to hide her so close to home.

On top of that worry, she heard whispers, not actual sentences, but fragments from centuries'-old ghosts. They wanted their messages heard, regardless of Lanie's situation. Her head had been full of these noises ever since they arrived. Even a walk in the quiet woods wasn't quiet in Feather's mind.

When Feather and Tug found Bev, not at her catering store but eating Christmas Eve dinner with her daughter, a policeman they didn't recognize was taking her statement. Autumn was due back with the catering van and when she didn't show or answer her phone, Bev knew something was wrong. She was pacing back and forth, stuffing chocolates shaped like presents into her mouth. "I'm so sorry. So sorry. I never should have hired that girl!" Bev cried.

It was obvious to Tug and Feather that Bev didn't have anything to do with Lanie's disappearance.

The next morning, Christmas morning, they'd all risen at the crack of dawn. Tug was off hiking the more challenging terrain with Cosmo and Truman. She and November were combing the section of woods they were assigned by Officer Holliday. At least fifty other community members searched for Lanie as well. Lanie was extremely well-liked, that was evident.

She felt her phone buzz in the pocket of her tangerine fleece. When she recognized the caller, she almost cried.

"Jayden?" She gasped. "You knew Lanie was in trouble. Oh, thank you! Please tell me where to find her!"

A low voice chuckled on the other end of the conversation. "And a Merry Christmas to you, Feather."

That's right. It was a day of celebration for everyone else. Not exactly the holiday any of them had expected. The hollowness they were all feeling made Feather wish it wasn't a day meant for joy.

"Sorry, Merry Christmas to you, Jayden. As you already know, Lanie has disappeared. We're all sick with worry. What can you tell me?"

Jayden sighed. "Not as much as you'd like, I'm afraid. I had a vision of Lanie struggling. She's in a fortress with someone she knows. When I try to focus in to find more information, a wall rises in front of me."

Feather's heart sank. Jayden's powers were superhuman. If she couldn't locate Lanie, no one could. "You taught me we are in control of our gifts, not the spirits. Can't you just tell them to step aside?"

"Usually. I've encountered a few who are skilled at keeping me from seeing what I need. That's the case here. But all isn't lost. I've got an idea."

Feather approached the remnants of a pine tree, most likely a casualty of the holiday tradition. She lowered herself down on the stump, feeling relieved for a few moments off her feet. After she'd made contact, she remembered the fierce rain from the previous night. Her backside would be covered in mud, a predicament that would upset Tug. He liked to keep her looking her best.

"Go ahead, Jayden."

"You've got quite a number of spirits surrounding you, Feather. Some of them have been there since the inception of Piney Falls, those who suffered tremendously throughout the century, and those who want to help you now. It's hard to keep them all straight. I'm sure you're feeling it too. It's probably coming through like a mishmash of words."

Tears slid down her cheek. She was exhausted, both physically and emotionally, so she couldn't be sure where it was coming from. No one understood her gift better than Jayden. Her friends from Charming—Gemini Reed, especially—were all supportive, but no one else understood the voices constantly bombarding her.

"You're right. Out here, walking through the woods, I hear constant whispers. They are driving me insane, Jayden. There was one woman I thought was helping me, but she's nowhere to be found now that I need her."

"Try this, sugar. Close your eyes now and put a face to her voice. I'm going to help you and call to her too. Her name is Fiona, right?"

She wanted to protest, that she wasn't capable of that level of communication. There was no sense in arguing with Jayden, though. She was always right.

She closed her eyes and concentrated. Fiona, from her brief vision, was a diminutive woman with intense green eyes and a kindly smile.

"No one is here, Jayden," she said, defeated.

"Shh. Just listen."

Feather dropped her shoulders and opened her mind, picturing a warm, sunny day in the same forest. She was walking with Tug, and they were smelling the pines and holding hands. They came upon a woman dressed in dark clothing with delicate features and kind eyes.

There was a crackling sound and Feather's eyes snapped open. In front of her was an apparition of a woman, dressed in a black, tight-fitting, button-up dress with a high collar. Her thick hair was held on top of her head with a large comb. The entity she'd seen before was there again and this time, her appearance was almost regal.

"Fiona? You're here?"

Aye, lass.

"Fiona, you have to help me find Lanie. She's in terrible danger."

Fiona moved closer and Feather could see her delicate features, small hands and impossibly tiny waist. She looked like she'd just walked out of a 1900s photo. The detail of this entity was unlike any other. She could stare at Fiona Scheddy forever, drinking in every detail.

Oh, my poor dear. You're worried and rightly so. I've been watching Lanie for years. She's been my champion, and now's my time to return the favor.

Feather wanted to ask what she meant, but she knew there wasn't time. "Where is she? How can we save her?"

There's an evil presence that's been wandering through these woods, watching for nigh a month now. But it isn't that one who's got you in a twist. 'Tis a living being whose set his sights on you now, Feather Jones.

"Me?" Feather's eyes opened wide. "Why me?
"You're a prize, dear sweet girl. Your gifts are highly coveted by those who see their potential for evil.

"Then why not take me?"

Because you're a stubborn one. It's served you well in life, but this one thought he'd have more leverage to make you comply if he took Lanie.

All day she'd felt depressed about Lanie's disappearance. Now that the short winter sun was waning, she was angry. How dare someone drag Lanie into their business with her?

"Tell me where they are. I'll offer myself if they'll let her go."

Fiona shook her head. *Not a wise choice. You give in and they don't need to keep Lanie anymore. They'll dispose of her and then you, when you've done their bidding.*

She wanted to understand what exactly their "bidding" was, but once again, she kept that thought to herself. "I have to do something, Fiona!"

Aye, you do. I'll be here to help you, lass. First thing you need to do is find that dear sweet husband of hers. Tell him you need to see her phone. She's been receiving calls for nigh a month.

Fiona's shape dissipated.

"Wait! What do I do when I get the number? Fiona? Don't leave me now!"

Jayden cleared her throat, reminding Feather of her presence.

"You found someone to help. I'm glad!"

"I've got to find Cosmo. Can I call you back later? I don't want to interrupt your celebration or—"

"Of course. Call me when you're stuck, but you won't be. You've got a strong entity by your side."

"Thank you, Jayden. I won't forget this."

Feather hung up and stood with renewed vigor. She wiped as much debris as she could from her pants and looked around. The voices, the living voices, were silent.

"November? Truman? Where are you?"

Her sense of direction had never been terrific. Once, as a child, she'd gotten lost going to a friend's house to play. Her mother instructed her to walk two blocks, then turn toward the sun, and then two more blocks toward Burgers Now, and she ended up in downtown Charming, at the Charming Drive-Thru Cleaners. The busy Nagasaki family was none-too-pleased to babysit her while they waited for her mother to come and pick her up.

"Truman? Help!"

She remembered he'd given his phone number to everyone in his search crew.

"It's Feather. Jones. I need to find Cosmo right away!"

Truman put his hand over the phone, though she could still hear every word he was saying. "It's that little gal staying at your place. She sounds frantic."

"Feather? Did you find her?"

Cosmo's strong voice faltered. Feather thought about Tug and how devastated he would be if anything happened to her. Fiona was right. Giving herself over to Lanie's captor wouldn't serve any purpose.

"No, I didn't, but I did have a conversation with someone named Fiona."

There was a silence on the other end she hadn't

expected. She thought, maybe wrongly, that Cosmo was completely supportive of her gift.

"Cosmo? Are you still there? This is important."

"Yeah, I'm here. It threw me off, I gotta tell you. Fiona is one of the founders of our town. I guess you're the real deal, aren't you?"

"I am. I need you to look at your app tracking Lanie's calls and tell me if there are any recent numbers you don't recognize."

She glanced around, realizing she had no idea where she'd wandered.

"I've never used this thing before. Seemed like a huge invasion of privacy. Give me a sec...Hmm. Yeah, I do see several. Always the same time of day. What does that mean?"

"Tug has a device similar to a walkie-talkie. We can talk in real-time, and it has a GPS. Could you ask him to come find me?"

She'd scoffed when he wanted to bring this useless toy along. *"Why do we need this? We're going to spend our week in the hot tub?" she complained.*

Now she would owe him big.

There were muffled words and this time Tug's voice on the other end of the line.

"Feath? Are you okay?"

"I'm fine, babe. I just need to see you and hold you tight. And I need to talk to Cosmo. But I have no idea where I am!"

"You don't have to worry about that. I have a tracker on your phone. We'll be there in no time."

He hung up and she was left wondering how long he'd kept this secret. Quickly, she opened her Lost Lanie app. There was nothing to show, so Lanie's phone was off. The last known location was at their home, when life seemed so simple.

Chapter Thirty — Lanie

"What's that smell?"

There was a scent I recognized in the air. Orange and mint, just like I'd smelled in Dash's room and when Autumn came to do the catering for our dinner. With what had transpired over the past two days, it brought bile up my throat.

I'd wiggled in my seat, struggling to find the least painful angle to place my body. The longer I was awake, the more details emerged from my capture. Autumn, the young woman I was planning to tip generously, came up behind me while I was cutting the cheesecake. As I turned to see what she wanted, I heard someone whisper, "Now!" and I was struck over the head. I tried to keep myself upright, but in addition to Autumn, someone else was fighting me.

In a matter of seconds, they'd bound me and tossed me in the back of the catering van. I struggled, rolling back and forth against the sides of the vehicle. When I had one hand free, they pulled over and covered my mouth with something sickly-sweet smelling and that was the last thing I remembered before waking up in this makeshift prison.

A sinister smile crept across his face, one of amusement at my discomfort.

"You still haven't told me why I'm here. Torturing me isn't going to make any difference if I have no idea what you want from me, Sylas."

"One thing at a time, cousin. The scent you're smelling is a new product. I'm expanding our holdings all the time, and we're testing a room air freshener scent that people can wear around their necks." He pulled a gold disk out of his shirt."

Joie d'Orange. All my employees are wearing one so that we can test the distance at which the scent can be smelled. Genius, don't you think?"

"No, I don't think. This makes absolutely no sense. Why did you kidnap me?"

My knees were knocking.

I'm usually not afraid of much, but after what had transpired, I couldn't control them. My teeth were chattering as well, making a strange cacophony of sounds emanating from my body.

My cousin drummed his fingers on his desk. "You were interfering with my movie. I can't have that."

There was simply no way to be comfortable in this chair that Mr. Masked Face forced me into. I was trying desperately to regain the feeling in my foot, but part of me wondered if it was even worth it, if they were going to kill me soon.

"Usually, your investigations involve someone in Piney Falls, am I correct?"

I nodded wearily, too tired to argue.

Under normal circumstances, I would relish the chance to tear this dirtbag apart. But I'd been knocked around. What wasn't swollen on me was achy and defeated, unlike my usual, upbeat self. I closed my eyes, trying to imagine the smells of Christmas in my home, with my family smiling at me.

"Lanie?" He reached across the desk and poked my forehead with his pen. "It's much too early for you to check out. We have to finish our conversation."

I opened my eyes, incredibly sad by my reality. That really was my cousin sitting across from me. Sylas Anders, traitor. And Lanie Anders was just dumb enough to fall for it.

"Two years ago, I was invited to a séance. It was a corporate getaway, lots of drinking and all that." He made a swishing motion with his hand, as if we would have a meeting of the minds on this topic.

"A spirit came through who promised me great wealth if I followed his instructions implicitly," he continued. "Immediately, I convened a group of writers to compose an anthology based on this spirit, as per his wishes."

"Stanford Aisley wanted you to feed his ego and you were just the guy to do it."

I didn't try to hide my disgust.

"As you know by now, the anthology was such a success, it cried out for its moment on the big screen. I went to another séance, asking for this entity's help again." Sylas leaned back in his chair, completely oblivious to my discomfort.

"This time, the entity suggested I kill off the authors, one by one." He chuckled. "It was absurd, on the surface, but then I started to imagine a movie within a movie, where the authors died in real life just the way their main characters had in the anthology. It was brilliant."

He sat forward and clasped his hands together on the desk.

"Everything went perfectly with Elle and Ivy, but Dash was a problem from day one. First, he refused to sign over his rights to the movie until I paid him more than the others. I told him he could have a bonus for getting everyone on board. Then he got greedy and wanted more." Sylas sighed. "I should have expected it, I suppose. I knew his reputation before we began.

I searched for signs of humanity in his face, but found none.

"Just as in life, in death he was also troublesome. He refused to die as his character did, so my little elf had to improvise. You were supposed to find his body in order for you to be a suspect in his death. That's what happened in his story, you know."

"So you orchestrated all of this," I snickered. "You're starting to bore me. Can I go back to my cell now?" I couldn't believe what I was hearing. The times we'd video chatted, Sylas seemed so intelligent. Now he sounded like a complete moron. I didn't want him thinking I was in awe of him anymore.

"With Dash's refusal to sign over his rights, I changed course. I thought it was you I wanted as the star. The amateur detective, caught red-handed at the murder scene. But then you invited a delightful little starlit into your home and, as they say, the plot thickened."

"What?" Now I was alert.

"She's got a gift I find valuable. Not only for this picture, but many more to come. Brain Gravy is going to thrive with her under my tutelage."

My head throbbed, making this conversation even more difficult to follow. "You're saying that you want to force Feather to help you run your business? I still don't understand why you kidnapped me, and why did you send the creepy present?"

"Oh, I don't know. I kind of like games, don't you? Remember our conversation last month about the word games?"

I'd opened myself up to this stranger, telling him about my daily word puzzles and memories of my childhood. All so he could use it against me now.

"Where's Eloise?" My heart was racing. "What did you do with that poor little girl?"

"She's safe." He used his hand to push aside my concerns. "Toys and candy. That's all it takes to entertain the young ones."

"Whatever you want, I'll do it. Provided you

deliver Eloise to her grandparents, without a hair on her head disturbed."

He let out an uproarious laugh. It gave me a moment to study his features. The man had no chin to speak of. Enormous, puffy cheeks, a bulbous nose, and no chin. He didn't resemble any of the Anders, at least the ones I'd seen in pictures. I don't know why I'd missed it during our video chats. Maybe he wasn't as closely related to me as I'd thought?

"This is how things will work, dear cousin. I'm going to enjoy a nice holiday dinner with my companions. Tomorrow, when you're ready to listen, I'll tell you what comes next. It is the holiday, after all. We bought a nice bottle of Sassy Lasses Merlot from the vineyard down the road. I'm sorry you can't join us."

There was no sense in letting him get to me. No sense, but also, I had no thoughts on how to escape. For now, the best thing he could do, ironically, was to send me back to the silence of the cold room. At least there I could think.

I struggled to my feet, expecting Mr. Black Mask to appear. Instead, someone else, considerably taller than Mr. Black Mask, wearing a navy-blue mask entered the room. It was humorous thinking about the monochromatic look, one Vem would appreciate. If she were to become a career criminal, her wardrobe would work well.

He grabbed my arms and began to zip-tie me again. "In the morning, you'll be the guest of honor,"

Sylas said with a sneer. "The brunches here are like none other."

"The guest of...what? You've beaten me to a pulp, my dress is torn, I can barely talk with this swollen lip. How in the world am I supposed to enjoy food with your family? And Sylas, what is this about a movie?"

"Who said anything about my family?" He motioned slightly with one finger. "Tomorrow, sweet Lanie. I look forward to dining with you."

The man in blue jerked me away and led me back down the hallway, where he opened one of an endless set of doors and shoved me inside.

For the second time today, I was in shock.

Chapter Thirty-One — Feather

Officer Holliday's superior called in back-up officers from up and down the Oregon Coast. Once he explained the situation, they gladly gave up their Christmas feasts to help. Boysie Lumquest, local police chief, was still away with family and unavailable by phone. An extensive search of the woods had turned up nothing, and now police and volunteers alike were going door-to-door searching for Lanie Anders Hill. Though it didn't seem possible that anyone was left at home.

Those who weren't actively searching were making meals, printing flyers or finding other creative ways to help. November, after an unsuccessful session in her room of top-secret toys, held a special moaning session. Moaning for My Bestie included Lanie's favorite stretches as well as a group howl at the end of the session.

After an exhaustive all-day search, Lanie's

husband, Cosmo Hill, refused to leave his bedroom the next morning. Feather tapped on the door, offering to make him breakfast or even call their daughter, but he said no thank you to both.

In addition to the disappearance of their host, Feather was tasked with finding the murderer of the *Strung by the Fire* authors all by herself. November Bean was lost in her grief, dealing with it by conducting a twenty-four-hour moan session. Feather felt a duty to finish this investigation for Lanie, if nothing else than to take the burden off her plate if she was found.

When. When she was found.

After sending Tug off for a morning jog up to the Piney Falls, she settled into a chair on the back porch to gather her thoughts. She felt a little guilty, enjoying the sounds of birds chirping and the sight of the tall trees as she drank her coffee. Lanie was probably locked away in a trunk somewhere.

On this unusually sunny winter day, Feather closed her eyes and opened her mind, hoping desperately that the right spirit would make contact.

Did you forget?

She felt a chill run down her spine.

"Stanford Aisley? Tell me where Lanie is!"

A skill she was most proud of was imagining herself as a superhero, pushing evil spirits like him away. But recently, Stanford Aisley had shown her just how powerful he was.

Don't wait.

Feather stood up, pulling her compact body up to its full five feet and two inches. "Look, buddy. I'm not putting up with your–"

At that moment, it occurred to her that this spirit may not be Stanford at all. Lately she'd been unable to discern his energy from Fiona's. They were both strong, on opposite ends of the spectrum. She made a mental note to ask Jayden about that later.

This spirit was trying to help.

"We were looking for them the day that Lanie disappeared. All three of the authors still living from the anthology. Is that what you mean? Do I need to contact them again?"

Pick up the phone.

She rushed inside and found her phone. Yesterday when she'd encountered Fiona, she'd insisted that Feather look at the calls Lanie received in the days leading up to her kidnapping. Feather got all of those numbers from Cosmo and then forgot about them.

The best idea in situations like this was to research each person carefully to ensure they weren't a danger. With Lanie having been gone over twenty-four hours now, that was a luxury she couldn't afford.

"Hello? I...need to speak with Lanie."

She'd hurried to make the call, but forgot to think about what she might say.

"Who is this?" The voice on the other end asked suspiciously.

"I'm a...friend of Lanie's," she stuttered. "I really

need to talk to her. We're planning a New Year's Eve party together, and—"

"You didn't hear she's been taken? What kind of a friend doesn't know that?"

It was definitely not the person she needed to speak with.

"No! I didn't! When did this happen?"

"Christmas Eve. The poor woman just sat down to dinner when men dressed in black entered their home and captured Lanie. Cosmo tried valiantly to fight them off, but he was no match for their strength."

Feather resisted the urge to correct the person on the other end of the line. Small town gossip twisted words into situations they were never meant to be.

"That's frightening. Who might have taken her?" She asked, playing along.

"Well, we have some ideas. All the gals at the beauty salon think it's one of the criminals she's put in jail. You know she's done her part to keep Piney Falls safe. They must've escaped and come after her."

"Hmm."

All she needed now was to get off the phone.

"I should call Cosmo and see if I can be of help."

"No, don't bother the poor man. Alma called the bakery this morning to find out if there was any word and Doris said he hadn't come in and wouldn't answer his phone. He's probably off in the woods, hunting or doing something else therapeutic."

Feather glanced at his bedroom door, knowing full well that Cosmo hadn't left his room.

"Thanks for your help. I need to go now." She hung up and moved on to the next number. This time, she thought out ahead of time what she was going to say.

When someone answered, she clenched her body into the hard, defensive stance she imagined this persona to be.

"Hi, this is Lanie. I know you've been calling my phone for almost a month. It's time we quit playing games. What is it you want from me?"

She waited for a response.

"I...um...it's time for your annual teeth cleaning. I thought I left that message, numerous times."

Again.

This time, the number she called came up as "unknown caller" with a California area code.

"What?"

Feather paused, giving herself time to get the words out.

"I'm a friend of Lanie Anders Hill. She's currently missing and I've been asked to look into recent calls. Can you tell me the nature of your relationship with her?"

"Sa-sa-sa-so, you found me."

That wasn't the answer she'd been expecting.

"Of course I did. It wasn't that hard, Wendell. Where is Lanie?"

"She's not here."

Feather stifled the anger she felt. Too many times, people in her life had misjudged her. They believed she didn't have the strength or intelligence to take them on.

"You're going to tell me where Lanie is, and then I'm going to get her. This isn't a game you want to play, not with the powerful people involved now."

Silence.

"Is she...ma-ma-ma-missing?"

"Stop it! We're not doing this!" Feather stomped her foot, though she knew it would make no difference to Wendell, who had dismissed her as insignificant the first time they met.

"Okay, okay. I'm sorry. Let me ma-ma-move to the bathroom so we can talk."

She waited patiently for him to walk across the lobby to the bathroom. When she heard the door close, she asked, "Why would you and Lanie call each other so often?"

"We talked every day on my break. She was helping me with some fa-fa-family issues."

"You're going to have to do better than that, Wendell. I can have November Bean over there in fifteen minutes to grill you. My sense is that you don't want to mess with her."

"Well...My family has been giving me a hard ta-ta-time. They wanted me to join them in the family business, but I said no. Lanie asked me to call her at work, so they wouldn't know we were speaking. She's been a tremendous help."

Something about this didn't sound right.

"She's been counseling you? For how long?"

"Three months. She gives me the right words to use. Just last week, when my mother insisted I come over for Christmas, Lanie told me to stand my ground. She said, 'Wa-wa-wendell, you have to be firm with that woman. Tell her you've made other plans and you can see her at a later date.' That's our Lanie. She's always helping others."

Feather processed what he was saying. Lanie was his sounding board, but she'd neglected to mention that to her husband? They seemed so close.

"You're frightened. I can feel it."

"I ha-ha-have to go."

"No, wait!" She sensed there was more. "What else, Wendell? What did Lanie tell you?"

Silence. Was he coming up with a good story, or debating whether or not he was going to tell her the truth?

"She—she confessed to me that she'd been paid to ka-ka-kill Dash. I'm sa-sa-sorry, Feather."

Chapter Thirty-Two—
Lanie

I woke up, squinting as the bright light assaulted my eyes. I had no idea how long I'd been out, but my head hurt, reminding me of the previous day's events. I wiggled my fingers and toes, relieved they all still worked as they should. It felt like a massive hangover, though I couldn't remember consuming any alcohol.

Even more of a relief was the realization that I was no longer bound. I hadn't been returned to my previous cell, but to a bedroom. The furniture was slick, black lacquer with gold trim. The comforter was buttercup yellow daisies.

Now it was coming to me. Navy Blue Mask Man took me by the arm and shoved me inside. It was shockingly familiar. When I turned to ask Blue Mask why we were in Sylas and Tidbit's bedroom, he placed a foul-smelling cloth over my mouth. If only this came in pill form, I wouldn't have to fight these bags under my eyes.

At least my sense of humor was still intact.

Glancing around, I noticed a familiar piece of furniture, the dresser that featured so prominently in my talks with Sylas, Tidbit, and Eloise. Sylas mentioned numerous times that it was a part of my story. There were bottles of perfume and a pearl-handled brush sitting on top of a cream-colored doily on top, exactly as I remembered them. The dresser, the bed, and me. All props.

"Okay, so, the rest of this torture will be mental. You want me to think I'm crazy," I said out loud, half-hoping someone would respond.

Chuckling to myself, I was reminded of how much everything hurt. My arms, my legs, and of course, my head. The wider awake I became, the more I realized two important things. First, I was starving to death. It was hard to know when last I ate. Time was at a standstill in my current surroundings. I could go for one of Cosmo's famous square scones. I wouldn't even complain if he gave me one of the poorer sellers. The thought of prune and cream cheese, oozing with extra prunes, made my mouth water.

The other unwelcome fact was that I smelled. The once-sumptuous dinner odors lingered in my hair, now stale and distasteful. I must've fought hard, because I could also smell sweat, the kind I accumulated from a healthy hike up the mountain with Vem.

We went last week—at least I thought it was last

week—in celebration of Fiona Scheddy's birthday. The co-founder of our town was a woman of incredible strength I'd admired ever since learning her story.

Vem hummed one of her made up songs, "Ruta-beg-ya but don't give in," as we trounced through the woods. More than once, I was ready to give up.

"Can't we just say we made it to her grave? I'm pooped, Vem."

She put her hands on those tiny hips and clucked her tongue. "Lanie, Lanie, Lanie. Do you really think she's not watching? Would she say, 'Oh, that's okay, don't bother reaching my grave. I sacrificed everything so that you two could poop out at the halfway point, but I don't mind if you're lazy.' No, I don't think so. This is why you were supposed to attend my morning Moan for Misery."

"First of all," I said between heavy breaths, "Fiona won't be watching us at all because she's dead. That's kind of the point here. The woman doesn't know we're here. It was your idea to honor her today, remember? It's our own tribute, our living person tribute. We could just as easily say something nice in my back yard and donate some books to the school library."

I stopped, not caring a fig if she kept going.

She did.

"And secondly," I called, after I'd regained my breath. "A moan about being miserable will only serve to make me MORE miserable, not less."

I placed my hands on my hips, trying to assess if my tired body was really capable of going any further. I closed my eyes, trying to feel the presence of Fiona Scheddy.

In my mind, I saw the hardworking mother of three I'd read so much about. She was busily preparing for Christmas, wrapping gifts for her own children as well as her sister's. She was no doubt, also wrapping gifts for the children of cannery workers.

"There's no misery in the holidays, Lanie."

I jumped at least a foot.

"Vem! How did you do that?"

"I circled around. If you'd come up here with me more often, you'd know I found a nice trail of rabbit droppings to follow. It's a diversion from the boredom of the normal pathway."

"I hike with you almost every day. I just don't come up here."

It was no use; she'd already taken off again.

The holiday was over. The table I'd spent months decorating just so, was no doubt still full of dishes. Vem would be involved in a meditation or a moan, or whatever she thought would bring me back. *Poor Vem.* She had no idea what she was dealing with. And Cos— I couldn't allow myself to think about his pain.

The door swung open, and a new face appeared. One that I recognized from our Christmas Eve gathering. "Autumn! You kidnapped me! Why?" I didn't bother disguising the hurt in my voice.

It was all making sense now: The orange scent, her interest in Dash, and in Feather's abilities; she was part of this horrid plot.

"You're awake, then." It wasn't a question, but a statement made by someone with no emotion. She was not the cheerful young lady I'd met a few days earlier. Was she here under protest as well?

"Autumn!" I was still shocked by this revelation, that she'd been in my home, and I never suspected a thing. "If you'll let me go, my husband and I can help you. If you need to get out of town, we can arrange—"

She opened a closet and shuffled through until she found what she was looking for. Autumn turned and tossed a grey dress toward me that reminded me of the old movies featuring an imprisoned woman. Fitting.

She dug around some more and found underwear the size of a beach ball and tossed those toward me too.

"Shower's through the door." She motioned to a door painted the same color as the wall.

"Oh, I hadn't noticed that bef–"

"You've got ten minutes. When you've finished, come downstairs and take the first left. Don't try to escape, there's plenty of goons here to stop you. Brunch won't stay warm forever."

She walked to the door.

"Wait! I don't even know your real name!"

The little I knew about being kidnapped came from movies, and the cap-tee was always trying to make friends with their captor, in order to trick them into thinking they were friends.

"Don't need to know it. You won't be here long enough."

Relief ran through my body, and then a sense of dread. "Why? Are you planning on...killing me?"

The woman pivoted, staring at me with hard, dark eyes.

"Probably not."

She closed the door, and I was left alone once more. I slid off the tall bed and went to the window, looking out at a circular driveway below.

Two fancy cars, both the same model but one was silver, the other, red, sat in the driveway. A handsome man of sixty, in my estimation, stood, talking to a woman wearing an expensive blush-colored pantsuit.

The more I stared at them, the more I realized they were actors. I think they were in a sci-fi series Cosmo talked me in to watching.

"It starts out a little slow, but you'll really get into it by episode six," Cosmo had said, elbowing me in the side as I tried not to doze off.

"Tell me who these people are again?" I asked, trying desperately to stay awake.

"That's Willow Jackson and the guy is Gregory Moss. They've been in lots of shows together. Rumor has it they are an item, but there has been no public comment."

I giggled at my husband's knowledge of Hollywood. "How does my handsome baker have time to learn all of this?"

He glanced at me sheepishly. "Bathroom reading material."

"Hey! I'm up here!"

I pounded furiously on the window. "Hey!"

I tried lifting it, with no success.

They continued their discussion without bothering to glance up at me. Discouraged, I found my way to the shower where the hot water pouring over me gave me new hope.

I dried off with a fluffy towel similar to one I'd purchased for our new guest house. The exact same kind, in fact. Never in my life had a shower felt so good.

After donning the atrocious clothing, I opened the door and walked timidly down a hallway that, if I didn't know any better, was part of a museum. Descending a spiraling staircase which wound around a giant Christmas tree it did feel like I was in a movie. What if I was being filmed right now? with

The irony of a warm holiday symbol amidst a kidnapping wasn't lost on me.

I could smell something wonderful. My nose didn't have any trouble leading me to the source. I entered the enormous kitchen where mounds of bacon, eggs, toast, and a large pot of coffee sat.

This may be full of poison, I thought. At that moment, I didn't care. I didn't even need a plate. With Vem-like vigor, I stuffed an entire piece of buttery toast in my mouth and swallowed.

Next, I moved to the bacon. Taking pieces in both fists, I shoveled them into my mouth so quickly I started choking.

I felt a hand on my back, patting gently.

"Careful, Lanie. You don't want to end up like the rest of the family."

I spun around, flinging bacon crumbs across the room, to see my cousin, Sylas, dressed in an expensive cranberry-colored sweater. It was far more upscale than anything the "humble" Sylas of our video chats would wear.

"What are you doing here?" I asked, through watery eyes and a gravelly voice.

"I already told you. I'm the head of Brain Gravy Pictures. Upstairs is my studio and business office. Downstairs are my living quarters."

My next conquest was the pastry tray. They didn't hold a candle to anything Cosmo made, but today they tasted like heaven. "Why didn't you tell me that before?"

He shrugged. "It didn't make sense. I wanted to gain your trust quickly, so you would help me."

"Why did you fake your own death? And what about your daughter? And Tidbit? Don't you care what happens to them?"

"Eloise is fine. You'll meet her soon, Lanie."

"How is it you were grooming me all of this time, but now I'm being used to lure Feather Jones here?"

"This is going to be delicious. I can't wait to share the whole story. I want to see the look on your face when I tell you. We need to do it in the best lighting."

Chapter Thirty-Three—
Feather

Feather was distressed by the notion that Lanie might be involved with Dash's murder. It wasn't the woman she'd come to know and admire during her short time in Piney Falls.

After she'd hung up from her strange conversation with Wendell, she went and knocked on Cosmo's door one more time. "It's Feather again. I wanted to ask...I wanted to ask what you know about these calls on Lanie's phone."

She was being selfish. It wasn't right to bother him when his wife was missing. Feather turned, preparing to leave when she heard the squeak of the door opening.

The sight in front of her was shocking. The well-groomed man she'd met and secretly found handsome was now a pale, unshaven, disheveled mess. He was still wearing his clothes from the search of the previous day and his pants were covered in crusty mud. "Yeah? What's this about a phone call?"

He ran his fingers through his thick salt-and-pepper hair, training his intense ice-blue eyes on her face.

"I...um...Lanie's phone had several calls to this number. Do you recognize it?"

She held the phone up to his face. He took it from her hands and squinted as he read the numbers.

"...five-four-two. Nope." He handed it back to her. "I'm not one to look at phone numbers, but that one doesn't ring a bell. Is it someone I should know?"

Feather closed her eyes and swallowed hard. Somehow, she had to ask this question without upsetting him.

"I just called. It's the front desk manager at Fallen Branch. He says Lanie had been counseling him for months."

Cosmo's face lit up. "Wendell? Doesn't surprise me on either end. He's a trainwreck with a mustache. And my Lanie would help just about anyone. She's too good for me, that's for sure."

He sniffed and turned his head away, presumably so Feather wouldn't see the tears. Tug would do the same.

"Tug is preparing your bakery orders, so you don't have to worry about those. November dropped him off on her way to parking patrol. She's helping the police by writing out parking tickets. Oh—and your daughter called. She said the flights out of the Bahamas are on hold because of a big storm. She doesn't know when they'll be able to leave, but they're having a good time."

He grinned, a half-smile that reminded her of a famous actor who always played ruggedly handsome cowboys.

"She's gonna have some good stories when she gets back."

"Do you want me to call her back and tell her about Lanie? I don't mind."

"No, let's not worry her. There's nothing she can do from her tropical paradise anyway. Let her have that and I'll carry this worry."

Their conversation concluded, he turned and shut the door.

She would wait until she had concrete proof that Lanie was involved with Dash's death before she told Cosmo. This poor man couldn't handle much more.

Feather decided to go for another walk in the woods, in hopes of connecting with Fiona Scheddy. She felt helpless and even if it didn't lead anywhere, using her skills as a paranormal investigator were all she had to offer.

An early morning rain left tiny droplets on the trees. The scent of pine filled her nostrils as she walked, calming her. It wasn't that they didn't have the same thing in Charming, but the trails near her were steep and treacherous. They were only to be traversed by skilled hikers.

She closed her eyes and tipped her head back,

inviting positive words into her mind. She pictured Fiona, just as Jayden had suggested. Fiona was sitting on a log, eating a peanut butter and jelly sandwich as her children played around her feet. *"Make me a pretty picture in the earth, lovies,"* she said with a sweet voice that sounded much too frail to be the strong woman she was known to be. Feather watched, warmed by the sight of a loving mother enjoying nature. When she heard rustling, she opened her eyes and looked around.

"Hello?"

She peaked around the trees beside her, seeing only more of the same. As she pivoted to return to the trail, she recognized a now-familiar sight.

"Fiona! I'm so happy to see you again!"

It was like welcoming an old friend. If they'd lived in the same time period, she was certain they would have enjoyed each other's company.

Feather still marveled that this apparition appeared so clearly, just as though she were a living person standing in front of her.

Your dear sweet man is in trouble, Feather, she warned.

"He's at the bakery. How can he be in trouble? Is there a problem? They just fixed the oven."

The repairman. He told you the repairman showed up out of nowhere?

Feather thought back. That day they'd been in a rush, thinking they would solve this mystery before the holiday.

"That's right. He did mention a stranger showed up to help."

Well, lass, the stranger was there to cause a commotion. You'll be receiving a call soon. A terrible accident, or so they think. Smoke and the like, and in the confusion, they'll skirt your handsome lad away.

She sucked in air. "Right now?" She pulled her phone out of her pocket and hit the button for Tug's number.

"Babe? Can I call you back? The oven's making a funny noise."

There were sounds of chaos in the background, people of varying levels of expertise discussing the problem and a solution.

"Tug, get out of there now! Hurry! Run to the police station!"

"What? Feath, are you kidding? I'm in the middle of–"

"DO IT!" she screamed into the phone. She'd never yelled at him before, at least not in anger. The force of her voice even scared her, giving her hope it would be unsettling enough to get Tug away from danger.

She placed the phone back in her pocket, unsure what came next. Looking up, Feather was surprised to see Fiona was still there. Often, the spirits delivered the message and then disappeared.

"Is there something else, Fiona?"

The apparition nodded. *You're in a bit of a bind, too, sweet lass. The only way to save your friend is to save yourself. Remember that.*

Feather had to keep her composure, no matter what was going on with Tug. There was no guarantee she would have contact with Fiona again.

"Fiona, what can you tell me about the authors who were murdered? Why did it happen?"

Fiona turned and walked away, her skirt dragging across the muddy soil without absorbing it.

"Please don't leave me here!" she begged. "I need you."

Even though she was used to spirits coming and going on a whim, she couldn't help but feel saddened by Fiona's abrupt exit.

Feather heard more rustling. She knew this time it wouldn't be an entity, the hairs on her arms were flat. Glancing around her, she found a large boulder and crouched down behind it.

Two sets of feet approached and stopped, directly in front of the place she was waiting. Feather's pulse quickened and she breathed through her nose, hoping to remain as quiet as possible.

"I did everything you asked. Even ma-ma-more. Do you know I had to miss my bra-bra-brother's holiday party?"

Ashes dropped on the ground in front of her. All she needed was to witness the beginnings of a forest fire without doing something to stop it. She looked around where she was sitting and found a small twig. Carefully, Feather reached for the white ash smoldering on top of a dead leaf. She pulled it slowly to her side, relieved when the two people speaking didn't seem to notice.

Her combat boots were a great help in situations like these, but they would be too noisy. Instead, she took her hand and placed it on top of the leaf, biting her lip as it burnt her. She let out a little yelp and then used her other hand to cover her mouth.

"What was that?" A woman's voice asked.

"You haven't lived here long enough to know there are critters running around the wa-wa-woods? Take a breath, girl."

"Where were we? Oh, yeah. You want to get paid. So do I, but Daddy says not until production is finished. The lead actress is still uncooperative."

"Do you bah-bah-blame her? Yanked from her home on Christmas Eve? Did the boss think she'd just roll over and take it? Kidnapping does funny things to people. I'd like to end my association with this whole ma-ma-mess."

This time it was an entire half-a-cigarette that dropped to the ground, still smoldering. Feather reached for her twig. Just as she was about to expose it and herself, a shoe came down on top of the cigarette, putting out the ember.

"You'll do as you're told," the woman's voice threatened. "You knew the deal when we started, so keep your cool. He doesn't forget traitors."

The man laughed nervously. "We're disposable to him. Even you."

More ashes dropped.

"You are, that's for sure. But not me. I'm family. Just do as you're told and soon it will all be over, Wendell."

"There's no shame in wanting a better life for yourself, dear. We ca-ca-could go to the police, and they would help us both."

She sighed. "Oh, Wendell. That kind of talk can get you a starring role in the next picture. And not the way you'd like."

"Forget I sa-sa-said anything."

They turned and began walking away.

"This was a good place to meet. Nice and quiet," Wendell commented.

"Yeah, other than the critters," the woman agreed.

Chapter Thirty-Four—
Lanie

"What is it with my family? Are we all a bunch of kooks?"

I still couldn't believe that my cousin had faked his own death. After all the relatives I'd encountered over the years who'd turned out to be deeply disturbed, I'd allowed myself to slip into complacency this time.

Sylas, his wife, Tidbit, and his daughter Eloise were seemingly open and kind. They shared photos of their vacations and Eloise's stick-people family drawings. We played long-distance backgammon and told corny jokes. They were the family I'd longed for as a child.

Now that he stood before me, dressed like the executive he was, I realized that, once again, I'd been duped.

"Lanie, I can assure you that I'm not a 'kook' as you so eloquently put it. I'm a successful businessman. You should be impressed that I masterminded this whole thing."

When he smiled, I noticed his small, yellowed teeth looked nothing like my handsome father's. His face was also pock-marked from acne, something I hadn't seen while we chatted online. It was sad to think about the details I'd overlooked in my desire to find a family connection. Whatever branch of the family he resembled, I certainly hadn't encountered before now.

"My husband is out looking for me, I promise. When he finds you, well, let's just say, they'll be finding bits of you in the woods for decades to come."

I'd often chided Cosmo for his menacing façade. He was a pussycat, no matter what demeanor he put on. He'd used it to protect himself for so many years, it became a part of who he was.

"I'm not concerned," Sylas replied gleefully. "They'll never find you here. This complex has been in existence for twenty years. I bet you've never seen it from the highway, though you've driven by hundreds of times."

I wracked my brain for any hidden fortress. Vem pointed out every dwelling as we drove past. Now I chided myself for ignoring her.

"Where, exactly? If you're going to challenge me, at least give me a chance to defend myself."

I helped myself to another marionberry-filled pastry. It wouldn't hold up to anything Cosmo made, but I was stressed and still had a vacant corner of my stomach that it filled nicely. It was a good thing I changed out of my party dress. By this point in my gorge-fest, it was doubtful it would fit any part of my body.

Sylas placed a chocolate croissant on his plate. "Mm. I always forget how good these are. You should try these next, cousin. And I'm not telling you where we are."

As I watched him shovel large bites into his mouth, I sat my own pastry down and rubbed the sugar off my fingers. I didn't want to resemble him in any way.

"Where is your wife? I suppose Tidbit is a part of your plan too."

"Oh, she's dead." His eyes twinkled inappropriately. "Weight. She's dead weight, get it?"

I shook my head in disgust. I'd lost count how many times I'd done this already during my kidnapping. "You are nothing like you were online. I feel pretty stupid for trusting you, Sylas. So, poor Tidbit was a casualty of your big plan. And what about Eloise?"

My voice trailed off. I couldn't bear the thought.

"I'm not the monster you think I am." He helped himself to a cream cheese scone. "I would never harm a child."

"But you would kidnap your own cousin. Let's get to it—you want Feather Jones to help with your business and I'm bait. How, exactly, are we going about this farce? If you don't hurry up, she'll be back home in Ch–"

I stopped myself before I mentioned the name of

her town. I didn't know how much information he had on her, but if I could give her time to escape, at least she could contact her spirit buddies and figure out how to protect herself.

"Wait, it just occurred to me that you had no way of knowing Feather would be staying with me. You've been planning her kidnapping, and yet I'm somehow caught in the middle of this."

"This is where you're going to find me brilliant, Lanie," he bragged, pausing to lick the sugar from his fingers one at a time. "I loved the idea of authors dying the way their characters did, but one of the authors was a loyal employee. Nick Chestnut had been with the company since its inception, though we'd never met."

"Of course not," I scoffed. "Mister Big Head doesn't bother to mingle with the lowly employees."

Sylas's mouth twitched but he chose not to respond.

"We met at an office Christmas party =. He explained that in his spare time, he was an author. Being the generous man I am, I suggested he send me his work. Nick sent me some of his short stories and a novel he'd written and was impressed. When I was finding authors to write the anthology, his was the first name to come to mind. Of course, part of it was the subject matter too."

"Which was..."

"That he'd written a novel about Stanford Aisley. It was about his beginnings in the cannery industry, how his sheer genius got him to the top. " He looked at me for approval and when I offered none, he continued. "I suppose we're at the point of honesty, aren't we? Nick and I didn't meet randomly. When I went to the séance, I was told I had an employee who wrote a novel about Mr. Aisley. That and a shared love of brandy drew me to Nick. We've been in touch ever since. Brilliant, isn't it?"

I shuddered. "What does this all have to do with me?"

"The timing of Dash Vixen's death wasn't accidental. I wanted you to find his body, as the tragic sleuth in my story. I'm sorry that part of the plan didn't work. You've just been in the way ever since, so I created a plot twist."

"You already told me about—what plot twist?"

"The story must be told. I'm going to add another author, one who dies in a horrible way, as yet to be determined. I'm nothing if not adaptable."

I took a moment to gather my thoughts before continuing. I couldn't fall apart yet.

"Tell me more about Nick. You haven't mentioned his death."

He nodded vigorously. "*Sleighed by the Fire in Reel Time* is going to be such a huge hit, but I've come to value my friendship with Nick."

Sylas took a moment to slurp his latte in a very unmogul-like way.

"I sent him away to write another book. He has no idea, but I'm turning this one into a live-death movie too. Not Nick, of course, but his murder victims."

He raised one eyebrow, an act I found charming when we spoke online. Now it gave me the creeps.

"Why, Sylas?" I was growing impatient with this ugly little man. Playing the role of mouse in the game of cat-and-mouse was never my favorite role.

"Because I've never won a Poser Award for any of my studio's work. Doing something like this will put me in the running."

I thought back to our first few online visits. He was so eager to meet me that at first, I'd worried there was something wrong with him. *"Tell me more about your sleuthing, Lanie. That fascinates me."*

I wished I would have listened to that little voice of reason, instead of the big, dumb voice that said, *"It's the family you've always dreamt of, Lanie. Don't let your fears get in the way."*

I fought back tears.

"You never addressed why you need Feather for your sordid plan. Why not forget about her?"

"Dear, sweet Lanie." He smiled broadly, making me cringe.

"You don't know anything about Hollywood. It's a cutthroat business and I need Stanford Aisley by my side, not just during seances. Feather will provide that connection. She'll be my translator."

"No!"

"Don't be too hard on yourself. You've had a good run." He giggled childishly, something I'd never heard before today. The sound was out of place for a person who was so sinister.

"And what if Feather refuses to go along with this insanity? What then?"

"Oh, I guess I forgot to mention this part." He clasped his hands and leaned forward. Automatically, I leaned away.

"Tug Muehler's going to meet his demise soon. My team is out right now, laying the groundwork. The best love stories always end tragically. Feather will be so bereft, she'll be putty in my hands."

"Sylas, Tug comes from a prominent family. They won't stop until they bring you to justice. You won't get away with this!" I spat.

That first dinner together, Tug mentioned his father's company and the fact that he still hadn't visited all his family's properties. People like that didn't just turn a blind eye when one of their own disappeared.

"I doubt that, cousin. I don't make mistakes. You didn't even realize you were being filmed all this time. My sweet wife didn't realize it either, at least, until the end."

Tidbit, from all our video visits, was a lovely, well-mannered woman. There wasn't one hint that she knew she was married to a sadistic murderer. I was learning quite a lot about myself today. I was a horrid judge of character.

"Time for you to see my garden, dear."

"I don't want to see your stupid garden, Sylas."

I folded my arms across my chest and planted

myself firmly in the chair. If another big goon was going to manhandle me again, I wanted to be ready.

Sylas appeared hurt by my words, which delighted me.

"No, I don't want to see anything you've done, because I really don't care. You're nothing to me. I was just pretending to like you because I didn't have other family. The truth is, I have plenty of family. My husband and daughter and best friend and then the entire town of Piney Falls. I don't need you. I hope you got that all on camera."

He studied me. "You don't mean that. We'll be creating jobs for the community once our studio is open. We're in the process of clearing acres of trees and then we'll build an entire studio backlot. Not one person will be unemployed in your little hamlet. Your 'family' as you call them, will all benefit. Isn't that wonderful?"

I shrugged.

He took my elbow and pulled me outside, through French doors and onto a brick patio surrounded by flowering bushes and decorative fountains of different shapes and sizes. My eyes focused on a fountain depicting a woman leaning against a tree. The water fell around her, as if she were caught in a storm.

"Lovely, isn't it?" Sylas said as he followed my gaze. "Knowing your appreciation for old movies, I thought you might enjoy this area. All the fountains, the tables and benches, they all came from movie studio backlots.

Do you see that little round table, in the corner by the gate?"

It was almost swallowed by lush, green vines, but the ornate, white table and two chairs sat to the side of a lattice-covered gate.

"Charlie Chaplin insisted it accompany him on the set of each movie. He would entertain a starlet over sandwiches and tea."

Sylas waited for me to express awe or shock, or maybe both.

"I'm ready to go back to lock up," I said, trying to make it as clear as possible that I wasn't interested.

"Suit yourself, cousin."

Chapter Thirty-Five — Feather

She held him close, not wanting to let go.

"I could have lost you forever," Feather cried, sticking her nose into his red t-shirt. It was covered in flour, but she didn't care. She needed to smell the reassuring scent of her boyfriend.

"But you didn't, Feath. Thanks to you, I got out of there just in time. I gave the policeman on duty a description of the man who offered to fix the stove. He said it didn't sound like any repairman he knew." Tug gently rubbed his fingers up and down Feather's back. "I wish we could talk to Cosmo about all of this."

Feather pulled away. "Oh no, you can't. He's so upset, Tug. We need to leave him alone until we have a lead on Lanie."

"I guess you're right. His bakery wasn't damaged in the explosion. The damage was confined to the vacant building. As far as Cosmo is concerned, things are still the same."

She took his hand and led him to the covered patio swing, where a light rain was beginning to fall. They sat together, each watching their breath in the afternoon humidity.

"Are you going to tell me what happened? I mean, I know with you, there is nothing that surprises me now, but you must've gotten an incredible message. Please thank whoever it was for me."

"That's what we need to talk about. The strongest voices I've been hearing are two very opposite entities. One is Stanford Aisley. He owned a lumber mill when the town began. He was a bad man, Tug. Real bad. I get the impression he didn't care what happened to his employees or anyone else. He's been in the minds of whoever took Lanie. I think I've told you about him before."

"Okay."

Tug blinked rapidly, his sign that he wanted to trust Feather, but wasn't sure exactly what was happening. "How does this all connect to the author murders?"

"He's been inside the head–heads–I don't know if it's more than one person. But he wants his time in the spotlight, he feels history has forgotten him. All of the Christmas stories in the *Strung by the Fire* anthology contain at least a reference to him. I think he orchestrated the deaths and plans to finish off the rest of them."

Tug stared out across the forest. After a few minutes, he turned back to Feather.

"That's wild. I've heard of that sort of thing, but in all of the mysteries you've solved, not one of the entities had that kind of power."

"It is crazy, but the next thing I tell you will be even more unbelievable."

Feather hadn't given herself much time to think about the unique opportunity she'd been given. Jayden was right; it was life changing.

"I've been in contact with someone else. As evil as Stanford Aisley is, there's someone who is equally good. Her name is Fiona Scheddy."

"Who is she?"

"She and her sister were also here when the town began. I haven't been able to do much research, but they contributed to the schools and the canning industry. They were amazing women."

"Like you, Feath. You are an amazing woman. That's probably why she wanted to connect." Tug brought her hand to his lips and kissed it gently.

She felt a chill go down her spine. It wasn't the kind she got from spirits, but the kind that came from the intense feelings she had for this incredible man.

"Thanks, babe. The most unbelievable thing about Fiona is that I can actually see her. She's not in shadows or a light view, she's real. If I were walking down the street, I wouldn't know she was a spirit if I passed her. Well, other than what she's wearing."

Tug's mouth fell open. "That's insane! I mean, really insane! I wish I could see her too!"

"Maybe you will. When this is all done, I'll take you out in the woods where we meet and see if she'll appear for you. She saved your life, Tug."

"She's the one who told you about the explosion? I want to thank her!"

"As we were talking, I heard someone else, so I hid."

"Another entity? You've hit the jackpot," Tug joked.

"No, these were living beings. They were talking about kidnapping Lanie, and how she was supposed to star in some movie. It didn't make any sense."

"That's bizarre."

"It confused me, too, Tug. I knew the man. It was Wendell, who works at the front desk at the Fallen Branch Resort. We'd had a conversation earlier where he tried convincing me that Lanie had murdered Dash and the other authors."

"What?"

"Lanie has been helping him with some kind of personal problem."

"Wait—he's been going to her for help, and out of the blue, she confessed a need to murder? Something doesn't add up."

"That didn't hit me right, either."

They rocked back and forth on the swing, Tug's feet dragging and Feather's toes barely touching the ground.

"This whole situation with Lanie is horrible, and

Cosmo needs support, but we do have lives in Charming, Feath. We can't stay forever."

"I know. Just a few more days, I promise."

Chapter Thirty-Six—Lanie

I drummed my fingers on the glass table, hoping my disgusting, long-lost cousin would sense my disdain. I'd offered then pleaded to go back to the privacy of the bedroom he'd used as a movie set.

Instead, he continued reading the morning paper, as if I didn't exist.

Glancing at the front page, I was shocked to see my picture consuming the top half. I cringed, thinking about what that must look like on the computer, where people could zoom in and see my wrinkles.

Stop it, Lanie!

The picture was underneath thick black letters that read, "Local Entrepreneur Missing."

That only described the woman who moved to Piney Falls, not the woman I'd become. The person who hosted Christmas dinner for six in her lovely new home was so much more.

"Are you going to tell me what it is you're doing to

poor Tug? The boy will be putty in your hands once you threaten his girlfriend. There's really no need to kill him."

When he didn't respond, I grabbed the paper from his hands and tossed it on the floor. He looked up, my act of defiance barely registering on his face.

"Lanie, that's terribly rude. I was catching up on the sports. We may be getting a Triple-A baseball team here on the coast. They're talking about next spring."

By this juncture, nothing should have shocked me, but I couldn't help myself.

"How can you be so cavalier? You've ended some lives and ruined others. Don't you care?"

"Not really." His upper lip twitched. "You wanted honesty, and there it is."

I stood, placing my hands on my hips, and stretched, my body still aching from its mistreatment. I did my best thinking when I walked, especially in the forest. A disgustingly calm courtyard would have to do for now.

If I was going to be collateral damage once they obtained Feather, then maybe I could make myself more attractive to them. The longer I was here to help her, the better.

"What if I make you a deal, Sylas? You're a wheeler-dealer. At least that's what you led me to believe in our online chats."

Sylas dipped his chin so that his eyes stared upward. My father used to do the same thing when he was pretending to be impressed.

"You've got my attention. Please, elaborate."

"I was thinking, Feather will be a wreck once you've gotten rid of Tug. She's able to block spirits, you know. And that girl is as stubborn as me."

"And?"

"And...I can help you with that. Let us room together. I'll work with her until she's comfortable. You'll recall from our talks; I've got a background in marketing. Whatever the company needs, I can do."

I smiled, the act that normally closed the deal. Back in my heyday, I attended seminars at least six times a year. *Embrace the Face,* a seminar that emphasized drawing in your clientele with nonverbal cues, taught me the right time to bat my eyes and when to nod my head sympathetically. A perfectly placed smile went a long way. I slept with the presenter, Jonathan Mustard, in his VW van. I was still picking shag carpet out of my scalp two months later.

"Isn't that nice of you, cousin? I would have expected you'd come up with a clever way to make an exit. Is this an olive branch?"

"If you can't beat 'em, join 'em. That's how that saying goes, right?"

A housekeeper joined us on the patio, eyeing me with disgust. "You done eating, miss? If so, I've got to start on lunch. They don't give me much time in between."

"Ask him," I replied, gesturing to my voluptuous cousin, who had brought the last of the bacon with us on the patio.

"Yes, go ahead, Magda. Delicious, as always." Sylas shoved another piece of bacon in his mouth. "Oh, where are my manners? This is my cousin, Lanie. She's here temporarily. Lanie, Magda."

I approached her and stuck my hand out. "How do you do?"

Carrying a bowl of fruit, she shoved me aside and reached for the empty plate.

She could be an important ally if I could break through her crusty exterior.

"Did you have a nice Christmas, Magda?"

"Mm," she grunted.

"Magda has four grown children and sixteen grandchildren. They all got together at Magda's place for the holiday," Sylas explained, as though we were having a casual chat.

I moved in front of her as she attempted to set the bowl of fruit on the table. "Magda, how would you feel if you weren't allowed to be with your family on Christmas?"

She tried nudging me aside, but I'd regained my strength and she was no match for my mountain-climbing limbs.

Finally, she sighed in irritation. "Tell the woman to move!" she called without looking at Sylas.

"Answer my question and I will," I replied calmly. "How would you feel if you were kept away from your grandchildren on the one day you'd been planning for a whole year?"

"Lanie, you have grandchildren? You've never mentioned it!"

I shot Sylas a sharp glance but said nothing. He was toying with me, and I knew it.

"It's torturous to keep a family apart. Sylas doesn't care about his family. He let someone take his scared little girl away. Didn't bother him one bit."

Magda's brow furrowed and she glanced at Sylas. "What's she talkin' about?"

"Didn't he tell you? Which part, that he has a daughter named Eloise, or that he let the poor thing be dragged away from her mother?"

In the first show of emotion I'd seen this morning, Sylas jumped up from the table and grabbed my arm in one motion. He yanked me away from Magda and took the bowl from her hands.

"Lanie is overly excited. She's had a busy few days. Once she's calmed down, she'll be back to visit, Magda. For now, we've got things to attend to. Come on, dear cousin."

He set the bowl on the table and grabbed me by the neck like he thought I was a newborn kitten.

"Are you worried I'll tell her what's really happening here?" I asked, knowing full good and well that this kind of insolence could get me locked up again, or worse yet, killed.

"Magda requires a delicate touch, that's all. Why don't you relax by the pool until—"

His phone buzzed and he brought it up to his ear. "Oh?" His face displayed disappointment that made me deliciously happy. I managed to wiggle free of his grip and leaned up against the house.

"How did that happen? We planned it so carefully! No, don't grab him now. Someone must've tipped him off." Sylas glared at me. He couldn't be so stupid as to think I'd thwarted his plans. I'd been under his fat thumb all morning.

"I've got a better idea."

He put the phone back in his pocket and smiled at me. The flustered Sylas from a few moments ago was gone, replaced by the smarmy man I'd been forced to share my breakfast with.

"You're not seriously thinking I had anything to do with it. I can guess your plot to murder poor Tug didn't go as planned. He's a smart boy, I'm sure he figured it out."

"I know you have no means to contact him. Every room is thoroughly searched before you're allowed to enter."

I wrapped my arms across my mid-section, feeling vulnerable. "Then, what?"

"I'm not sure. We'll get to the bottom of it eventually. For now, I've got a better plan. I'm going to ransom you."

"What? My husband doesn't have any money! We just opened a second location and built a home. That's where our wealth is. I'm afraid he won't be turning over either one to you!"

The truth of the matter was much different. My husband would give everything he had to get me back

—his bakery, our beautiful home, he would spare no expense. I knew his devotion to me was as deep as mine was to him.

"No, it's nothing like that. I'm going to broker a trade. You for Feather Jones. It will make an incredible plot twist. We'll film it all, of course."

While the idea of seeing my husband again was appealing, I couldn't imagine living with myself if I agreed to this idea.

"No, Sylas. I refuse. I won't take part in your twisted plot." I crossed my arms and leaned against the wall, steadying myself in case he tried to yank on me again.

"Did you think I was going to give you a choice, Lanie? No, it's this or your life. We can always find a way around you."

He pulled a bedazzled phone—my phone—out of his pocket and handed it to me.

"Now isn't a good time to try something funny. Put it on speaker. Remember, at this point, this is your only value to me." He produced a gun from the back of his pants and set it on the desk in front of him. "In case you need more incentive. I could always film your death with your husband listening in."

My eyes darted back and forth, trying to find something on this patio to use as a point of reference, some way to tell my husband where I was being held. They paused and came to a rest on an item I hadn't notice before.

Now, I needed to remember his number. I hadn't

actually typed out the numbers before. I took a deep breath and cleared my throat, ready to put on the best performance of my life .

"Lanie? Oh, God. Where are you? I love you, honey!"

"Cos?" It came out shakier than I'd planned. Sylas frowned, clearly displeased.

"I'm fine, babe. I need you to do a couple of things for me. First, you need to bring Feather to Quimby's Quick Mart off Highway 101. Tomorrow morning, at ten. I'll be exchanged for her. She'll need to keep her phone on, awaiting further instructions."

It's a trap, Cos. He's planning to kill us both once he has Feather.

I glanced over at my despicable cousin, who nodded in approval.

"And second, if you take your car, be sure to get the registration from my glove box. I just renewed it and forgot to put it in your car. Got it?"

"Lanie, why would that even matter? It's not due to be renewed till..." He paused. Cosmo knew my thoughts almost better than I did some days. "That's right, I remember now. I'll be there at ten."

"I love you, Cos," I whispered as tears slid down my face. Sylas grabbed the phone from my hands and hung up.

"It's a pity your leading actress role didn't work out. That was masterful. Must be in the genes."

Chapter Thirty-Seven — Feather

"Yoo-hoo! Are you two crazy kids decent?"

They sat upright as November Bean hopped up the wooden steps.

Today, she was wearing a fluorescent orange jumpsuit with a matching headband and glasses frames. She was also sporting a fluorescent green vest and orange shoes. She was almost too bright for this gloomy day.

"Have you come up with a plan to save our Lanie?"

Feather shook her head sorrowfully. "I was just filling Tug in. Since we saw you last, I did overhear a couple of people in the woods. They were talking about Lanie."

She didn't want to upset November by telling her that it was suggested her best friend was a killer. Not yet.

November placed her fists on her hips and stomped in circles. "That's enough to put my giblets in a twist. What did they look like?"

"One of them was Wendell. I don't know who the other person was because she was wearing a hood, but it was a woman."

"Wendell? Are you sure?" November performed some sort of interpretive dance, flapping her arms wildly.

"I'm releasing my anger, kids!" she called, by way of explanation. After the emotion had sufficiently dissipated, she pulled up a patio chair next to Tug, their knees touching. "Wendell is in big trouble once I get my hands on him."

This next bit of information would require care, and the last thing she wanted to do was upset November.

"They talked about putting Lanie in a movie, as crazy as it sounds. Before that, I'd spoken with Wendell. He implied Lanie was responsible for Dash's murder."

November jumped up, smacking her forehead with her palm, and began pacing in a circle again. "Oh, this is bad. So bad. Why would they want to pin a murder on her? She's too pretty for prison."

"Well..." Feather hesitated, trying to formulate the best sentence. "Well," she repeated. "I think they're planning to kill her too. That's just my sense. Maybe it has something to do with her killing Dash and their movie."

November stopped and looked up, her eyes as big as saucers.

"What did you just say, young lady?" In an instant

she was in front of Feather, almost nose-to-nose. She placed her hands on Feather's knees and stared at her menacingly.

Feather leaned back as Tug wrapped a supportive arm around her.

"Feather is just the messenger, Ms. Bean. None of us really believes Lanie would kill someone, right, Feath?"

"Yes—I mean, no–of course not."

November took a step back, her features softening. "How are we going to find these people and Lanie? Any ideas?"

"Someone just tried to kill Tug, or at least create a diversion while they took him. I'm certain it has something to do with wanting me to help them."

November pointed down at Feather's combat boots and raised her finger up to Feather's multicolored hair. "You have a keen sense of style, but besides that, what are they after? Do you have that elusive Farnham's Department Store cookie recipe?"

"I've had contact with—"

"I almost forgot. I'm a speed reader," November interjected. "You should probably know that. Last night, before I went to bed, I read through the rest of the anthology. Dash's character, Brit Fudge, died from strangulation. Doesn't make any sense that he was conked over the head with a book."

"What?"

"Elle and Ivy were killed exactly like their victims in the anthology. But Dash should have been strangled.

I'm not sure why." November snapped her fingers. "In all of this chaos, I've forgotten to warn the other two authors. We started working on this before Christmas and then things went haywire. Can you do your ghost thingy and find them?"

"It doesn't work quite like that, Ms. Bean," Feather replied solemnly, though she might try asking Fiona for help.

"Oh, well. It's not going to be spirits that help her. It's going to be all of us. I think you should join me in a chant for success." Without waiting for an answer, she grabbed both of their hands and pulled them to their feet. "Repeat after me—"

Tug looked over his shoulder, where Cosmo had quietly joined them.

"Cosmo, what do you know?" Tug asked, dropping November's hand with relief.

Feather noticed he was wearing a clean shirt and had brushed his hair.

"I just got off the phone with Lanie. Her kidnappers want an exchange—Feather for Lanie."

Tug and Feather looked at each other with fear in their eyes.

"Cosmo, I can't sacrifice Feather. I know you miss your wife, but..."

"No one is being sacrificed here. I've got a plan." He pivoted toward his nemesis. "November, we'll need one of the toys you purchased at that big military equipment sale."

"Cosmo Hill, we've just made our own plan,"

November retorted. "We need to contact the other two authors in the anthology because they will be murdered next."

Cosmo trained his angry gaze on November. "I don't care about your stupid mystery game. Those people can take care of themselves. I need to find my wife. Now." He held up a crumpled piece of paper. "Lanie gave me a clue. She told me to look in the glove box, where I found this."

November yanked the paper out of his hands and read aloud, "One remote control Freddy's Firework Launcher. Company discount for Work Ahead Office Supplies, the Most Successful Office Supply Chain in the World. Total, four-hundred-eighty-five dollars and twenty cents."

She glanced up, her brows furrowed. "Why didn't Lanie tell me she still got an employee discount? And when did an office supply store start carrying firework launchers?"

"So? How does this help us find your wife, Cosmo?" Tug asked.

"She's being held near Truman's home. She bought this firework launcher for him and he mentioned over dinner the other night that it was missing. I know how to save her."

Chapter Thirty-Eight—
Lanie

As strange as it seemed, I was giddy about seeing Cosmo again. It was like I was back in high school, waiting for the good-looking boy after football practice. No, this was not the same at all. However, I took it as a positive that I still had those exciting feelings about Cosmo.

I took another shower, by now, feeling immense gratitude for the water, the soap and shampoo. After going just one day without them, I could only imagine how one would feel being deprived of these basic necessities long term. In the drawer, I found another set of grey clothing and gigantic underwear.

The fact that these particular items were here, in what was supposed to be a corporate headquarters, baffled me. They were the type of clothes a prison would provide for the inmates.

As I stepped in the underwear, it hit me. In the sci-fi series Cosmo watched, the women all dressed like prison matrons. These clothes came from a movie wardrobe.

After I'd dressed, I glanced at the clock. Seven-fifteen. In my years in Piney Falls, I'd allowed myself the luxury of sleeping in until at least nine.

Cautiously, I crept into the hallway. It was unusually quiet. Feeling giddy, I was confident could find my way out. The endless corridor made me uneasy though, and the next best plan was to locate a room with a window, so I could see how high up I was.

Tiptoeing in the opposite direction from the stairs, I pushed gently on doors until I found one that opened with ease. Inside was a desk piled high with files. I moved to the window behind it eagerly, where, to my disappointment, it overlooked a large, empty parking lot. There were no landmarks, as I'd seen the other day when I watched the man and woman getting into the car.

Turning my attention to the desk, I soon discovered the files were all names of movies:

The Beast of Belleview
The Dahlias of Damned Driscoll
Blood, Bones and Misery

Cheery, I thought to myself. There was a large bookshelf beside the desk, which was full of books, old and new. I recognized the Christmas horror anthology, as well as several other books by those involved in the anthology. At the end of that row was a familiar photo, one I'd seen in our local museum. It hung right beside the one of Mrs. Bonitam, State Fair Pie Champ, four years in a row.

Aisley family reunion, 2015.

Removing the picture, I studied the faces with interest, hoping to gain insight into the people who would work for such a monster as my cousin. They all had the same toothy grins, just like they'd been taken out of the box looking that way.

The man and woman I'd seen from my window were standing in the second row, and I recognized Elle Vanashelve from her website photo. Dressed in a shimmering silver gown, she was standing next to Sylas, holding onto his arm like she knew him well.

What an odd coincidence.

That's when the truth struck me right between the eyes.

"Lanie! Didn't anyone tell you it was rude to snoop in people's homes?"

The shock of his voice caused me to drop the framed photo and the glass shattered into a million pieces.

Without turning away from me, he pinched a small microphone on his shirt and yelled, "Autumn! Come up to my office! And bring a broom and dustpan, please!"

"That was very unkind, Lanie. It's not how you should treat your cousin."

"But you're not my cousin. Your name isn't even Sylas." I smiled wryly and pointed to the photo on the floor. In the center was this man standing in front of me, grinning the same plastic smile he'd used with me these horrid few days. "You're Elle Vanashelve's husband."

His face turned crimson. "I was going to tell you eventually."

"Did I *ever* have a cousin named Sylas, or did you manipulate my DNA results too?"

He stepped inside the room, looking more like his usual cat-who-caught-the-mouse self. "Of course not. You have a cousin named Sylas. He works for me."

"Well, that figures," I grumbled. "The real Sylas is just as devious as the fake one. Make sure you leave that in your movie."

"Nothing of importance will be left on the cutting room floor, I assure you."

"My friends and I have been studying your relative, Stanford Aisley, Mr. Rudolph. Or may I call you Brooks?"

"We both have relatives with secrets, it seems, Lanie." Brooks replied tersely.

"Now what would you know about that?"

Your cousin Sylas is my employee, but he's also one of the authors in the anthology. He goes by Nick Chestnut in the literary world. He wrote *Krinkled; a Krunchy Christmas Nightmare*."

Chapter Thirty-Nine — Feather

During their first Christmas together, November had given Lanie the gift of a new phone. It wasn't until three months later that she confessed she'd already loaded a tracking device to keep tabs on her in case she was ever in trouble.

At the time, Lanie was incensed. "That's invasive, Vem."

"Oh, Lanie put the Lanie Locator on my phone too, Cosmo." Feather reached into her pocket and pulled out her phone. Cosmo opened the Lanie Locator and quickly discovered where Lanie was when she made the phone call telling him about the exchange.

"Okay, now we're getting somewhere." Cosmo handed her phone back and rubbed his hands together, as though he were about to create the biggest, most exciting cake of his career. "Tug, when we were working the other day, Feather was able to contact you with a walkie-talkie device. I'll need you to get that out and show me how it works. I don't want any of us out of touch."

"Back in a minute. "Tug jumped up with even more energy than normal and bounded to the guest house.

Cosmo pivoted toward Feather and smiled. "Feather, it's no secret why they want you. The abilities you have could really cause some damage, if placed in the wrong hands. I'd like you to contact Fiona and Stanford."

Feather nodded. "I'll do whatever you need me to do, Cosmo." She was eager to help, but the thought of purposely contacting that awful man made her skin crawl.

"I want information from him, and maybe Fiona can help us decipher it."

"I've only ever called to one spirit at a time. Given they are complete opposites, I'm not sure it can be done."

Cosmo's face fell and all the stress of the past few days made him appear worn and haggard.

"I'll try though."

He smiled. "Good girl. Lanie is being held out near the Sassy Lasses Vineyard, which is a twenty-five-minute drive from Quimby's Quick Mart, where we're supposed to make the exchange. We'll leave Feather's phone at Quimby's. With that app you and Lanie share, they'll be tracking your location. I'm sure they want to make sure we're not trying anything funny."

He gazed at a concerned Feather. "Don't worry, you won't be there. In fact, I'm planning to use the life-size dummy Lanie bought last year for Halloween. Vem insisted the hair should be a bright red to scare away the pigeons, so luckily, we have a wig. For once, your hair-brained ideas are paying off."

November remained uncharacteristically silent.

"The kidnappers know by now that Lanie has one on her phone to track Feather, but they won't know about Tug's device, or yours, Bean."

"Excellent thoughts, Cosmo Hill. But what if they send someone early to case the joint?"

"That's why we're heading out there soon. Quimby's doesn't open until six. Truman has a standing order for a coffee at six, and because the employees are sometimes late, they gave Truman a key to get his own coffee. He'll set up the dummy then."

"Color me impressed," November said, bowing formally.

"If we can use that drone you bought at the military sale, we may be able to spot something that isn't visible from the road," Cosmo continued.

"Don't you think they've got security there? What if they just shoot it down?" Feather asked.

"We'll wait for it to get dark and then send it up. We'll do short bursts, so it's not obvious it's there. You read the instructions, Bean?"

She glared at him. "No instructions needed, Mr. Hill. It comes with its own pilot."

Cosmo huffed. "As long as it works, you can tape your voodoo doll of me to the top."

When her mouth dropped open, he quipped, "Yes, I know about that. Lanie and I don't keep secrets."

"We're going to ambush them at their gates, and anyone watching the restaurant will see that *"Feather"* is sitting with her back to the door. What happens if we are waiting for them, but they have too much manpower to stop?"

"That's where Tug comes in. We're going to leave him somewhere nearby, and when I give the signal, he'll blast them with, 'You're surrounded. Don't move!'"

"Now, about the spirits?" Feather asked. "I can't summon them at the same time, but someone else could summon Stanford. I'm not sure Fiona will talk to anyone else, but Stanford will appear to anyone who will listen to him."

"I'll do it. Tell me what to do, and I'll do it."

Though she was sure he was willing to do whatever it took to help his wife, Feather was less sure that Cosmo's mind was currently strong enough to fend off Stanford's evil suggestions.

"He thinks he's good at manipulating women. I think it would be a better idea to find a strong woman willing to contact him."

"Oh, no. Not–"

All sets of eyes landed on the strongest woman in the room.

"Say no more, Feather Jones. November Bean, reporting for duty!" She saluted Feather, dressed coincidentally today in navy blue.

It was the scenario she wanted, but she didn't have a way of telling Cosmo without hurting his feelings.

"Are you sure, November? He's tricky. He'll try anything he can to get you to do his bidding."

November posed, her muscles firm on either side of her head. "The body AND the mind are solid. There's no way he'll find a weak link."

Cosmo leaned against the doorway, chuckling to himself. "I have to admit, she's right. If this devil can penetrate that nutty brain, he was never human to begin with."

"I choose to ignore your insults today, Cosmo Hill. I know you're grieving and that gives you a pass." She clasped her hands together and stretched them out in front of her. "Okay, Feather, tell me what to do."

"Cosmo, what is it exactly you'd like to get from Stanford?"

"I want to know whose mind he's in. If he has been controlling them, he'd want to brag about it, right? I want names, what he's convinced them to do, and anything else he'll say. I don't want any surprises today."

She didn't want to disappoint him, but that was much more specific information that she usually got from the spirits. "We'll do our best. They can be very finnicky about the information they choose to share."

Cosmo shook his head emphatically. "I won't accept that. My wife's life is on the line."

"November Bean is on the case. There's no spirit able to withstand my persuasive methods."

"First, we need to find a quiet space where we won't be disturbed."

Cosmo held out his hand. "That means I need your phone, Bean."

She rolled her eyes and dug it out of her pants pocket, flopping it in his hand. "Don't be making naughty phone calls. I know your email password and have no problem filling out a form to be a crossing guard on your behalf."

November pointed to the deck, where just a day before, Feather sat contemplating what came next.

They sat facing each other as the birds tweeted in harmony around them.

"Lanie loves this time of day. When I practice my bird calls, she says, 'Vem, I love those sounds. I think I should listen to the real thing first so I can do a bird call myself.'"

"Put your hands on your knees and close your eyes," Feather instructed. "Now, I want you to take several deep breaths in and out."

"That's how I start all of my classes too. We take deep breaths, and–"

"No talking, Ms. Bean. We have to listen for Stanford. Now, I want you to think of his name and what he represents to this community. Lanie mentioned the other day that the two of you researched his family. Think about all of that without emotion, if you can."

Feather closed her eyes as well and felt the hairs on her arms rise immediately. She sensed a heaviness in her chest as a dark entity approached her, and imagined herself standing, combat boots firmly planted on the ground. She stuck her hand out. "Stop! I'm not letting you through. Feather pointed beside her, to November Bean. "There is your human today."

After several tense minutes where she stood her ground, her chest felt light once more. The dark cloud was gone. She opened her eyes and glanced over at November, whose brows were knitted tightly together.

It didn't seem right, purposely inflicting this kind of torment on another person, but they were desperate, and Cosmo seemed so sure of his plan. Feather glanced down at her arms, where the hairs still stood at attention.

November mouthed words and clenched her fists. Feather stood, ready to yank November back to the human world. *Let her go, lass. Trust this odd woman.*

Fiona was here. Good.

She allowed November to continue, and to distract herself, she scrolled through her messages. She hadn't checked them since the drive down. There was one from a permanently disgruntled client, *'Don't care for this style. I'll be in next week for a re-do.' 'I need more blonde,'* and another from her best friend, Gemini.

'Merry Christmas, Feather and Tug! Relax and Enjoy! Love you both!'

November shot up to a standing position, her eyes bulging out of her head. Her face was covered in sweat and her mouth frozen in a grimace.

Feather jumped up and rushed to her side, shaking her.

"Ms. Bean? November? Come back to me! I'm right here, on Lanie's porch. Please! You've been somewhere else, and I need you to return to the living world."

Noting that she hadn't made any progress, she took the glass of special iced tea November had made for her and threw it in her face.

In an instant, November's demeanor changed. Feather took her shirt and wiped November's face dry. "Are you all right?"

November stared at Feather, her eyes glazed over.

Cosmo's plan backfired. Stanford Aisley claimed another one.

A smile crept over November's face and she tilted her head to the side, allowing tea droplets to run down her navy jumpsuit. "That man is no match for the superpowers of the Bean."

Feather threw her arms around November and hugged her, not caring a bit that she was soaked in tea when she'd finished.

"What happened? What did he say?"

"This is all a novel. Stanford Aisley's novel. He's using someone named Brooks to create it."

"I know just who that is," Feather replied, setting the empty glass on the table. "What else did he say? Fiona is here and she's ready to help."

"Stanford wants to create a death scene for Lanie and Cosmo." November glanced at Cosmo apologetically. "Sorry, Cos. I'm just repeating."

Cosmo grimaced but said nothing.

"Is that all?" Feather asked.

"He said something about righting a wrong."

Fiona?

The man's deranged, lass. He thinks his death wasn't his fault. He wants his descendant to triumph in this battle.

"She says Stanford wants this to be his defining moment. He's planning on a real bloodbath."

Tug returned from the guest house, winded from the jog. "What'd I miss?"

Chapter Forty — Lanie

"Let me get this straight. You're NOT my cousin Sylas. My cousin Sylas is NOT my cousin Sylas, but Nick Chestnut."

He chuckled and stepped over the glass into the office. "That is correct. I'm the head of Brain Gravy Pictures and my name is Brooks Rudolph. You might have seen some of my films, back when I was an actor. And Sylas is still Sylas, but his pen name is Nick Chestnut."

Brooks stood up a little taller.

"Nope. Not one movie. I guess that makes it easier for you to pretend you're my cousin though."

"I quite enjoyed that. It took me back to my acting class days. Tidbit and Eloise, they were actors too."

I thought about our last video conversation. Eloise mentioned they were playing pretend. Now it all made sense.

"Can you back up and explain why the elaborate ruse? And who, exactly, burned in Sylas's car?"

"Of course. I do owe you that. The bodies in the car were actors who badmouthed me to other studios. My props department did an incredible job creating the right hair color and clothing so that they would look similar to Sylas and Tidbit. They were uncooperative when I told them about my idea to create a movie in real time. I couldn't have them going around telling people about it. Think how many other studios would try and steal it?"

I wondered how they hadn't been reported missing, but I didn't want to stop him, so I just nodded.

"It all started at a writer's conference I attended with my wife. Elle Vanashelve? You may have heard of her." Brooks pointed to his bookshelf, where a copy of *Strung by the Fire* had been sitting all this time.

"Stanford asked me to choose six writers for the anthology and I'd already chosen Nick. My wife was seated with other Christmas horror authors, and as these authors became more inebriated, I suggested the anthology to them. It was mostly Stanford's idea, though it was my idea to catch them in their most delicate phase. My wife was resistant, but once I promised to use her story for all promotional material, she was putty in my hands." Brooks rolled his eyes. "Always full of herself, that one."

Elle Vanashelve. Died in her bathtub, electrocuted by Christmas lights.

I gasped in horror. "You filmed your wife's murder?"

"Not me! That would be vulgar. When she refused to go along with my plan, my daughter Autumn, who has always despised Elle, agreed to drug her and then put the lights in the tub, while her boyfriend filmed. We've been trying to keep it at one month intervals for the sake of the plot, but things have changed.

"Autumn, the girl who kidnapped me, is your daughter? You're not going to convince me that she participated in all of this willingly. She's sweet, deep down, I know it."

I shuddered, trying hard to keep that picture from taking center stage in my mind. "Stanford told you to kill your wife?" I asked.

"Let me back up. On Elle's birthday, shortly before we attended the writer's conference, I invited a paranormal expert to help us with a séance."

"You already mentioned that. What I'm asking is why Stanford would ask you to kill your own wife, and why you would agree?"

"Stanford was my relative. I'd done some family history research and became fascinated by him. He was the most successful man of his day. That's what drew me to Nick. I read his novel and realized success ran deep in our family. Sadly, my dear wife didn't understand that."

"Because she figured out you were crazy?"

Brooks chuckled. "Lanie, you're a treasure. Elle refused to continue the line. She didn't want children with me. I suggested we go about it a different way and she was against that too. Stanford was right about her; she was only holding me back."

If my lip hadn't been puffed up, my mouth would have been hanging open.

"Sy—I mean, Brooks, he's been manipulating you. Once you let that evil into your head, it doesn't leave unless by force."

"I'm very aware of what I'm doing, Lanie. It's given me the most fulfilling months I've ever had."

I thought back over the past six months, trying to wrap my head around this giant farce. "What about the emails Sylas sent me?"

"We were at a dinner party for the studio, and I invited Sylas, as we'd become good friends. He mentioned his cousin was an amateur detective, and recently this cousin contacted him. He wasn't sure if he wanted to have contact with you. That's when I knew I had to find you. Adding an amateur sleuth to my cast was just the ingredient it was missing. My IT department hacked into his emails to communicate with you. I had Sylas and his family sent on, let's say, an extended vacation."

"In this little twisted situation you've created, what happens to the sleuth? Does she get to the bottom of the mystery?"

"I'm here to clean up," Autumn announced.

"What's he doing to keep you here, Autumn?" I asked, shooting her a disgusted look.

Autumn appeared confused by my question. "Daddy? What's she talking about?"

"Nothing, darling. It's time for you to go to the Fallen Branch. You're clear on your assignment for today?"

She smiled, her brown eyes sparkling. *His daughter.* I shuddered at the idea of him parenting a goldfish, let alone an actual child. In other circumstances, I would find her endearing. *Poor thing.* She must've been manipulated by her father too. I couldn't place the blame for my abduction at her feet.

"I'm going to eliminate Wendell, after he's finished his lines."

"My darling daughter came home and told me about Feather's abilities. That's when I knew she had to be part of our production." He smiled proudly at her. "I'm giving Autumn a producer's credit. Her very first one."

When Autumn left, Brooks pivoted back to me. "You asked what happens to the sleuth in my live-action movie?" He took a deep breath and put his hand to his chest, as if he were getting ready to recite from Shakespeare. "She fought valiantly, but in the end, she failed to realize it was all a trap. She and her husband died in a blaze of glory."

Chapter Forty-One — Feather

"It isn't that I question your abilities, Cosmo Hill, but—"

"We don't have time for me to list the number of instances that's happened, Bean," Cosmo snapped. "You're going to have to trust me on this. My plan will work. Officer Holliday said he'd meet us at Truman's farm so we can stage from there. I want to get the dummy set up as soon as possible."

He started to walk away, but then pivoted back. "Oh, did you bring the disguise I requested?"

"Of course! It's in my trunk. Also acquired a few goodies from another secret auction." November winked at Feather, and if Feather wasn't mistaken, made kissing noises.

Tug appeared with his mini *find-me* device. "I'm ready. I have night-vision goggles back home. Sorry I didn't bring them now." He glanced at Feather. "You said they weren't needed."

"I didn't think we'd be out searching for a kidnap victim, babe," she replied apologetically.

"I've got all of that. I took the liberty of loading my car with everything we'd need, in addition to midnight snacks and energy drinks," November said enthusiastically, like she was planning for a kid's slumber party.

"We're supposed to meet the kidnapper tomorrow morning at ten a.m. that gives us plenty of time to find out where they're located. Officer Holliday has the Tellum police and the county sheriff on standby. Any questions?"

They all shook their heads in unison. "Okay, November, you drive Tug and Feather, so they know where to go."

"You just want me in a different car than you, so you don't accidentally leave me in a ditch somewhere," she retorted.

"I just wanted to warn you two. Anything November offers you to eat or drink should come with a warning label," Cosmo said.

Feather nodded as she felt the hairs on her arms rising. *Meet me in the woods, lass.*

"November, I'm sorry. I need to speak with a spirit in the woods. It won't take long, I promise."

November nodded.

Cosmo walked toward the back door placing his hand on the knob and paused. "Ask your spirit friend to tell my wife I've never felt love like I have with her."

Feather dipped her head slightly, holding back the tears as much as she could. She was glad when he left, and she could let them spill. She didn't have time to waste on emotions, so she wiped her face on her sleeve as she headed out to the back door.

When she reached their usual spot, she didn't have to wait long before she heard the rustling of Fiona's skirts.

I already told you, this is a trap. This imposter wants you for his own.

"I know, but I can't risk losing Lanie. I have to go.

'Course you do, lass. I wanted to give you the armor you need. This man isn't Lanie's cousin. And he's warkin' with Stanford Aisley. The two'a them plan to keep killing. You can stop them, though.

"How?"

Believe in the power of your friendship.

"Huh?"

There was a rustling in the woods, what turned out to be a curious rabbit. When Feather turned back, Fiona was gone.

"Fiona! Don't leave yet! I need you!"

Somehow, she didn't think Fiona would return.

Fiona's brief appearance angered Feather. Nothing about this was fair. She tromped on the ground, smashing dead leaves and any miniscule living creature that crossed her path. All she got were riddles from this spirit. She'd selflessly given up her vacation to help Lanie. Didn't that count for anything?

When she reached November's car, Tug was sitting in the passenger seat and November was doing cartwheels around the vehicle.

"Sorry. I had to clear my head."

"Oh, that's fine. I was just doing a little stress reliever myself. I'm sure I'm gonna need it by the end of the day." November jumped up and down in place ten times before opening her car door. "Let's roll!"

Feather slid in the back seat, squeezing Tug's shoulder on the way by.

"What did you find out, babe?" He asked.

"I have to trust Lanie and the rest of our little group, but no one else." She folded her hands in her lap and tried preparing herself mentally for whatever lay ahead.

"That's not very helpful. But November Bean is on the case. My drone is up in the air now. I just got confirmation."

"November, may I ask what happened between you and Cosmo? Did you have a fight?" Tug asked.

She glared at him in her rearview mirror. "Not a fight, exactly. We went through some dark times together and he blames me for his end. That's all you'll get from me, Mr. Muscles." She made a zipping motion across her mouth.

"Did you pay someone to send up the drone?" Feather asked, wanting to change the subject quickly. It seemed dangerous to involve someone else in their rescue mission, especially since Fiona said to trust no one.

"I told you, he came with the equipment."

November put the car in reverse and stepped on the gas, causing their heads to snap back and forward.

"I've got the latest in technology. It's very quiet and undetectable with radar. At night, no one will see it unless they're really looking for it. You'll be impressed."

Feather leaned forward and put her head between the seats. "What, exactly, is our plan? No one really told me."

Tug glanced over at November who was humming an unfamiliar tune, evidently wrapped up in her own thoughts. "We're going to use November's drone to find the general location. As soon as the building is located, we'll get as close as possible and then the Lanie Locator will show us where she was when she phoned Cos. We'll be waiting for them in the morning when they leave to make the exchange. Officer Holliday promised to provide backup, along with the full support of the police up and down the coast."

"And then I'll pull out my Vem Vaporizer," November added. "It's only in the testing phase, but it knocks the unsuspecting criminal unconscious with a sharp thwack to the back of the head. Not only does it knock them unconscious, but also administers an immediate dose of Flaminol, a drug that will keep them asleep for hours. Eventually, the Vem Vaporizer will include a puff of Vem's Morning Muck, a cloud of disgusting-smelling gas to further disable the criminal. That will distract them long enough for me to grab our Lanie."

A tiny smile crept over Tug's face. "Of course. You're not to be messed with."

Chapter Forty-Two — Feather

The ride out to Truman Coolidge's farm was a silent one. Feather would have enjoyed the full moon and the light, coastal breeze, if this were a normal evening. It was anything but.

As they pulled into Truman's driveway, illuminated by the heads of presidents crafted into lightbulbs, Feather noticed a rather large aircraft parked in a field behind his house. She couldn't quite make out the shape, but it didn't seem the right shape to carry passengers.

"What's that?" she asked, pointing to the mystery shape.

"Oh, that's my drone. Kelvin—he's the pilot—is probably done surveilling by now." She shut off the car and turned around. "He's hot, but not really my type. Too clean cut, too normal."

"When you said you had a drone, I thought you

meant the kind you fly with a remote control," Tug remarked as he opened Feather's door for her.

November covered her curly hair with a helmet containing a light on the front. "I have one of those too. This one flies at fifty-thousand feet. Since we don't know how much intel these kidnappers have, I didn't want to take any chances." She stopped and pivoted, facing them both. "Besides, I like to take it out for a spin once in a while. Bought the thing at a private government auction in November. It's like brand-new. Kelvin rents it and himself out for parties."

Nothing November Bean said should have surprised them at this stage.

As they made their way up the driveway, they heard voices from the backyard. November turned on her headlamp and lit the way. When they reached the patio, they found Cosmo, Truman, and Kelvin making small talk.

"It's about time, Bean," Cosmo said, irritated.

Ignoring his angry words, she marched over to Kelvin. "What did you find, dashing man?"

"H'lo, Ms. Bean."

A man in his thirties wearing a military-issue jumpsuit stuck out his hand.

November pushed it aside and pulled him in for a hug. Feather couldn't see the expression on his face, but she was sure it caught him off guard.

Kelvin cleared his throat, signaling he was done with her version of hello. "Now that the necessary pleasantries are over, I'd like to show you the magic of a drone."

Truman handed out flashlights to everyone but November and they circled Kelvin.

He pulled out a device that looked like a tablet and showed them a well-detailed map. "Over here, in this clump of trees, you'll notice there is the outline of an underground building. When I zoom in," he took two fingers and widened the image, "you can see that it says Rudolph Productions over the door leading inside. It's genius the way it's tucked away in the side of a hill. I suspect there are rooms receiving daylight too."

Feather leaned in as close as she could and stood on her tip toes. Down two flights of stairs was a door that looked like the door to a bank vault. "This is incredible!" she marveled.

Kelvin grinned. "Just wait." He took his finger and flipped through the pictures until he found one that showed 'smudges.'

"What are those?" Feather asked.

"Those are called hot spots. That's where the people are."

As they all studied the image, Cosmo said, "I say we go in where the majority of the hotspots are and take them all out. That way, we can get to Lanie without worrying they're coming after us. We won't even need the dummy."

"Do you mean you're going to kill them?" Tug asked.

The dramatic silhouette of Cosmo's face glowed in

the moonlight like he had been plucked from a black-and-white Hollywood detective movie. "That's exactly what I mean."

"Let's don't stand around and think about it, let's go!" November urged. "You guys know how to shoot a gun, right?"

"Nobody is going to shoot anything."

Entranced by the picture show, none of them had noticed Officer Holliday as he joined them.

"Oh, good, you're here. Did you bring back up?" Cosmo asked.

He nodded. "It's all taken care of. What I want is for you folks to sit tight and let the police handle things from here."

The energy of the group dropped with a thud.

Cosmo placed himself inches from Officer Holliday. "If you think I'm just going to sit here and wait for word of my wife, you've got another thing coming."

Officer Holliday motioned for Cosmo to step back. "That's exactly what I'm saying, Mr. Hill. Everything is taken care of. It's a beautiful night. Why don't you folks make a fire and tell stories? Maybe toast some marshmallows."

The absurdity of his statement was shocking to all of them. Feather felt her arm hairs rising.

If he isn't for ye, he's agin' ye.

"Officer Holliday, where are the others?" she blurted out.

"Yes, I'll second that question," Truman added. "You can't go in all by yourself now."

"They're already at the location," he replied, his voice faltering.

"But you couldn't have known where that was. We just found it ourselves with hi-tech equipment." Truman moved over to Officer Holliday's side and leaned around behind him. "And now that I can see clearly, yours is the only car in the driveway."

In one swift motion, Officer Holliday grabbed Feather and removed his gun from its holster, pointing it directly at Feather's head. "Do as I say, and nobody gets hurt."

His voice was at least an octave lower than the kindly one he'd been using to help them before.

"You're working with the kidnappers?" Cosmo asked in disbelief. "Why?"

"Why does anyone do anything?" He snickered. "For money, of course."

November took a giant sniff of the air. "Deceit. Should have known that wasn't coming from the cows next door."

"Officer, if you're going to hold all of us hostage, we'd at the very least like an explanation. How did you get involved in all of this?"

"After the incident with Sheriff Frost's pig, my boss refused to give me any hours. Basically, I came in once a week to write parking tickets. That's how I met Brooks. I was writing a parking ticket one day for this fancy black car, when the owner came up and tapped me on the shoulder. I was ready for him to make a scene, but instead he said, 'How would you like to make real money working for me?'"

"So, with dollar signs in your eyes, you said yes," Truman harrumphed. "Same old story."

"It was more than that. My talents are being wasted here. He promised if I helped him with his projects, that he'd let me direct a picture."

"The one based on the murders of six authors? How do you know you're not next?"

"Because I..." his voice trailed off.

"Because you were there, weren't you? Did you kill Elle, Ivy, and Dash?" Feather asked.

"Not by myself!" He protested. Feather could feel his grip loosen slightly and she struggled to free herself. When he realized what was happening, he moved his arm up to her neck and held her in place.

"I had help," he continued. "Autumn, my girlfriend, drugged her stepmother, Elle Vanashelve, with wine. That made it easy. He wanted it all staged to look just like the cover of the book, so we took—"

"Cranberries, strung on twine, and wrapped them around the body." November crossed her arms and huffed. "So amateurish."

"For Ivy's death, we had to bring in Wendell. Autumn sent Ivy's neighbors a gift card for dinner that had to be used on that night. Once they left, Wendell and me got on their roof and sawed the ornament off. I held it until she radioed me that Ivy was coming down the street. That was a nightmare for the camera crew. We hired a few camera operators, even though the bulk of the movie is being filmed via our hidden cameras."

Feather shivered at the thought.

"And Dash required a little more work. The boss wanted to frame Lanie for the murder, just as Dash's main character had framed a detective. Autumn went to his door with towels. She was supposed to ask for an autograph and when he went to sign the book, she would stab him in the neck with a pen containing a solution to paralyze him while she strangled him."

Feather thought back to the first time she met Autumn. She went out to retrieve the pizza box, taking far longer than she should have. "Your girlfriend wrote that number on the pizza box, the one we thought was Dash's code?" She wheezed, trying to force the words out of her restricted vocal cords.

"O'course she did. Are you gonna let me finish?" He rolled her in closer to his body, causing Feather to wince with pain. Both Cosmo and Tug lurched forward, but Officer Holliday pulled Feather to the side of him and pointed the gun directly at Tug's head. "Don't try it, son!" he warned.

"You folks don't have good listening skills," he growled. "Anyway, Dash caught on too quick, and they struggled. Autumn took the book and hit him over the head, knocking him to the ground. She's a quick thinker, my girl, so when she'd hit him enough that she knew he was dead, she used the twine to strangle him. She hoped her father could recut with Lanie's face to make it look like Lanie killed him just the way his character died. After wrapping the cranberries strung on twine around his body, Wendell called Lanie to that room for an emergency. We had no idea Boysie Lumquest was already in the building."

"Wendell has been working for that creep? This whole time?" Cosmo's voice weakened. "Lanie tried helping him and he betrayed her like this?"

"Wendell came to the project late. He overheard a phone conversation between me and Autumn and threatened to go to Boysie, and that's when she told him he wouldn't live long enough for that. Seeing as how his life was on the line, he made a deal with her. Wendell got to breathe for another day, and he would receive fifty-thousand dollars for his cooperation."

Now it all made perfect sense to Feather. The feeling she had the first day they met, it was Stanford Aisley's evil oozing out of all of his pores. She glanced around the group, trying to gauge their reactions with only the full moon as light. With so many of them and only one of him, she hoped the same thing had occurred to them that was running through her mind now.

There was no time to think.

Chapter Forty-Three—
Feather

Spinning inward so that she was facing Officer Holliday, she was able to loosen his grip enough to get away. Tug taught her that self-defense tactic.

Luckily, her friends' reactions were just as timely. November Bean did an impressively high kick, targeting Officer Holliday's gun. It went sailing into the air, visible only in the full moonlight. It fired as it hit the ground with a thud.

Cosmo and Truman took advantage of Officer Holliday's loss of balance and brought him to the ground. As he struggled, they held him firmly in place.

"Get his cuffs, Bean!" Cosmo shouted.

Luckily, November wore her head lamp that evening. As she bent down, her light shone on his pocket where his cuffs were attached to his belt.

Witnessing all this left Feather in awe of their capacity not only to work quickly and efficiently, but together. It was almost as if they possessed the power to read each other's minds.

All this time, she'd not thought about Tug. Glancing to her side, she didn't see him, so she looked the other way, where, to her horror, he was kneeling on the ground.

She screamed when she saw him, unsure of the extent of his injuries. Just like the three of her companions could read each other, she and Tug could sense when the other was in danger.

"One, two, three," Cosmo and Truman heaved Officer Holliday up and into one of Truman's patio chairs. When they'd sat him down, Cosmo immediately fell to the ground next to him.

As she moved closer, Feather realized it wasn't Tug who got hit, but Kelvin the man piloting the drone.

"Buddy, where'd it get you?" He asked calmly.

"I...I'm not sure. I can feel the blood, but there's no pain."

"Oh, that's bad," November remarked. "If you've ever watched a movie, you'll know that happens right before the victim kicks the bucket."

Feather put her hand over her mouth.

"Bean, stop terrorizing the girl and bring your light down here!" Cosmo barked.

She kneeled next to Cosmo, moving her head around until she found the wound. His chest was covered in blood, but as they opened his shirt, they discovered the wound was actually on the top of his arm. Inside his shirt, they also found Tug's tracking device."

"Kelvin, the bullet looks like it went through Tug's tracking device before hitting you," Cosmo explained. "The device is basically shot, but I'm willing to bet your arm will be easily fixed."

"I knew it. He's too pretty to die," November remarked.

"Truman, go into your place and get some towels."

Quickly, he rushed in through his patio doors and returned momentarily with the towels, placing them over the wound.

"You've got to go in before dawn," Kelvin whispered.

"We're not leaving you here, Kelvin," Tug replied solemnly.

"He's right. We need to get there before they figure out we're on to them. When Officer Dunce over there doesn't show, they're going to figure that something is wrong and Lanie could be in trouble," Cosmo said. "Tug, you and Truman need to hold on to our prisoner while I relieve him of his shirt and jacket."

November didn't wait to be asked to help, and plopped down on Officer Holiday's lap as he made an "Ugh" sound. He didn't struggle.

"Someone is going to have to stay here with the prisoner and wait for the ambulance," she said.

"I'll do it," Truman offered. "I've got a stun gun from the Presidential Goodz website that I've been anxious to try out. That work for you, Officer?"

Officer Holliday didn't reply.

"I'll call an ambulance. You folks hurry up. Our Lanie needs you."

"They know we're coming now, Tug stated. "What do we do?"

All eyes fell on Officer Holliday.

"Your career in law enforcement is over, effective immediately," Cosmo said sternly. "But if you want to see freedom by the time you're fifty, you need to speak up now."

When he remained silent, Feather bent down next to him and whispered in his ear.

He glared at her before uttering, "The code to the gate is nineteen-twenty-two, the year of Stanford Aisley's death. But you'll never get inside the building. Mr. Rudolph has cameras everywhere."

He stuck out his jaw in defiance.

"Tell Autumn it wasn't my fault. Tell her I did everything she said!" Officer Holliday called in desperation. "I would never betray her!"

"Oh, we'll be glad to pass along a message. Just not the one you want," Cosmo quipped.

As they made their way quickly to the car, Tug asked, "What did you say? A message from an angry relative?"

"No, I just told him I'd personally make sure he was on the Sheriff's Department's Wall of Shame if he didn't cooperate."

Chapter Forty-Four — Lanie

Though I was grateful to have a bed, there wasn't much sleep happening. Sylas, or rather, Brooks' admission that we were all nothing more than unwilling actors in his movie was disturbing. I could only imagine the trap he was setting for poor Cosmo, given the fact that he was planning to make us disappear.

And then there was Feather. Had she been informed of the trap by her spirits? Fiona Scheddy seemed like a decent sort, and if she had been communicating with Feather, she must feel protective of her. Fiona would save her, wouldn't she?

I opened the door slowly, and as I had the previous day, stuck my head out. There was no one guarding me or this area, so I snuck down the hallway, moving as quickly as my still-aching parts would allow.

When I reached the elevator, I let out a sigh of relief that I'd made it this far without detection. It was too risky to let the doors open and close, so I searched for a nearby staircase and found one. It led me to the kitchen, where I'd eaten the day before. The strange combination of offices and home must've all been a part of Brooks' plan, including the bedroom that looked so familiar. Everything in life was a movie set to him.

A familiar scent wafted to my nostrils, making my stomach growl. It was breakfast cooking, eggs and bacon, and something baking. My heart sank, realizing I wasn't alone. As I moved closer, the sound of Christmas tunes assaulted my ears like it was the middle of July. It was Magda, humming away as she stirred something in a bowl. If she was cooking, someone had to be awake to eat.

There was still a chance she might be distracted enough that she wouldn't notice someone passing by. The garden Sylas—Brooks—had been so proud of was through the formal dining room, just beyond the kitchen. If I could make it that far, I could make a run for it.

Moving swiftly, I hid behind the formal dining room table. As Magda moved around, I realized she was wearing earbuds. *Good.*

The French doors were open, maybe so she could enjoy the fresh, early morning air. I couldn't believe my good fortune. I slipped outside undetected and made a beeline for the gate. To my disappointment, it was locked.

Vem had been pushing me to take a combat

training course with her. I explained my body had no intention of climbing up one side of a wall and flopping over the other. Why did she always have to be right?

With a quick glance to Magda, who was dancing and singing to Jingle Bell Rock, oblivious to the attempted escape on the patio, I took one of Charlie Chaplin's chairs and placed it in front of the gate.

I was able to hoist myself over the top and lower my weary body to the ground.

Freedom!

There were stairs directly in front of me, which was my only option. When I'd reached the top, I looked around, uncertain of what to do next.

It was like going from day to night. As opposed to the lush greenery of the patio, this was completely brown and barren: an undeveloped area without even a tree to dot its landscape. In the distance I spotted a large parking lot which meant I risked seeing Brooks or one of his goons.

The way Brooks spoke, this complex was off the beaten path. The fireworks launcher meant Truman's farm was near, but in farmland terms, that could mean miles away. *Cosmo, I hope you understood my message.* Finding a road might not lead me to civilization, at least not right away. I turned and began walking left, for no reason other than the pocket of cloudless early morning sky.

After thirty minutes, I came to a cluster of tall evergreen trees. Never had they looked so beautiful. At least there was some cover here, so I stopped to rest. My feet hurt. My achy bones still hadn't recovered from their mistreatment. It seemed wrong to sit out in the open, but I didn't have any options.

Leaning against a tree, my eyes quickly grew heavy. I was hungry and tired, but I could only tend to one need. I dreamt Cosmo and I were dancing in an open field of wildflowers. He kissed my neck, and I nuzzled my face in his hair, drinking in his familiar and comforting scent.

Fiona Scheddy, the version of her I'd seen in her wedding photo, appeared at the edge of the field, waving her arms wildly.

Careful, lass! Keep watch!

I tried protesting, that I wanted just one more minute with my husband, but when I turned around, he was gone. My eyes snapped open, and I had no sense how long I'd been asleep. It was fully daylight now and my absence would be obvious.

It occurred to me at that moment that Brooks recorded everything. There was no way he didn't see me sneaking out. I chuckled. "Your butt falling over that fence may be on the next movie poster for Brain Gravy Pictures."

He recorded everything.

I sat up straight and looked around. He was probably watching me right now, enjoying the fact that I was lost in the trees with no way to get home.

My stomach growled again, just to make sure I

hadn't forgotten how long it had been since I'd gorged myself on Magda's pastries.

Out of nowhere, I heard a vehicle. There wasn't a road that I'd found. Where was it coming from?

I heard a door open and then slam shut. I slid around to the other side of the tree, away from the sound.

"Oh, cousin?" Brooks called mockingly. "I know you're here! You're being very rude. We've got filming to do today!"

My throat tightened.

"I've got a crew of big, burly men with me. The three of us searching for one, middle-aged woman, well, you understand those odds. Why not make it easy on yourself and come out now?"

For a split second, I thought about it. If he was going to capture me anyway, why put myself through all of this?

But then I remembered Feather's bravery in the face of Stanford Aisley's tricks. If she could stand up to a powerful entity, then so could I.

Moving as quietly as possible, I walked backwards. When my foot hit something solid, I stopped. It was a trip wire, probably one that caused the unsuspecting person to fall to their horrible, gruesome death.

I stepped over the wire and felt momentary relief, until I realized there was a second trip wire, and I was standing on top of it.

Before I had time to think, two hands grabbed my

wrists and yanked me away from a giant log suspended by ropes, heading right for me.

"Thank you for saving me."

Turning to see my savior, I found evil instead.

Fiona Scheddy, if you are truly watching me, now is the time to help.

Chapter Forty-Five — Feather

"I'm not going to repeat my objections to your plan, Cosmo Hill, but if you want my opinion—"

"I don't." Cosmo snapped, holding the car door open while November jumped out. He tugged on Officer Holiday's pants uncomfortably. They were roughly the same height, but Cosmo was much more muscular.

The sun was just peeking over the horizon and soon it would be time to meet the kidnapper and pay Lanie's ransom.

"I'm going in, by myself. You all will wait out here in case they leave before I find them. Because our police friend threw a wrench into the plans, there's no decoy at the quick mart."

He glanced around nervously. "This place looks like something from my Sci-Fi show. It's hard to believe it's a movie studio."

Pivoting away from his friends, he turned 360 degrees, viewing the giant, empty parking lot. Just inside the gate was a staircase with a small sign above it that read, Brain Gravy Pictures. When he reached the keypad, he punched in the numbers Officer Holliday had given him. A big gate slid open slowly and he gave them all a thumbs up before heading inside and disappearing behind a large, white truck.

When he was out of sight, November Bean placed her hands on her slender hips and declared, "I don't know about the rest of you, but I'm not going to just sit out here and wait for my two best friends to meet an untimely demise."

Feather and Tug gazed at her warily.

"It's not that we don't want to help, Ms. Bean," Tug began. "It's that we're not sure where to go once we get in. Us wandering around without any direction could be more of a liability than a help. Since my miniature walkie-talkie was crushed, we'd only have our phones for communication. They could easily track those."

November huffed in frustration. "Fine! I'll do it myself. But don't come to me when something bad happens to your hosts and you were out here twiddling your thumbs instead of helping."

She opened the trunk of her car and retrieved a complicated-looking weapon, smaller than a gun, but with three barrels.

"Wait!" Feather yelled. "Give me a minute. I can find out where to go."

She turned away from them both and walked in a circle on the other side of the car, pleading with the spirits——any spirits—to come to her aid.

"We don't have all day!" November called after her in frustration, though she made no attempt to leave. Her phone played *Good Morning Gorgeous,* and she put it up to her ear. "Did they capture you, Hill? If you'd...oh, I see. We'll come back and get you when we're done."

She put the phone back in her pocket, shaking her head. "Cosmo is always working, even when he's not. I guess he found the kitchen and he confronted the cook. She gave it up right away, that Lanie escaped, and her cousin Sylas went after her. He's got her restrained and has taken out two guards. He wants us to pick him up on the other side of the building.""

In a matter of seconds, Feather returned to them.

"We have a weapon, too, by the name of Fiona Scheddy." She gave Tug a shy smile.

"Well? Don't keep us in the dark, girlfriend! Where is she?" November demanded.

"Fiona described where she's hiding, it's a wooded area not far from here. We don't have any time to spare."

"What about Cosmo? We can't just leave him here!" Tug pleaded.

November transferred her weight back and forth between her feet. "Ooh, I knew this day would come. I have to make a choice—save my Lanie, or rescue someone who hates me with a fiery hot passion. How can I be in two places at once?"

"You can do both," Feather said.

"How?" November grabbed Feather's arms and shook her. "We've got to get to Lanie right now!"

Chapter Forty-Six—Lanie

"Sylas, or Brooks, or whoever you are—I'm not worth all of this. Let me go and I'll keep your location and your secret movie plans to myself."

I watched as his eyes darted back and forth. In the seminar, "Read Their Eyes if you Want Their Dollars," I learned that people's eyes often darted back and forth when they were contemplating a moral dilemma. It could be as simple as deciding if this purchase was purely selfish, or if it was needed. I could tell his thoughts were much deeper.

"Brooks, this dark energy you're feeling isn't you. It's all Stanford Aisley. He wants to control you."

"No one controls me," He huffed. "I own a motion picture studio."

I struggled against his body, trying to sit upright so I would have more leverage against his firm grip.

"You may feel that way right now, but I can tell you

adored your wife. The Brooks who fell in love and married Elle Vanashelve would never have arranged her death. Your body language is honest even when your words aren't."

The smirk on his face melted away to expose a sadness. His grip on me loosened slightly.

"That wasn't Stanford. That was me. I don't let anyone make decisions for me," he said quietly.

"It wasn't your fault. He's the strong—the strongest—entity Feather has ever encountered. Someone with a weaker will would have gone on a killing streak, ending the lives of everyone in Piney Falls."

I hoped that by giving him an excuse for his abhorrent behavior we could connect, and he might let me go.

I was wrong.

Brooks squeezed my wrists. "I see what you're doing. This is all a mind game to you. It won't work. Ever since I contacted Stanford at a séance, he's been more than accommodating. People like you have laughed at my creativity my whole life. He understands me because we're cut from the same cloth."

His hot breath was oppressive. I tried turning my head to the side to escape it, but it was no use.

"You're nothing, a nobody. You aren't going to destroy my masterpiece," he continued with a hatred he hadn't displayed before. "Stanford assures me this groundbreaking film will win all of the awards I'm owed after being the industry laughingstock. We're going back to the studio, and I'll turn on the camera while we re-enact this. We can do it against the green screen, so it will appear we're in the woods. Face it, Lanie. I've outplayed you at every turn."

He wasn't wrong. I was exhausted, both from the ordeal of these past few days and a body that needed rest and healing. I was out of ideas.

"If I agree to—"

"Lanie? Sister-friend, I know your scent. You don't have to hide, it's me."

"Vem! Don't come any closer! It's a tra—" I yelled before he let go of one of my hands and clasped his hand firmly over my mouth.

His evil smile curled around his bulbous cheeks, just as I imagined Stanford Aisley's would. "This is perfect. I couldn't have scripted it better," he whispered menacingly.

The sound of the underbrush moving with her every step was agonizing. In my mind, there was a picture of Vem sniffing out my location. When she got close enough, she would trip over the same wire that I did. But instead of being caught in Brooks' arms, she would fall to her death. It was more than I could bear.

I squeezed my eyes shut as tightly as I could. If I couldn't block out the sound, I could at least avoid the sight of my best friend's demise.

Help is on the way, lass.

My eyes snapped open. There was no one around us. I was still lying on the ground with Brooks astride me. He seemed to relish my horror, as he leaned closer to my face and whispered, "This one is for Stanford."

His head hit my forehead and for a moment, I thought my life would end with one painful head butt. Instead, his hand fell off my mouth and I screamed, "Vem! Help!"

Brooks' body suddenly rolled off mine, leaving me with a clear view of my beautiful best friend, impressive weapon in hand.

She blew on the barrels of her weapon. I could see yellow lettering on the side that read, "Vem Vaporizer. Test Version."

"Lanie, you don't have to yell. You should have known I would rescue you."

My adoration was short-lived. "Vem! This is a trap! Watch out!"

"Oh, you mean this?" She moved casually to the trip wire and kicked it, causing a large section of ground to open up. It was far enough away from us both that we weren't in any danger.

"How did you know?"

She pulled me to my feet and dusted off my ugly gray dress. "You forgot, I've got all sorts of neat gadgets from that big auction I attended last month in California. She pulled her helmet off her head and pointed to a light. "Infrared," she explained.

Vem bent down and rolled Brooks to the tree I'd hid behind. She pulled zip-ties out of her pocket, why she had them I didn't dare ask, and affixed his hands to the tree over his head. "That should hold him until Boysie arrives," she said with satisfaction.

"Make sure those are good and snug, Vem."

The last I knew, the Lumquest family was off in California. "Isn't Boysie still on vacation?"

"Gladys checked in with Urica Jollopy, who was watering her plants. She told Gladys all about your kidnapping. The Lumquest family hightailed it out of California and they should be back soon."

Once on my feet, I found myself too wobbly to walk. "Vem, I'm afraid I can't..." my voice trailed off. She never understood people who weren't at her elite fitness level.

"Carry you? No problem."

Before I could protest, she'd hoisted me off the ground and over her shoulder like a large bag of soil.

"If you feel like passing gas, go ahead," she said through a plugged nose. "I'm putting dose plugs in."

In this somewhat embarrassing position, it occurred to me that the rest of our party was still unaccounted for.

"Where's Cos? And Feather and Tug? Truman? I know they're with you."

"We're picking up Cosmo and then I'll take you home and place you on my examining table. The others require more explanation..."

I was too tired to protest.

"November, what if there are more of them at the studio? What if we're walking right into a trap?"

My brain was beyond processing anything being

said, so I did my best to listen as a casual observer. As she chattered on, we reached her car and she lowered me to the ground. Tug and Feather rushed to my side and helped me into the car.

"I need to call—"

"No!" Tug and Feather yelled in unison. "Tug's walkie-talkie was destroyed, and Cosmo already called us. If they have the capability to track his calls, they know exactly where he is. We don't want them knowing we're there too."

There was a period of silence. Because of my current condition, I had no idea if it was one minute or one hour.

My eyelids, held down by the weight of exhaustion, refused to open when I heard, "That's Autumn. She's the one I overheard in the woods. She's dangerous."

I tried forming the words to tell them exactly who Autumn was, but my mouth and brain were no longer connected. A vehicle drove down the road, or flew over our heads, I couldn't be sure.

Indistinguishable mumbling.

The door opened and closed and I felt familiar, strong arms around me as well as the scent of thyme. "Don't try to sit up, sweetheart. I've got you. You're always safe with me."

Chapter Forty-Seven — Two Days Later

"Vem, can you check and see if that's Truman coming up the driveway?"

I pulled the turkey out of the oven, grateful my job only involved warming it up.

"Sure. Make sure you set aside a plate for Kelvin. I'm taking it to the hospital when we're done. I think he's interested in dating me. I can tell he has a thing for older women." She tilted her head to the side. "I don't look a day over thirty-seven-point-five, do I?"

"You're ageless, Vem," I agreed.

After I'd had a soothing shower and fallen into bed, I had a panic attack. I jumped out of bed and ran to the kitchen, returning with an envelope. By now, Cosmo was sitting up with the light on beside him, rubbing his eyes.

"What is it, babe? Do you need an aspirin?"

I crawled back into bed gingerly, making sure none of my sensitive parts hit the mattress. "No, nothing like that. I just remembered that I never had a chance to give you your Christmas gift."

"Lanie, you don't need to—"

"Just open it, Cos. Life is short and we're both exhausted. I won't be able to sleep until I know I was able to share this with you."

He grabbed his readers from the night stand and perched them on the tip of his nose before opening the envelope and pulling out the letter.

"Read it out loud, please." I rested my chin on his shoulder, waiting for his reaction.

"Dear Brother,

Your wife and I have been conspiring for months. We know you haven't had time off since your wedding, and it's high time you do. Therefore, we've planned a trip to San Diego. The bakery is in good hands, as you know. You'll spend four nights in a resort, with every food option your picky palate can dream up. Oh, and you'll be seeing me so much you'll need a vacation from your vacation!

Merry Christmas, Cos. I love you more than life.

Sincerely,

Cedar."

He dropped the letter and rolled toward me. "I don't know what to say. You and Cedar...Oh, Lanie."

Cosmo took me in his strong arms and held me tightly. I didn't care that it made everything on the outside hurt. On the inside, I was warm and comfortable. His embrace was always home to me.

The next morning, Boysie called Cosmo with more good news. Brooks, his daughter, Autumn and Officer Holliday were sitting in the county jail. They were denied bail, so they would be Boysie's guests for the foreseeable future. Wendell agreed to testify against them in exchange for a lighter sentence. Vem and I planned to appear on his behalf. He was coerced into this position, after all.

Brain Gravy Pictures would no doubt be sold to pay for their mounting legal bills. I planned to email my cousin Sylas—the real one—when I knew how to explain all of this. He was still under contract to make a movie from his anthology story.

After we'd come home and slept for hours, there was a knock at the door. Cosmo, refusing to allow me out of bed, answered and then called, "Lanie, you'd better come see this."

Our entire porch was full of holiday delights. There was a note attached to one bag that read, "Cosmo and Lanie, you missed out on your Christmas Eve dinner, so we've all made something for you. Please enjoy! We're so happy you're safe. Signed, Your Piney Falls family."

It took four trips with both of us carrying to bring it all into the kitchen. While I would have preferred to wait and celebrate with our daughter, who would be arriving in two days, Tug and Feather deserved the holiday they came for.

I could hear the front door opening and Vem greeting Truman with her usual energy.

"If you need a stomach stretch before we begin, I can help you," she offered.

"Well now, that's very kind of you, November Bean. I expect my stomach is well stretched, even for a meal fit for visiting White House dignitaries."

Truman appeared in the kitchen, sporting his best green holiday overalls. "Merry Christmas, Lanie!" He kissed me on the cheek and set a paper bag on the counter, finding a space I didn't realize was there.

"What's that, Truman?"

"After all we've been through, it didn't seem right to come empty-handed to our big celebration. I brought something called, 'muddy pigs.' Chocolate covered bacon, to be exact. President Lincoln was a fan. I order them from a specialty store back east every year. This seemed like the best time as any to share them."

There were salads of every kind, mashed potatoes, sweet potatoes, three kinds of gravy, two kinds of stuffing, a fancy bean dish, six pies and of course, the turkey. The table was as much a feast for the eyes as it would be for our stomachs.

Still nursing a bruised body, it wouldn't be as formal an affair on my end. I was wearing sweats and I invited our guests to do the same. There was another knock on the door and Feather and Tug entered.

I rushed, as much as my hobbled body would allow, to hug them. "I'm so happy we get to spend our holiday with you!" I said after a big hug. "You're family now. There's no way out!" I joked.

If I wasn't mistaken, Feather wiped away a tear. "Lanie, this week has been crazy, but Tug and me, we're just glad you're okay and we can all be together."

Tug rubbed my shoulder carefully. "You've taken such good care of us. If you don't watch out, you'll have your own bed and breakfast here before long!"

"Thank you, Tug. The next time you two come to town, you'll be staying here, whether you like it or not. Come sit down, everything is ready!"

"Can we wait a few minutes?" Cosmo asked. I'd noticed him pacing around the living room earlier, but I'd been too busy to question him.

"While I'm very grateful for all of this wonderful food, it takes nothing short of a miracle to have it all the proper temperature at the same time." I kissed him, touching my tender lip afterward. "Whatever you're planning, can it wait?"

His ice-blue eyes stared at me plaintively.

"Okay," I sighed. "I'll give you five minutes."

At that exact minute, our laptop buzzed.

"What in the electronic wonder?" Vem asked, examining the screen closely.

Cosmo shoved her out of the way. "Don't touch that, Bean!" he barked, picking up the computer and placing it on the counter. He clicked a series of sites and then three happy faces appeared on the screen. Immediately I recognized one. It was the face of my father, at least the one I'd remembered from my childhood.

"Sylas! Is that really you?"

All three of them nodded, beaming.

"Cos, how did you..."

"It wasn't just him, Lanie. He asked if I could track them down with all of my fancy schmancy equipment. So I did," Vem said proudly.

Cosmo elbowed her in the side.

"Ow!" she complained, rubbing the offended body part. "Yes, Cosmo and Truman helped. They sent an email to Sylas, telling him what had happened. And then Feather and Tug called to make sure he was willing to meet you. So we all helped."

"Lanie, now that we know the whole story, we're just so sorry," Tidbit said. She looked every bit her name, a tiny person with delicate features and a whisper of a voice. "We thought it was a great promotion when Sylas was offered this opportunity to work in Europe. We had no idea Sylas wasn't receiving his email any longer."

"I am concerned about one thing. With all that you've gone through, I hate to ask, but we were informed of a bank box containing incriminating information about each author. When you're feeling better, could you find out exactly what that is? I haven't done anything illegal, but any one of us have done things that, in the wrong hands, could be misconstrued."

"Already taken care of," Feather said.

I turned to her, surprised. "How?"

"The numbers in Dash's ring? They unlocked the box at Flanagan Savings and Loan. I took Tug to meet Fiona in the woods and that was her final gift to us."

"You got to meet her?" November asked. "I'm so jealous." November took Tug's arm and walked into the other room.

"Tug and I went there this morning and took everything out. We burned it." Feather said.

"Cousin Lanie," a young girl who claimed her mother's dainty features and her father's intense brown eyes interjected. "Feather told me the fake Eloise drew you a picture of her family. I'm not much of an illustrator."

This Eloise was much more sophisticated than the young girl I'd met online. Still, I felt a little sad knowing I'd never have occasion to speak with her again.

"That's perfectly fine, hon. I look forward to getting to know you!"

"Well, I'm not much of an artist, but I decided to try a picture of my family anyway." She produced a detailed picture of her father, mother, Eloise herself, Cosmo and me.

"Eloise, I don't know what to say. That's wonderful." I choked up, unable to contain the emotion of this past week.

"We'll have more time to talk soon. Cosmo invited us to stay with you next month, when your daughter is home," Sylas continued. "I hope that's all right with you?"

"More than all right, cousin." I sniffed and turned

to grab Cosmo's hand. "This is the best Christmas gift ever!"

When we'd ended our conversation, promising another soon, Truman cleared his throat.

"What is it, Truman?" I asked, knowing this was his sign for posing uncomfortable questions.

"I never did hear how Cosmo escaped. Oh, and Feather, what happened to Stanford Aisley? Do we still have to worry about him?"

Chapter Forty-Eight— Two Days Ago

COSMO

I learned how to hide from the bad guys when I was a kid. So many bad things happened, my young brain couldn't comprehend them, so I made a safe place.

At first, it was a picture with a loving family around the holiday table. I saw them in magazines on the rare occasions I was allowed to go into town. When that no longer quenched my thirst for normalcy, I hid physically.

I trained myself in shallow breathing and I could stand in the same place for hours, my mind off somewhere more pleasant. Today would require one of those skills.

After I made my way on to the grounds of Brain Gravy Productions, I hid just outside the French doors leading into the kitchen. Barely breathing, I started to wonder what would happen when I encountered someone who knew the real *Officer Nitwit*. and my uniform would only bring more questions.

Lad, we need to save your Lanie. But you'll have to follow my instructions to the letter.

My head whipped around so quickly I heard my neck crack. Resisting the urge to rub the pain of a frequent trouble spot, I used only my eyes to survey the yard. Just inside the doors, an older woman was humming as she stirred something on the stove. Birds tweeted and fought for rim space on a bird bath. No other activity.

You know me. We don't have time for the formalities. Your Lanie is in trouble but help is on the way. Unless we get rid of Stanford Aisley for good, he'll be in the minds of the weak forever.

Now I understood. It was a ghost of some kind. Must've latched on to me in the car.

"Not sure I believe in this hocus pocus, but I'll play along. What can I do to get rid of this stuffed shirt?" I asked.

You'll have to go into the kitchen and ask Magda for thyme, red pepper and sage. She doesn't know everyone who works here. When you've gathered those things, you'll bring them back here to your hiding place.

What, exactly, am I making? Do I need a pot? Is this a witch's brew?

Don't be sassy with me, lad. You're making a potion to send Stanford back from whence he came. You'll be closing the portal.

This was way out of my wheelhouse. But without any way to know what was happening with the rest of the search party, my options were limited.

"Okay. How much do I need?"

A handful of each.

I stood, listening to my knees crack, then rubbed the back of my neck. Lanie's soft fingers rubbing out the kink flashed through my mind and then I pushed away my selfish indulgence.

Whistling a Christmas tune, I sauntered through the French doors. Magda spun around, her eyes as big as saucers.

"Another new one? The boss needs to tell me. I've got to have a head count for meals or I won't make enough. Doesn't he realize that?"

She shook her head and returned to her stirring.

"Yeah, I'm new. I'm here to get a few spices for..." Nothing came to mind.

Magda clucked her tongue. "He's doing that dark magic again, is he? I don't believe in any of that. What do you need this time?"

She turned around, wiping her wrinkled hands on a red apron.

"I need thyme, red pepper, and sage. A handful of each."

She looked me up and down like a holiday turkey.

"You're better looking than most of them. Are you married?"

I nodded solemnly.

"Too bad." She reached into the refrigerator and

pulled out the requested items." My daughter is divorced. A year now. All she finds is them bar boys who want a good time and a drink." Magda placed everything in my hands.

"What are you making?" I asked, trying to divert the conversation.

"Filling. Tonight, it's meat pies with mashed potatoes and vegetables."

"You'll need a little more of this sage in your mix," I said, tearing off a few leaves and handing them to her before I walked outside. "Thanks for your help."

Returning to my spot behind the bushes, I crouched down. "Now what?" I whispered.

It will take stronger conviction than Stanford possesses, Cosmo Hill. I believe you have just that. Squeeze everything together in your hand and repeat after me:

Stanford Aisley, I banish you. Your otherworldly powers aren't as strong as my love for my living wife.

I took one more glance around the yard. If November Bean was pulling one over on me, she was going to be in real trouble this time. When I didn't see anything new, I closed my eyes and recited her words with everything held tightly in my hand. A tear rolled down my cheek as I whispered, "...aren't as strong as my love for my living wife."

Now you say, I'm closing this portal door, both good and evil dead must leave.

My eyes popped open. "Does that mean you're gone too? How will I find Lanie?"

Tell Magda you've been instructed to take her vehicle to the wooded area to help the boss and ask her for directions. I know you lads aren't keen on asking for directions, but this time, you'll do as I say.

I resisted the urge to argue with her and did exactly as I was told. Damned if the air didn't feel lighter when I finished.

Magda gave me her keys and directions without question and I drove like hell to find my wife. Heading down the dusty road, I saw the strangest thing. It looked like transparent people, floating up and disappearing into the sky.

"Did I do that?" I asked, out loud. Of course, no one answered.

When I reached their car, November Bean was emerging from the forest, carrying Lanie on her back. I couldn't help myself, I chuckled out loud.

Feather came running over to me as I stepped out. "There's been a change in the spirit world. Stanford is gone! I felt his energy leave!"

"I know. I'll explain the whole thing after we've got Lanie safely home. But Feather, your Fiona helped me. When I got rid of Stanford, she was taken to the other side too, or whatever it is you paranormal types say."

Her gaze dropped to the ground.

"Hey, this is a good thing." I took her chin and lifted it gently. "The last thing she told me was to give you this message."

Feather glanced at me hopefully. "Really? What did she say?"

"That you're doing good work. You're helping both the living and the dead by relaying their messages. And that you're a brave lass."

Feather threw her arms around me and began to cry.

Chapter Forty-Nine—A Day of Celebration

"You know it's a rough day when I don't share my war stories with you," Cosmo chuckled.

"Stanford is gone, thanks to Cosmo," Feather announced. "And everyone he had under his spell is in jail."

He shrugged his shoulders with indifference. "I don't know about that. It wasn't me, so much as all of us." Cosmo lifted his glass. "Even November Bean. Cheers."

Vem gasped but said nothing, clinking his glass before downing the entire serving of wine in one gulp.

"As we sit down to eat, I can't help reflecting on our harrowing experience," Lanie said, pausing a moment to gaze affectionately at each face around the table.

"We're all here, together, because of a series of awful events," Lanie continued. "What brought us together was horrific, but we found our way home.

None of us would be here today without that ability. She swallowed hard, her voice faltering. Cosmo put his arm around her shoulder protectively.

"Do you need to lie down?" he asked. "We don't have to eat now."

"No, Cos. I'm fine. I need to get through this without losing my cool. I didn't put on all of this makeup for nothing." She touched her bright red lips.

"I've never regretted the people who've joined me around this table. I'm so lucky to have you all here and call you the most powerful word in my vocabulary—family."

Everyone lifted a glass and then clinked theirs with the person next to them.

Vem hopped up from the table and bounced into the kitchen.

"We're eating without you, Bean!" Cosmo called after her.

She reappeared, holding a dish covered in foil. "We forgot this!" Vem took the foil off and took a big whiff. "Looks like cranberry salad."

I glanced from Cosmo's face, to Truman's, to Feather's, and then Tug's. In unison, we said, "Throw it away!"

Acknowledgments

Each successful writer needs not just one but many people in their corner, helping at all stages of development. I'm especially fond of the team of people I've assembled; each an expert in their own way. I'm fortunate that you are willing to share your personal areas of expertise with me. Keder Readers, you are the best Advanced Reader team. I'm certain you are the cream of the crop when it comes to marketing and passing the word about new publications. Special thanks to Doug, Mackensie and Meghan, Thomas and Barb for your help with all sorts of odd questions and for being supportive of my chosen writerly lifestyle. Please don't ask to look at their search histories.

About the Author

USA TODAY Bestselling Author, Joann Keder raised a family and taught piano lessons on the Great Plains of Nebraska, all the while secretly dreaming of a career as a writer.

At the age of 35 she timidly took her first college course, unsure if she had what it took to go much further. At the age of 42 she received her Masters Degree in Creative Writing, creating her first novella, *The Something That Happened in Pepperville* as her thesis.

An abrupt move to the Pacific Northwest and much personal trauma lead to a re-examination of who and what she was meant to be.

Today, her passions include hiking, writing and chocolate, not necessarily in that order. Find Joann on social media:

Also by Joann Keder

PEPPERVILLE STORIES

The Something that Happened in Pepperville

The Story of Keilah

Secrets and Sunflowers

Franniebell and Purple Wonder

PINEY FALLS MYSTERIES

Welcome to Piney Falls

Saving Piper Moonlight

Tales of Naybor Manor

Lavender's Tangled Tree

The Twisted Stitch Society

CHARMING MYSTERIES

Oceanberry Blues

Tangerine Troubles

Perilously Pink

EMORY BING MYSTERIES

Ebook only

Be the first to hear about new releases! Sign up for my newsletter here:

http://www.joannkeder.com

Made in the USA
Middletown, DE
18 October 2022

12964161R00208